Bewitching Benedict

Also by CE Murphy

The Austen Chronicles
Magic & Manners * Sorcery & Society (forthcoming)

The Heartstrike Chronicles
Atlantis Fallen * Prometheus Bound (forthcoming)
Avalon Rising (forthcoming)

The Walker Papers
Urban Shaman * Winter Moon * Thunderbird Falls
Coyote Dreams * Walking Dead * Demon Hunts
Spirit Dances * Raven Calls * No Dominion
Mountain Echoes * Shaman Rises

The Old Races Universe
Heart of Stone * House of Cards * Hands of Flame
Baba Yaga's Daughter
Year of Miracles
Kiss of Angels (forthcoming)

The Worldwalker Duology
Truthseeker * Wayfinder

The Inheritors' Cycle
The Queen's Bastard * The Pretender's Crown

Stone's Throe
A Spirit of the Century Novel

Take A Chance
A Graphic Novel

Roses in Amber
A Beauty and the Beast Story

The Lovelorn Lads
Bewitching Benedict

& writing as Murphy Lawless
Raven Heart

Bewitching Benedict

Book One of the Lovelorn Lads

C.E. MURPHY

a miz kit production

MKP

BEWITCHING BENEDICT
ISBN-13: 978-1-61317-137-0

Cover Art & Design: Cora Graphics / coragraphics.it
Editor: Mary-Theresa Hussey / goodstorieswelltold.com
Copy Editor: Stephanie Mowery

For M.C. Beaton
who has given me many hours of
reading enjoyment

Chapter One

The Season had, in Miss Claire Dalton's estimation, come early, and come directly to her. It had arrived—or was soon to arrive—in the form of her cousin Charles, whom she had not seen since childhood. More interestingly, it was to arrive in the form of two of Charles's friends, young men *he* had seen only a few times since leaving for the Coalition Wars more than seven years ago.

Claire's mother had warned the Lads would be much taken with one another, but had not stopped Claire from dressing in the finest gown appropriate for home. She was consequently adorned in a white gown embellished with a rather high collar that nearly brushed her jaw but left the hollow of her throat exposed. The day was warm, and she had foregone a wrap, satisfied instead with the splash of pink allowed her by the ribbon of a deep straw bonnet that protected her skin from the weakening September sun. She felt quite pretty, with dark ringlets brushing her cheekbones as they fell free from the bonnet, and if her steps minced due to the slight gather at the gown's hem, then at least she was ladylike and not striding about like a man.

It would be more suitable, she supposed, to await Charles's arrival in a sitting room, pursuing her needlepoint or reading...or singing, or painting, or Italian, or any one of the myriad applications well-bred young women attended to. She had spent the morning engaged in similarly appropriate activities: calling upon the widow down the road with her mother before stopping in to visit friends and discussing, in breathless anticipation, the arrival of Charles and his Lads. The only pall that lay over these enjoyable duties was the absence of Claire's elder brother, recently commissioned and off to the Peninsula, but in their way, the morning engagements distracted her from that as well.

And if she wished to spend the afternoon pacing—not that she was pacing; she was merely taking a refreshing stroll up and down the precise length of the garden walk from which she could still see the drive—then that was her business and hers alone. Her mother's mouth had not, Claire was sure, twitched with amusement when Claire had announced her intention to take some air. Nor, surely, was her mother now watching from an upstairs window with poorly-concealed laughter on her features. No, she was merely smiling at her only daughter, and nothing more. Claire was determined, if not actually certain, of this, and carefully didn't look toward her mother's well-cut figure in the window for fear of dislodging her own determination.

Some little while ago dust had risen on the road, lifting Claire's spirits with it. In due time, though, that dust had ejected not a trio of young men, but a wagon filled with victuals intended to sustain three strapping youths over the course of four days. Claire's spirits had been hopelessly dashed. Now she presented an expression of complete indifference to a new cloud rising from the end of the drive, though her heart beat at an unnatural pace and her fingers were white about the knuckles where she strangled a trembling sapling with her grip.

Charles had, in her memory, been *quite* handsome: tall and with the promise of shoulders that any maiden would swoon for. He looked a great deal like their grandfather, or at least like the paintings of that gentleman (in, of course, his youth) which now adorned the halls of the Dalton residence in Town. It stood to reason, then, that Charles's friends would also be handsome, as they were all gentlemen and surely like called to like. Claire's first glimpse would tell all, and that was well worth skulking about in the garden.

Not that she was skulking. She lacked the opportunity to re-form that thought into a more pleasant interpretation before the carriage—no, the riders!—appeared. All three of the young men rode ahead of the carriage, so far ahead of it that its dust cloud had become a distant lie about their approach. They were *so* far ahead of it, in fact, that although she had been watching for them for three hours, their arrival came as a surprising thunder of hooves and laughter.

All of them sat beautifully upon their horses, with buckskins and Hessians, round-fronted tailcoats and light, capeless great coats all of such fine quality that in the rush of their appearance, not one man could be said to stand out from the others. Two of them had dark hair and the third, light, but beyond that, there were no immediately distinguishing characteristics. Hardly worth peering through the hedges for, Claire thought with a sniff of irritation. She took a single step back, and in doing so, attracted the attention of one of the riders. He had been in the lead, but without warning he spun his horse—a fine bay gelding —so that he circled the other two and came up behind them. He was not, though, attuned to his companions, but rather to the gardens beside the drive. Appealingly, he was framed, as if deliberately, by a slender archway in the hedge that allowed egress and exit from the garden to the drive.

Claire saw at once that he fell short of devastatingly handsome—a slight weakness of chin in profile stole that from him, though as his gaze came around to her, it became evident that his jaw had all the necessary breadth from the front to disguise its minor lack in profile. His nose, though, was perfect, and his cheekbones so sharp as to have been carved by a razor. Black hair was worn full of height and swept forward so that the fringe softened the width of his forehead; sideburns accentuated both his cheekbones and the length of his jaw.

Their gazes locked and a jolt of excitement stopped Claire's heart, only to have it start again at a racing pace as a wickedly sly half-smile slid over full and sensual lips. His eyes were as blue as a lightning flash, and Claire stood as though struck by them, unable to retreat or advance. It made no matter: he had seen her, his smile was for her alone, and he would sweep her into his arms, unguarded against passion, and within hours he would ask to speak to Claire's father privately, neither of them able to wait a moment longer than necessary for consummation of the fire that even now burned in both their breasts —

"What ho!" this vision of manliness cried, "Charles, there is a mouse in the garden!"

The girl herself, truth be told, was barely visible within the long confines of a poke bonnet. Her bonnet, though, glimpsed through the tangle of branches and changing leaves that lined the drive to the Daltons' country home, made so strong an impression of a mouse's quivering nose extending from a hole that Benedict Fairburn spoke before he thought. The words had barely left his lips when he saw the girl more clearly through the green archway that separated drive from garden. Dismay clawed his voice, and any amelioration he might have made, away.

Beyond the bonnet, a prim and old-fashioned dress did so little for the girl's attributes that it could only have been chosen to disguise them, or by a servant grateful to wear the outdated cast-offs of a wealthy mistress. He had shown poor enough manners by calling attention to her. It was worse yet to tease someone of such obviously lower rank than himself. His companions wheeled about, already laughing. Flushed with embarrassment, Benedict did his best to wave them off. "Never mind, it was a mean jape, let us ride on—"

Charles, a man of more genial nature than his wartime reputation suggested, chuckled agreeably and clicked to his horse, bringing it around again. Evander Hewitt, though, somewhat meaner than Benedict remembered from school, urged his forward a few steps, ducking to peer through the arch at the young woman. "Looks like a mouse to me, Benny. Shall I be the cat?" He pressed the horse forward, moving implacably toward the girl.

Just beyond Hewitt's shoulder, Benedict saw the girl's expression clear to such forthright astonishment that the vividness of her green eyes became visible despite the bonnet's depths. She did not, he thought with surprised admiration, look afraid. But then, she could withdraw easily enough: they were in a garden, not an alleyway, where Hewitt's horse would block any avenue of escape.

Still, it had already gone far enough. Benedict said, "Hewitt," at the same time Dalton, more firmly, said, "Evander," but neither man's voice stopped their third. He advanced, smirking with anticipation of the girl's oncoming fearful break.

Instead, she held her ground, small jaw set within the confines of her bonnet. There was hardly anything to her, Benedict thought. She was a slight and delicate creature, not much larger than a mouse after all, though there had never been a mouse with such a forthright gaze. The set of his shoulders said even Hewitt lost confidence in the face of her calm. Pride kept him urging the horse onward, though, until the girl, who had not moved a step, put her hand up with slow and gentle certainty to take the animal's bridle at the cheek piece. The horse blew a lippy breath full of commentary as it lowered its head. Hewitt's spine, already stiff with his riding posture, went positively rigid.

The girl took no notice of him at all. She could not, Benedict realized with slow horror, be a servant, regardless of how unfashionable her gown was. No servant, not even Dalton's valet Worthington, who ranked among the most unflappable men Benedict had ever encountered, could remain so arrogantly collected in the face of three gentlemen and their horses. He was not surprised, then, when the girl placed a gentle hand on the horse's nose and murmured to it in cultured, dulcet tones, "What utterly appalling creatures you travel with, my beauty. I don't suppose you would care to dump the one astride you into the garden pond? Well, yes, I'm certain you would, but you are far too well-mannered a beast to do such a thing, aren't you? What a shame."

She lifted her gaze then, to look through Hewitt as if he were not there at all, to disregard Benedict as if he were something too unpleasant to acknowledge, and to lance Charles with disgust. "Cousin Charles. I'm sure you are welcome to my father's house. I expect you remember where the stables are. Perhaps you and your companions could take yourselves there, tend to your horses, and before dinner is announced, do something about the dreadful smell of horse embedded in your clothes and skin. Good afternoon." With another gentle touch to the horse's nose, showing clearly that it stood highest in her estimation of the gathering before her, the girl turned, walked away, and did not look back.

All three men gazed after her, mesmerized, Benedict with the heat of bad manners scalding his cheeks. He had not yet scraped together an apology to Charles, much less attempted to form one to offer to the young woman, when Hewitt barked, "Well! Good thing we're not here for the society, isn't it?"

"That was badly done, Evander," Charles said quietly. Dalton never spoke loudly, not anymore, Benedict thought. He'd been hotter of head in their school days, but not since his return from the front. Now he was always reserved, even in his sensibility, and yet his mild tone caved even Hewitt's stiff posture.

Sullen, he muttered, "Thought she was a servant. and I'd put a scare into her, that's all."

"It is almost worse to terrorize a serving girl than a gentlewoman," Dalton said in the same softly chiding voice. "A lady might have the education, self-possession and wit to stand her ground, as my cousin did, whereas a servant could only quake and tremble for fear of losing her position if she dared defend herself. Fear is no way to live a life, Evan. Come. We have horses and, if Miss Dalton is to believed — and I dare say she is — bathing to attend to."

With the faintest uncomfortable suspicion that the smooth waters of Dalton's tones could turn suddenly dangerous and rough, and that Miss Claire Dalton might well be a topic that could set those rough waters a-boil, Benedict followed after his host and tried not to think too long on the green-eyed girl.

His cousin had not, it seemed, grown much in stature, though she had retained the boldness he recalled from her girlhood. Dalton smiled as he led the Lads toward the stables, where, despite Claire's pointed suggestion, they handed the beasts over to the stable-boys rather than tend to the animals themselves. He was, indeed, smiling still when he met the other two at the stable doors, and Fairburn blushed to see Dalton's humor still engaged.

"I'm ashamed of myself, Dalton, I truly am. I'll apologize to Miss Dalton—"

"If she'll let you," Charles said with an upward flick of his eyebrows. "I remember Claire as a proper little thing, Benny, but deuced if she didn't hold her ground once she'd made a decision. She may go through the forms, but whether she'll forgive you, that's something else entirely!" Still with uplifted eyebrows, he added, for clarity's sake, "*You*, Evan, will apologize."

Hewitt's lip curled. "You've just said she wouldn't accept it."

"And yet." Charles offered one of his gentlest smiles and watched with a trace of sorrow as Evander Hewitt's shoulders bowed slightly, as if the smile had the weight of a blow.

Evander had been generous in boyhood, a generosity made easy by an income guaranteed to him as both only child and beloved son, and by good looks that artists loved to paint. Things had changed since their school days, though, many things, and where generosity had once flowed, meanness now too often ran in its stead. Several of the other lads—not just lads, but *the* Lads, half a dozen of them in all who were closest to Dalton's heart in friendship—didn't care for Hewitt, but thus far they were all willing to tolerate him for Dalton's sake. Dalton himself had lost too much to give up on this Lad, and so Hewitt remained.

He also nodded, muttering an agreement to apologize, and to Dalton's way of thinking, all was once again right with the world. He fell into step between the Lads, momentarily aware that he stood—if they were to measure men as they did horses—a full hand shorter than the other two. Claire's diminutive size was something of a family trait, although Dalton considered his friends tall, rather than thinking of himself as short. The three of them passed through the stable doors together before Dalton took the lead, though anyone could see the pathway to the main house.

It was a fine-looking manor, not ostentatiously large and set into well-kept lawns and gardens that had not yet lost the jeweled colors of summer. A chicken yard and vegetable garden, attended by a white-capped girl who dipped a curtsy as the Lads passed by, lay between stables and house. The whole of it made a pretty picture, the very essence of a quiet, comfortable country life. There were lands enough to hunt on—indeed, that had been much of the appeal in agreeing to his uncle's invitation—and there were, aside from Claire, no young women to confuse a lads' holiday with the never-ending Society nonsense of matchmaking. Charles had returned from the Peninsular War some weeks ago only to be accosted by his parents' hopes of a swift and suitable marriage, a barrage as ceaseless as the guns of war. He consequently spent as many waking hours as possible in the Lads' company, avoiding not only his mother's unsubtle hints but what few parties and socials that nice society held in the autumn. His Uncle George's offer of a country visit had been a respite Charles both desperately desired and felt was ideal for the time of year; London was dull in September. All this reflection took him in companionable silence around the chicken yard and toward the front doors. Just before they swept open, Benedict seized Charles's arm and spoke in a tone of nervous concern.

"Cease your musing, Charles, and tell me what to do if Miss Dalton refuses my apology. I'm unaccustomed to insulting young ladies."

"Brave it out, man," Dalton said in surprise. "She won't be rude, and aside from meals, there's no call to speak to the girl. We're here for a bit of sport, not to fuss over whether a country miss has had her nose put out of joint. Besides, it's Hewitt who tried to intimidate her and from whom a proper apology is necessary. You only made an unfortunate remark."

"But one that needs redressing." Fairburn straightened his shoulders, earning an eye-roll from Hewitt before the doors opened and all three Lads were ushered in.

Dalton was drawn directly into an embrace by his short, sweet-faced aunt, whose dress, he noted, was no more fashionable than that of her daughter's. The house, at a glance, gleamed and was well-kept, suggesting their lack was in a sartorial sense, not funds, though it was possible a commission for their son had set them back farther than they might care to admit. But, no: in thinking about it, it seemed to Charles that even when he was young, his aunt's fashion sense had been some years behind the times. Having a daughter of marriageable age had not, it seemed, improved the matter. George Dalton, a man of middling height and little hair, was not badly out of fashion, but men's styles changed less rapidly than did women's.

"Charles Edward," his aunt, oblivious to his thoughts, said with real pleasure. "What a delight to see you again."

"Aunt Sylvia. You look well. Uncle George." Dalton shook the latter's hand, then, smiling, allowed himself to be drawn into an embrace there as well. The elder Dalton gentleman rumbled a greeting, surprising Charles, as always, with the unexpected depth of his voice from such an unprepossessing man. "And George Arnold?"

"In Spain." Sylvia Dalton put visible effort into not allowing a shadow to cross her smiling face. "Not at the front, or not last that we heard. And these are your friends?"

"Yes, of course. May I present you to Mr and Mrs Dalton, my beloved uncle and aunt. Aunt, Uncle, these are Benedict Fairburn and Evander Hewitt. You will recall me speaking of them, perhaps, from my school days."

Hands were kissed and shaken with polite murmurings as Aunt Sylvia said, "You would be Benny and Evan," with a smile. "How splendid to finally meet you. Claire mentioned you were all in dire hope of a bath before supper, so I've had hot water sent up. I hope Worthington won't be too put out." Her light blue eyes sparkled, bringing a laugh to Dalton's lips.

"I see you remember him too. Well, he's traveling with the carriage and our belongings, so he can't protest too strenuously if I'm clean before he arrives. I have no doubt our dinner wear will be laid out and presentable, all at his able hand, before we're out of the bath."

"Knowing Worthington, he may well somehow have it done before you're in the bath. Best hurry before he proves me right." Uncle George's words were made droller yet by the depth of his voice.

Charles felt Fairburn and Hewitt exchange a surprised glance as they heard George's voice properly for the first time. As a footman escorted them up to their rooms, Benedict breathed, "He ought to have been a politician, with that voice."

"I believe he was slated to be," Charles murmured in response. "But he fell quite in love with my aunt rather than make the fortuitous marriage my grandfather had arranged for him, and in pique the old man cut him off. They retired to the country to live on Aunt Sylvia's younger brother's sufferance, but he died in a riding accident when I was only a child. There being no others of her lineage, she inherited this house and lands. It nearly gave my grandfather apoplexy to have his disinherited son come into such comfort."

"Charming family," Hewitt muttered.

Charles chuckled as they were led into their separate rooms. "Cast no stones, Evan. Heaven knows what we all are, beneath the surface."

For a country estate with no pretensions at grandeur, Worthington decided the Dalton house was tremendously well presented. The room appointed to his immediate employer, young Master Dalton, was spacious enough to house a large bed and wardrobe with a vanity without crowding, yet small enough that the generous fireplace would easily warm it on a cold winter's day. Even the uppermost corners were clean of cobweb and soot. The leaded glass windows fit snugly into their frame, and the shutters were padded to hold in heat. The colors were, if not fashionable, at least pleasant, and were kept up; there were no faded patches in the duvet cover or on the upholstered chair, and the mirror above the fireplace reflected wallpaper of handsomely striped cream and burgundy.

He had been suitably welcomed by the staff. The butler himself had shown Worthington the way to Charles Edward's room while the three footmen carried luggage to each of the young men's rooms. When the footmen were gone, Worthington had, in a politely conspiratorial voice, wondered if there was anything within the household of which he should be aware. He was informed in an equally conspiratorial tone of the set-to betwixt Miss Dalton and the Lads upon their arrival, observed, the Dalton's butler murmured, by a maid watching from an upper window. Worthington extended his gratitude for the bit of knowledge, and butler and valet alike had shared the brief, expressionless look perfected by servants the world over that spoke volumes about the ladies and gentlemen they served without ever betraying a word or a thought of it on their faces. Both parties departed the discussion with the satisfaction of knowing they could work comfortably with the other man.

The young master's clothes were, of course, unpacked, and a suit pressed and laid out for the evening before he emerged from the bath. For some reason that caused Charles Edward to laugh, but laughter had been rare enough from him in the past months, and Worthington was glad to hear it. He now helped Dalton slip a deep blue, double-breasted tailcoat over his shoulders as the young master observed himself in the mirror, Worthington an unremarkable shadow in its background. Dalton turned twice, examining the fall of the tails to the backs of his knees and the admirable upward nip of the front, then brushed his thumbs down the lapels with satisfaction. "I believe that will do, Worthington, thank you. Tell me, is my aunt and uncle's house a tight ship? Do you approve?"

Worthington lifted his eyes to meet Dalton's in the mirror, his own non-committal brown; Dalton's a lazy hazel. "Of course, sir." He took precisely enough breath after the last word to leave things unsaid, and Charles Edward, of course, seized upon them.

"But?"

"It wouldn't be my place to say, sir."

"Oh, please, Worthington. I know we're back in civilized territory, but must we return to all that prattle?" Dalton shook off Worthington's hands so he could face the valet with all the laziness gone from his hazel eyes. "Haven't we been through enough to forgo the niceties of society, at least in private?"

"What is practiced in private cannot be forgotten in public," Worthington replied, but held up a hand to forestall his master's complaint. "Very well, sir. I may have heard that your companions, Master Hewitt in particular, were badly behaved toward Miss Dalton."

"Oh, that." The laziness came into Dalton's

eyes as he waved the concern away. "I've spoken to them already, Worthington. They'll apologize, both of them. Anything else?"

Worthington hesitated, examining his employer's features. Dalton was monied, of course, his parents having easily afforded a commission that the young man had not necessarily required. Nor had he needed to serve at the front; he might have had a safe and respectable desk job that no one would have sneered at, but such caution was not in Charles Dalton. Serving had been a passion; serving well, an obligation to that passion.

Similarly, Worthington might have stayed behind, sending a more adventuresome valet in his stead, or indeed allowing Dalton's person to be cared for from within the military ranks. But Worthingtons had served Daltons for over half a century, and James Allen Worthington would not be the son to abandon his duty. He had grown up with—or near, at least—Dalton, who was only a few years his junior; they had been man and servant since Dalton's eighteenth year, just under a decade now. There had never been any real question that Worthington would join Charles wherever he went.

Nor was there any question that if Worthington felt strongly about any topic that he should, in time, be able to make his employer aware of it, though that was in Worthington's opinion the duty of any valet. It was somewhat less expected, perhaps, that a man of Dalton's stature might deign to listen to his valet's opinions, but listen he did.

That did not mean the moment was always right to express one of those opinions. Worthington, judging Dalton's pleasantly curious guise, concluded that this was not the time. The softness had already slid once from Dalton's gaze, and Worthington knew well what dangers the harder edge in Dalton's eyes could unveil. So rather than pursue topics that could ignite a fire, the valet straightened the tall and slim lines of Dalton's ballroom cravat and, with a step back, said, "Nothing, sir, now that I've got that tidied."

"Very good. I'll call for you after dinner, Worthington. I think I can manage until then."

"Probably not, sir," Worthington said dryly, "but I'm sure you'll muddle through."

Dalton grinned, the familiar and friendly smile of an equal, and clapped his hand to Worthington's shoulder before hastening to the dinner call. Worthington trailed a few steps behind, retreating as the other Lads came down an opposite stair to meet Dalton at the landing. Worthington, silent and attentive, might have been no more than another sculpture.

But he watched Evander Hewitt, and as the Lads departed, Hewitt's sharp gaze met Worthington's neutral one. The valet lowered his eyes as was appropriate to his station, and knew that Hewitt could not read the mistrust that Worthington felt in his bones.

Chapter Two

Claire threw her bonnet onto her bed as if the offending article's mouse-like attributes might be vanquished if dashed with sufficient force. They were not, of course, and all pleasure in her appearance fled. She didn't bother to change for dinner; there seemed no purpose, when she was already as well-dressed as she could be and yet still worthy of sneers from gentlemen.

Inevitably, she regretted that decision upon entering the waiting room: Charles was bedecked in a navy tailcoat and trousers, and the other two Lads were irritatingly splendid in black. The bolder of the two wore a waterfall cravat whilst the other's jaw-tracing collar improved the line of his chin. The truth was they were rather formidable when presented together, while Charles Edward looked small and dashing between the two dark-haired Lads, who were so alike they could be brothers.

Her parents had not yet arrived, leaving Claire to feel alone and plain as the gentlemen bowed and she curtsied briefly in return. "Claire," Charles said with a note of apology, "I'm afraid I failed to make proper introductions earlier. May I present my friends Benedict Fairburn and Evander Hewitt? Gentlemen, my cousin, Miss Dalton."

"Miss Dalton." Fairburn of the slightly weak chin, a minor defect that seemed vastly more pronounced and unforgivable than it had been upon first sight, stepped forward immediately, his blue eyes beseeching. "I wish to extend an apology for my rudeness earlier. I cannot think what came over me, save for too many hours with my gentlemen friends and not enough time with the gentler sex."

"Mr Fairburn." Claire allowed him to take her hand, grateful for the gloves they both wore preventing their skin from touching. "With all due respect to my cousin, if your gentlemen friends are all so poorly raised that exposure to them causes you to forget your manners, perhaps you should consider finding new friends."

A pained line appeared between Fairburn's brows. "I shall take your suggestion under advisement, Miss Dalton. Let me again extend my apologies."

"They have been extended, Mr Fairburn. Let us not embarrass ourselves by dwelling on them." Feeling rather proud of herself, Claire turned her attention on Hewitt, who had all of Fairburn's looks without the fatally flawed jaw. He was, in fact, preposterously attractive, and flashed a smile so white and disarming that, could she not vividly recall the meanness of his mouth as he advanced his horse on her, she might have been swept away immediately. Fortunately, she thought coolly, she was a more sensible creature than that, and so rather than cowing her, the memory brought to mind the spine-stiffening rage she had felt earlier.

She could not know that her remembered anger brought a becoming flush to her cheeks, nor that her eyes were particularly green as she fixed Hewitt with a scathing and expectant gaze. She only knew that her dress, so admirable earlier in the day, now seemed dowdy and that she would not, under any circumstances, let any of the Lads know she felt her lack of fashion keenly.

Hewitt put forth a hand; she placed hers above it, not so much as touching glove to glove. To her surprise, he didn't take her fingers in his. Instead, he bowed extravagantly over her extended hand, never taking his eyes from hers. "I am a cad," he said with an air of rote duty. "I would beg your forgiveness if I thought there was any hope of earning it. Rather, I shall freely admit my faults and hope that you will either be kind enough to overlook them or that I shall be sufficiently unobtrusive throughout our visit as to permit you to ignore me. All that prevents me from a lifetime of sleepless nights with guilt gnawing at my soul is the perfect conviction that the very moment I leave these halls you will never think of me again, so meaningless and irrelevant is my imposition and callow behavior in your life."

It was delivered with such egregious insincerity that Claire, to her horror, found it necessary to bite the inside of her cheek to keep from smiling. Charles found it equally necessary to look elsewhere, a hand suddenly moving to cover his mouth as if a cough wished to escape. Only Fairburn showed no signs of humor at all, which made it funnier. Claire, employing steely control, refused to let her amusement show, saying, "I am sure you are correct about that last, Mr Hewitt, and here are my parents, so I believe we may go in to dinner now."

It had, in truth, only been their footsteps in the hall that she had heard, but announcing them gave her the chance to not quite accept Hewitt's apology, just as she had not quite accepted Fairburn's. With a sense of satisfaction —of self-reliance—she curtsied to each of the men and accepted her cousin's arm to follow her parents into the dining room.

It was intolerable that Hewitt had been forgiven and he had not. Any fool could see that Miss Dalton had been unable to retain her fury in the face of Hewitt's outrageous performance of an apology. Benedict's forehead settled into a furrow every time he forgot to school his features into pleasantry. A headache built behind that furrow, and to stave it off he drank a little more wine than was wise, followed, in the study with the other gentlemen, by a great deal more port than was wise. By the end of the evening — which came on tremendously late indeed, with the foyer clock ringing so few chimes he lacked the wit to start counting their number before they ended — by that time he could no longer remember precisely what had angered him. All he knew was that he liked Hewitt even less than usual, and that Miss Claire Dalton had become, through the haze of drink, a positively bewitching creature.

Morning came with violent brightness, autumnal sun somehow borrowing its midsummer strength to pierce Benedict's eyelids when an unforgivable servant whipped the curtains and shutters aside. An entirely too familiar voice with no hint of sympathy for his delicate state proclaimed, "You will be late for the luncheon, Master Fairburn, and as your compatriots intend a vigorous afternoon of shooting, Master Dalton feels strongly that you should be roused and fed at all costs."

Even the least sensible of men could call the sound Benedict made no less than a moan. He rolled, searching for a pillow with which to block the light, and felt it plucked from his hands by Worthington's ruthless grip. "They cannot be well enough to hunt," Benedict protested, but if Worthington had been sent there was no hope for it: he would be dressed, fed and sat upon a horse whether he felt able or not. A resigned groan followed the moan, and within appallingly little time, each of those terrible things had come to pass. Astride his bay, Benedict didn't dare look back for fear of seeing the valet — Charles's own valet, as though the gentleman's gentleman of the house was insufficiently trusted for this duty! — dusting his hands as if satisfied with a job adequately done.

Dalton and Hewitt were aggravatingly well, leaving Benedict to wonder how much of the port had gone down his own gullet the night before, when he'd thought they were partaking equally. But Hewitt's smile said otherwise, and Dalton rode forth to shoot without a care in the world for Benedict's sensitive skull. Benedict gave grim attention to gold-and-green trees on the near horizon rather than the painfully brilliant blue sky, and so it was Benedict who saw another rider coming toward them with a seat and skill so confident that it was enviable even in the distance. A cloak fluttered around the rider's shoulders, warding off what little chill might be imagined in the golden autumn afternoon, and a hat of dramatic proportion shadowed his face.

"Your uncle's joining us, Dalton." Benedict strove for good nature and cheer in his tone, and to his own ear barely escaped despair. Surely Mr Dalton had drunk as much as Benny had, and would be as sensitive to the fowling pieces' reports as Benedict was. Perhaps they could retreat to the house, there to...begin drinking again, Benedict concluded, unable to think of a cure more appealing than the hair of the dog. So intent was he upon this fantasy that he half-missed Dalton's response, and then, unable to fully believe what he had heard, was obliged to say, "Beg your pardon?"

"I said that's not Uncle George; it's Claire. Uncle rides like a sack of potatoes, but Claire has always had a flair for it. Showed her brother up by the time she was eight. Shot?" He hefted the gun, offering it to Benedict, who took it absently and peered over its gleaming barrel at the oncoming rider.

Deuced if it wasn't Miss Dalton, at that. Unforgivable. The cloak had disguised her figure and the foppish hat was, in fact, her hair, half-undone by the wind's greedy fingers as she rode. Benedict flushed, suddenly taken with envy for the wind and a curiosity as to how soft those dark curls might be.

At his ear, Hewitt bellowed, "Quail!" and despite the too-bright day, despite the distraction Miss Dalton provided, despite no intention what-so-ever to pull a trigger when his head already swam with the residue of last night's drinking, Benedict straightened in his saddle, swung the fowling piece around, squinted against the blue sky, and fired. A brace of birds fell even as Benedict twisted his mouth against the redoubled ringing in his ears.

A brief, impressed silence was broken by Dalton's, "Bloody good shot, Benny, bloody good. Didn't think you had it in you today."

Benedict muttered something even he failed to understand and handed the gun to Dalton. "Thanks. If you don't mind, I think I'll call that my contribution to tonight's dinner and..."

He was uncertain whether his plans were to ride with Miss Dalton or retreat to the gamekeeper's house, but neither was to be allowed. Miss Dalton, somewhat to Benedict's dismay, rode up to them as he searched for a method of escape, and with her words sealed any hope he had of departing unscorned: "Not a bad shot, Mr Fairburn. I wonder, Charles, if I might have a go?"

"No," Charles replied without a hint of chivalry. "I recall clearly that it was barely tolerable that you could out-ride both myself and George by the time you were eight, as a fine seat on horseback is a gentlewoman's trait. I also recall that you were in very near danger of out-shooting us both by the time you were twelve, and my ego cannot bear to find out how badly you have now outstripped me."

"Ladies do not shoot," Benedict said with such surprise that he sounded to himself like the worst of old aunties, not the rough-and-tumble brassy women of the previous generation, but older even than that, so decrepit their childhoods were long since lost to memory.

Hewitt, as blandly as he had apologized the night before, handed his gun to Miss Dalton. "Show Charles up, Miss Dalton, and shock poor

Fairburn. I, for one, am eager to see it."

Benedict's ears flamed. "My apologies. I didn't mean to suggest — it's merely unusual — I have no objection — "

"How terribly kind of you, Mr Fairburn." Claire Dalton accepted Hewitt's gun, examined it briefly, reloaded it, then with a casual air dipped her hand into her saddlebag to withdraw a small stone. The bag shifted in such a way as to suggest there were more of the same within it, but before he could pursue curiosity on that topic, Miss Dalton rose a scant inch or two in her saddle — sidesaddles were not as suited for standing in as his own — and proved herself to have a remarkably good arm as she threw the stone into the tall grass of the pasture before them.

Quail erupted upward. She lifted Hewitt's gun, sighted and shot thrice, each shot bringing a bird to earth. All three men watched in respectful, slightly astonished silence. Benedict could hardly take his eyes from the girl. She seemed an entirely different creature from the one he had embarrassed the afternoon before, and he could hardly imagine how he had thought her a mouse. He had never met a less mouse-like lady in his life, nor even imagined one whose interests might align with his own so closely.

That thought lay perilously close to a path of commitment that might delight his mother but which held no interest at all for Benedict himself. He shuddered slightly, throwing off the very idea, and in so doing, noticed a dog he had not seen before. It had, he feared, come with Miss Dalton, suggesting she had intended this encounter all along, for it now rippled through the grass, collecting birds as Charles let forth an explosive sigh. "I knew it. Claire, you outshine me in every regard. You ought to have been born a man."

"If I had been born a man, my poor mother would never have been able to bring me into this world," Claire said with shocking humor, "and had I been born a boy, which you no doubt meant, cousin, well then, as a second son I would have been destined for the church and would never have learned to shoot."

"How *did* you learn to shoot?" Benedict burst out, unable to contain his curiosity.

Miss Dalton's eyebrows lifted. "With practice, Mr Fairburn, just as anyone might."

"I recall," Dalton said dryly, "that she was as contented a miss as ever there was, attending to embroidery and chattering with her friends. A pretty half-dozen there were, with hair of every hue. But her girlfriends only visited, whilst her brother George was with her at all times. He is five years her elder, and I believe Claire was determined from infancy that she should be both entirely at home with the ladies and yet never left behind by the lads. I fear my own visits only spurred her onward."

"You gave me another mark to match myself

against," Miss Dalton agreed. "With George gone to the Peninsula I've recently been obliged to teach a few of my girlfriends to shoot, though none of them are as fond of it as I."

"Well, I tell you what, Dalton," said Hewitt, "if all the Empire's daughters can shoot like that, we ought to be sending them up against Bonny while our lads stay home and tend the fires."

"I am sure I could not shoot at a man," Miss Dalton said in a quiet and civilized murmur as she returned Hewitt's gun to him. "It is little enough sport to put a bird on the table, but men shoot back, and I would never cast aspersions on the bravery of soldiers such as Charles by pretending I might stand among them. And now that I am put in mind of it, this seems little sport to me indeed. Excuse me, gentlemen. I believe I shall return home and write to my brother."

Upon this announcement she nodded to each of them, conveying a note of formality that might do a duchess proud, then rode away with her spine straight and the dog trailing after with three birds dangling from its jaw.

"I believe she did that on purpose." Fairburn's usually pleasant tones were strained.

The corner of Charles's mouth twitched, though he did his best to respond evenly. "I believe she may have done, yes. All of it, although she could not have anticipated

Hewitt offering her such an opportunity to castigate him on the matter of warfare. The reminder that George is at war was masterful." By the end of this speech he could no longer help himself, and smiled openly. "But by the deuce, Benny, you should have seen your eyes pop at her aim. Yours too, Evan. I did say she was better than I."

"You intimated she *might* be," Hewitt protested. "You couldn't expect me to believe it."

"Do I often mislead you, Evan?" Charles asked genially. "I find the truth generally more efficient than prevarications. It hardly matters now, gentlemen. I believe we have been thoroughly put in our places, and I can hardly imagine Claire will bother herself with us any more, now that we are all assured that she is by some considerable measure the superior being amongst us. Benny, will you shoot again?"

Fairburn took Dalton's gun this time, but watched Claire's retreating form. Well, Charles thought, hardly retreating; that implied defeat. Fairburn watched Claire's *departing* form, then, and looked a trifle dejected when she chose not to look back at the men. No confident victor would need to, though, not when there was no chance of attack from behind. If her brother George Arnold had half her poise and cunning for engagement, he would do well in the war.

Tension drew Dalton's shoulders together, pinching his spine. He let his eyes close languidly, exhaling to release knots before they formed, then reawakened his gaze to the bright afternoon. The entire purpose of a country holiday was to put thoughts of the war aside. It was too much spoken of in London, and too few imagined that a man might not wish to tell tales of what he had seen and done, or why a fit man in his prime might have been sent home when the battles still raged on. The Lads had not pressed him, though even now Hewitt slid a considering glance his way, as if questions lay unspoken on his tongue. Perhaps it had been a mistake to bring Hewitt without Vincent or O'Brien along; their presence as men who had fought alongside Dalton kept Hewitt's curiosity at bay. But there had been other reasons to single Fairburn and Hewitt out. They were his school friends, representing a time and an innocence Dalton was loathe to lose. Was eager to reclaim, even, if such a thing was possible.

"The birds, Benny, are the other direction," Dalton said wryly, before Hewitt had got up the courage to breach the topic of war again, close as it lay to the surface. Fairburn blanched, then blushed — Dalton didn't remember him so inclined to obvious emotion, but then, it had been a long time, and sensibility was highly in fashion — and turned back to the meadow.

"I ought to have borrowed Miss Dalton's bag of stones to flush them out. Your cousin is well prepared, Dalton. She'll be formidable when she has her Season." With that alarming statement — not one of the Lads ought, in

Dalton's opinion, be considering young women or the Season—Fairburn nudged his horse into a quick trot that startled another group of quail, and brought down two more before they settled. "I say, has your uncle stocked these fields for us? The shooting is more than fair. I'll have to offer him my thanks. But we need at least five more if we're to make a meal of them. Hewitt, did you intend on shooting, or just handing your gun off to—"

"Mice?" asked Hewitt archly, and only pulled a thin smile when Dalton gave him a quelling look. "You're right, Dalton, she had it over all of us. I'll call her my little mouse now if I want to, but I won't mistake her for a creature without teeth."

"You will not in my hearing," Dalton said, "nor, if you are wise, will you do so in hers. Particularly, I think, if you are inclined to call her *your* little mouse. No, I should not do that, if I were you. Now, Fairburn is right. It's well past time you aired more than a brag, and brought a few quail to the table yourself."

"I haven't noticed you bagging anything," Hewitt said with a sniff. Beside him, Fairburn, who had bristled amusingly at Hewitt's threat to call Claire *his* little mouse, now shifted in such a way as to speak of wary stillness, as if he saw Hewitt's latest comment as treading increasingly dangerous waters. Interesting, Charles thought, with a softening of his heart. In school, he would have called Evan the more sensitive of his two friends, but since Charles's return from the war, Benny seemed the more able to recognize topics he didn't want to discuss. More to the point, Benedict appeared to recognize when conversation began to turn too closely to those topics. *He* would not have commented on Charles's failure to take aim, and indeed, now he spoke, voice light.

"It's a shooting holiday meant for *us*, Evan. Be embarrassing, wouldn't it, if he had to make up the numbers himself? Come on, now. Miss Dalton managed three. You can at least match that, can't you?" With a sigh so dramatic it mocked, Fairburn hefted Dalton's gun again. "I suppose I can bring down another brace myself, if you're unreliable."

"How dare you call me unreliable! I might call a man out for saying such a thing, Fairburn!"

"That seems unnecessary, doesn't it?" Fairburn leaned over a few inches, as if to confide in the other man. "Go on, then. I'll flush them out. All you have to do is shoot." He rode forward, startling more quail into the air. Charles, smiling, followed along behind the two men, listening to them bicker between the echoes of gunfire.

Miss Claire Dalton sat at her writing desk in the library, a pose she had taken up the evening after the shooting and retained throughout the following day, particularly when there was any chance of the Lads seeing her. There was a ferocious precision to her attitude and a constant gentle scrape of pen against paper, but it did not escape Worthington's notice that the inkwell rarely needed refilling, nor did the stack of papers upon which she wrote much diminish.

It was not, of course, his place to comment, or indeed to even behave as though he had observed, and so he did not. Instead, the evening after the hunt, he merely made himself...*available*, by way of stopping a polite distance from where she sat prettily framed by a large window that reflected her slender image in its darkness.

Several minutes passed before she lifted her head, though Worthington had no doubt that she was aware of his presence since his arrival. Still, he was not her servant, and as a gentlewoman she was not expected to attend to the needs of the serving class before her own. When she did look at him, though, it was with her full attention, which grace was offered to very few of those who served. She was not a beauty — pretty, yes, but not one who would stop men in the street to gape at her — but the fullness of her regard made her attractive despite the perfectly dreadful high-necked gown she wore. Even if the pale puce had suited her (and it did not; a woman of Miss Dalton's complexion should wear jewel tones at all times, if only convention would allow it), the dress would make a sow's ear out of silk. Yet Worthington nearly forgot the horror of a dress as Miss Dalton examined him with a forthright green gaze, and he concluded if that was the case, properly attired she could have London at her feet, merely pretty or no.

"I remember you," she said unexpectedly. "From when we were young. From when Charles last visited. He was twenty or twenty-one, and you could not have been more than a year or two older. Worthington, isn't it?"

"Miss." Worthington nodded as much to indicate her correctness as to hide his own surprise. "I'm honored to be remembered."

"You were exceedingly proper," Miss Dalton said with a smile, "and exceedingly patient, and you rode better than Charles, but were careful to hide that when he was with us. You were kind," she concluded with a note of curiosity.

"Miss?" An absolute world of inflection could be put into a single repeated word, and with this one, Worthington invited her to satisfy that curiosity.

"Well, you didn't have to be, and I wonder why you were. Kind, that is. Proper and patient are to be expected from a valet, and I remember that your father was—is?" She smiled swiftly at Worthington's nod, clearly relieved to have not tread on a sorrow as she continued. "Is Uncle Charles's valet, and so I might have expected pride. Lots of servants, especially ones with a long history of serving a single family, are proud. But you were kind. To Charles, to

George, even to me. I fell once and the boys laughed and left me, but you stopped to help. I remember." She blushed suddenly, as if realizing she had been speaking for some time, and fell silent with a glance at the blank pages beside her. "Please," she added awkwardly. "You want to speak with me. Won't you sit?"

"I think not, Miss, but thank you. Kindness costs me nothing," Worthington said after a moment. "My father told me that when I was very young: that kindness costs me nothing, but can be worth a great deal to those it is offered to. I remember that you fell, that I offered you assistance. I did not imagine you would."

"It was worth a great deal to me." Claire offered a shy smile and an upward glance through her eyelashes so devoid of guile and to such effect that Worthington cleared his throat. She was entirely wasted in the country, he decided. Something would have to be done. "What," she asked then, "did you want to say to me?"

"Ah. It is impetuous, Miss, and perhaps not in keeping with the kindness you remember me with. Perhaps I should not have come."

Miss Dalton's smile flashed. "You can hardly retreat now, Worthington. My interest is piqued. What, pray tell, do you have to say?"

Worthington made an economical gesture toward her papers. "Only that while I am certain your brother is delighted at your dedication in writing to him, that I would…

implore you, Miss Dalton, to spend no more time pursuing an attitude of such propriety on behalf of the young gentlemen staying here. I believe even young Master Hewitt has been put in his place, which I assure you is not an easy task, and Master Fairburn has spent an inordinate amount of time speaking of his concern regarding your opinion of him. They are all in dread of what you have already said to your brother, and I might suggest that to present yourself so piously for any longer could, ah, undermine your salubrious efforts."

A thoughtful smile curled the corners of Miss Dalton's full lips. "Is that so, Worthington? How convenient that I have just now finished my letter to George, then. I wonder, my good man, if you might be troubled to post it for me in the morning."

Worthington all but clicked his heels together in swift agreement. "It would be no trouble at all, Miss Dalton. Indeed, it would be my pleasure."

"Thank you." Claire Dalton had, it seemed, written a letter after all, and a lengthy one at that. She took a stack of pages that had been set aside and shuffled them together into tidiness, then folded them neatly before addressing them with an elegant hand, and offering the packet to Worthington.

He accepted with the solemn neutrality that suited his class, and took a step backward. "Your servant, Miss."

"Wait!" Miss Dalton pressed a hand to her throat as if to modulate the cry that had burst forth. "I wonder if I might trouble you for a little more advice, Worthington."

"Your servant, Miss."

Claire's voice dropped precipitously, and she leaned forward. Worthington took one step forward to make up the distance he had retreated, then a second to assume a pose of confidentiality. "What," Miss Dalton whispered, "should I do now? About the Lads?"

"Ah." Worthington straightened and allowed the briefest smile to crack his mien. "Ignore them, Miss Dalton. Ignore them entirely."

"Oh." Surprise, then understanding slipped across Miss Dalton's features. "Oh. Yes, of course." Her eyes sparkled, and Worthington thought again she was wasted in the country, with slim pickings for young men to marry. Her smile this time was slower and much fuller, and she rose gracefully to find a book with which to engage herself. Book in hand, she assumed an attitude of carelessness and waved him away. "Thank you, Worthington. You may go now."

"Miss," Worthington said a final time, and departed with a sense of satisfaction.

Something would have to be done.

Chapter Three

London was loud, noisome, soot-blackened, crowded, loud, and altogether the most splendid place Claire Dalton had ever been.

She had visited her aunt and uncle there twice, once as a child when Charles was away at school, and once only a few years ago, while Charles was at war. But it was one thing to visit and another entirely to be invited to be invited to Aunt Elizabeth's for the Season. Claire still was wont to clutch the letter in disbelief, though she had now been in London for three magnificent days. None-the-less, the letter remained to hand for re-reading and reassurance, as if without it as a talisman, London might slip away. She even slept with the wonderful missive beneath her pillow.

It had been expected that she would go to London for her Season, but there had never been any hurry about the matter. Italian romances might have passionate lovers of thirteen and fourteen, but young people of *her* class required permission to marry before age twenty-one, and Claire had only recently turned twenty. Mother and Father had intended to rent a house the following Season, once she had reached an age of majority, and conduct the business of marrying off their only daughter then. Aunt Elizabeth's letter had set those plans on their ear, for not only did she offer to host Claire for *this* Season, but insisted that she would take on the cost of appropriate attire for a young woman's first Season in London.

There was no doubt what-so-ever that it was a gift beyond expectation. The Daltons were a respectable family name, but Aunt Elizabeth had been the only child of a rich man, and was now the source of any fortune the Daltons might claim. George and Sylvia Dalton would put their daughter out respectably, but Elizabeth and Charles Dalton could do it with style. Claire had been bustled into Town, shown the house, then stood in front of a tall French dressmaker with large, confident hands, who clucked, winced, and twitched her way through Claire's wardrobe before finally turning to Aunt Elizabeth in sour disapproval. "This will never do," the woman—Madame Babineaux, announced, by Aunt Elizabeth, to be one of the finest private dressmakers in Town—proclaimed. "We must start over from the beginning." Her accent was dramatically thick, rendering each word a puzzle.

Aunt Elizabeth nodded agreement. With that nod, Claire began a three-day regime of being fed, walked in the garden as if a pet in need of exercise, and hustled into the upper rooms of the Daltons' fine townhouse. Madame Babineaux became increasingly comprehensible as the days wore on and Claire's wardrobe improved. Claire could not decide if she had become accustomed to the woman's accent or if it had become more decipherable as she grew more satisfied with Claire's appearance.

"There!" Madame Babineaux said with a sudden burst of energy. "That will do. Madame Dalton?"

Aunt Elizabeth, who besides being the source of the Dalton fortune, was also the source of any modest height that Charles Edward might claim, placed her book aside and unfolded herself from the leopard-monopodia armchair whence she had waited. She was not as tall as Madame Babineaux, but she had at least four inches on Claire and stood barely shorter than her son. The sensation of tall women surrounding her made Claire feel as though her own diminutive height was something of a failing.

If it was a failing, though, there was no sign of it in Aunt Elizabeth's approving smile. "*Magnifique*," she said to Madame Babineaux. "Much better. I would hardly know her for the same girl. Ah, no!" She waggled a finger at Claire, who had begun to turn toward the mirror. "No, let us call for my maid Marie to do your hair first, so you can receive the benefit of the full effect just as the young gentlemen of London shall tomorrow evening.

Sit, my dear."

"Surely there's no need to go to such effort today," Claire protested, though she also sat as Madame Babineaux put a chair behind her knees and went to the door to call, loudly and not at all genteelly, for Marie, who appeared so quickly that she must have been waiting nearby. "It is just family for dinner, is it not, Auntie?"

"A young woman given a new wardrobe should see herself in it for the first time at the height of her comeliness, so she understands what others will see. Marie, curl her hair high, I think, unless you believe it will make her forehead seem too broad."

Claire's fingers went to her forehead, which she had never once dreamed of as broad, and had her hand guided away by the maid. "If it were my decision, Mrs Dalton, I would clip her hair short, even if it is not in fashion, as it would make her lovely green eyes large and haunting."

"Very well, then, go ahea—"

"Wait!" Claire seized Marie's hand and stood to face her aunt with determination. "It is my hair, Auntie, and I am not prepared to have it all cut away."

"Don't be silly, child. Marie will save it and make a wig—"

"Auntie," Claire repeated more firmly, and Mrs Dalton's feathery, colored-in eyebrows rose minutely.

"Is this how you thank me, Claire?"

A blush climbed Claire's cheeks, though whether it was of mortification or anger she could not say. "My gratitude knows no bounds, Aunt Elizabeth, and I am nearly beside myself with excitement to turn and see this gown in the mirror. But I have never had my hair cut, and I do not intend to start on the whim of a maid whom, although I am certain knows her business, I do not myself know. If I am unbearably rude in this, then I beg your forgiveness, and I assure you I will find some way to repay you for the kindness and wardrobe you have already shown me, but I absolutely cannot accept any further assistance and shall call for my parents to fetch me immediately."

High dudgeon stood in Aunt Elizabeth's face, and for an instant, Claire was convinced that she had ruined her London chances before even being introduced. Misery rose in her breast, constricting her breath, but she would not back down, not about her hair, which she had long since imagined as her best feature. She bit the inside of her lower lip, suspecting she looked sullen but unable to keep from crying without the distraction of pain, and stared forthrightly at her aunt.

A rustle at the door distracted Mrs Dalton before her opinion about Claire's boldness could be made plain. All four women in the room looked that way; all four were surprised to see a nervous young maid, her skirts twisted between her hands, who hardly more than whispered, "Forgive me, ma'am, but Mr Worthington asked that you be informed that Master Charles has returned."

"Worthington." Aunt Elizabeth echoed the name with a brief glance at Claire, then sighed unexpectedly and released the aspect of insult she had held. "Thank you, Bridget. We'll be down momentarily. Very well, Claire, your hair remains. Marie," she suggested dryly, "arrange it so Miss Dalton comes around to your way of thinking."

"Yes, mum." Marie returned Claire to the chair and with hot irons, brushes, combs, and a ruthless lack of regard for Claire's comfort, pulled, tugged, curled and twisted her hair to such a degree that it was merely a matter of stubborn pride that kept Claire from pleading for her hair to be cut after all. Torture was not, she thought, what her aunt had meant with that remark, though her aching scalp said otherwise. Finally, Marie declared herself satisfied, and Claire was made to stand while all three women — for Madame Babineaux had stayed to observe the crown on her creation — studied her with such intensity that she began to feel like a wilting flower.

Surprisingly, though, Aunt Elizabeth smiled and stepped behind Claire to move the chair out of the way. "Turn, my dear," she suggested when the chair had been moved, and Claire, feeling tender and uncertain, faced the mirror.

The girl reflected in it was familiar, like a cousin often visited in childhood but unseen as an adult. She was, if not beautiful, at least very pretty, much prettier than the half-imagined cousin might have been expected to be. Her dark hair was drawn back farther than she was accustomed to, with only a few curls lowered to hide her hairline. It did, indeed, make her green eyes large and luminous in the afternoon light pouring through the window. Beneath those huge eyes, her nose was petite and her mouth full, all framed in a heart-shaped face given width at the chin by tendrils of curls at her nape.

Gone was the accustomed high-collared gown. Her throat, collarbones, shoulders, and a gentle swell of bosom were bared, all pale and delicate, so white in the sunlight they shone. In the old gown's place she had been clothed in emerald trimmed with gold, or so the rich and sumptuous colors seemed to her as they clung to her shoulders and encased her bosom before falling in soft, flawless folds toward the floor. Astonished, Claire pressed a hand against her chest, laughing in half-confused surprise when her reflection did the same.

"I do not know myself," she whispered, and in the reflection behind her, even the maid felt bold enough to smile her approval along with Aunt Elizabeth and Madam Babineaux.

ff

"Mother wishes to see you in the parlor." Amelia Fairburn, newly turned nineteen and the acknowledged beauty of the family, swept the library door open and made this announcement with the pleasure of someone anticipating trouble.

Benedict lowered his book to eye his sister over its top edge. "Why?"

"I'm sure I wouldn't know, Benny. She only asked me to fetch you." Amelia rounded her eyes as if to emphasize her lack of knowledge, then spun into the room with a swirl of skirts and auburn hair. She had, Benedict thought, the dignity of an Irish setter, and said so aloud. Amelia ceased spinning and fixed him with a piercing look that showed no effect from the twirls. "She has a letter from Great-Aunt Nancy," she said flatly. "It concerns you."

A hollowness opened in Benedict's belly, so visceral a sensation he glanced down to see if he could now see through his own body. He could not, but from that hollow rolled a chill as if a cold wind had invaded to replace the blood in his veins. He looked up again and in so doing caught a glimpse of his reflection, pale enough to make Amelia toss her hair with satisfaction. "I expect your days of ladding about are at an end. Charles will be heartbroken."

There was nothing to be said to this. Amelia was likely correct on both counts, but admitting it was tantamount to agreeing to a month's worth of reminders that he had said she was right. Benedict stood, wondering how it could be that Amelia had spun but *he* felt dizzy. Trying to restore a sense of equilibrium, he brushed imagined dust from his pale blue suit coat and buckskins. "Thank you for informing me. I shall attend her immediately."

He had hoped that would send Amelia off, but it was a hope born in vain. She fell into companionable step beside him, still sparkling with the anticipation of trouble in the making. "Did she call for you too?" he demanded.

Amelia only smiled. "No, but if your fate is to be decided, it's inevitable that mine will be discussed as well. Women can't wait as long as you men can, you know. By five-and-twenty our bloom is gone."

Very few, even in the family, might have heard the faint note of bitterness in that statement, but Benedict, despite their clashes, loved his sister. "Firstly, Amy, you are barely nineteen, and secondly, your bloom is unlikely ever to fade. You'll be a dowager of eighty years and still have young men paying court to you. Those cheekbones are not in vain."

"You only compliment yourself," Amy said with a sniff, but a smile colored her tone. Outside the parlor door she stopped him with a touch on his arm, then, as he had done, brushed imaginary dust from his clothes. "Don't let Mother force you into anything, Benny. Great-Aunt Nancy may be accustomed to having her way, but she doesn't have to live your life. Only you can do that."

"But you must admit it would be a great deal more luxurious with her fortune," Benedict said, and with a wry smile exchanged between siblings, they entered their mother's favorite parlor. Its vivid green chinoiserie wallpaper, lightly painted with large flowers and narrow, sparrow-dotted branches of differing shades of the same hue, dominated the upper walls; a chair rail of mahogany broke the wall, which was below painted with two subtle tones of green that complemented the wallpaper. The furniture had been recently re-covered in cream and yellow, with several chair legs replaced with the fanciful lion's-foot legs that were so in fashion.

At the heart of this space sat Mrs Delores Fairburn, who was proof in the flesh that Benedict's words to Amelia had not been merely idle flattery. Mrs Fairburn may have only been fifty-five, not eighty, but she had not lost even a trace of her youthful beauty. Instead, it had been refined, pared down, and perfected. If she lived to eighty, she would, Benedict believed, be such a source of raw beauty that it would be difficult to look upon her. Moreover, although she had always dressed well, the fashion for high waists and loose gowns became her in a way that clothes of decades earlier had not, though she had the wisdom to wear heavier cloth than was strictly in vogue, thus keeping warmer than many of the muslin-clad ladies of the younger generation. At the moment she wore deep red, which set her off from every article of furniture in the room; the eye was drawn to her instantly, and could not linger elsewhere for long.

She was, all in all, a formidable picture to be presented with, even without the thick letter that lay to one side on one of the room's small elegant tables. "Benedict," she said fondly, and with a trace of genuine amusement, "Amelia. I'm astonished you didn't locate your brothers and sister on your way to find Ben."

"Had you not impressed upon me the urgency of your summons, I might well have darted across town to collect Linda," Amelia said placidly, "but I could not in any likelihood have taken myself into the clubs and saloons that my brothers are likely to inhabit at this time of day. You'll have to be satisfied with us, Mama."

"And not merely with Benedict, who is the only one of my children with whom I actually need to speak. Very well, sit down, both of you. Tea? No," she said after examining Benedict's expression. "No, I see we will go straight to the meat of the matter. I have it here in plain language, Benedict. Aunt Nancy is dying, and she is inclined to leave you her fortune."

The hollowness in his belly reasserted itself, this time driving air from his lungs. Benedict coughed quietly and steepled his fingers before his mouth, faintly aware that it must look as though he was trying to prepare himself for a blow. "Inclined. Provided...?"

"Provided you marry before she dies."

This time Amelia's breath left her, a more incredulous sound than Benedict had made. "How much time does he have?"

Mrs Fairburn lifted an eyebrow, not wrinkling the skin of her forehead as she did. "He, or she? Surely you're concerned for your great-aunt's health, Amelia. I have a letter from her doctor," she continued without awaiting Amelia's response. "She is old and her strength is failing. He suggests that she will not last the Season."

"The Season," Benedict echoed, and was aware that his mother spoke again, but could not discern the words through a rush of sound in his ears. Lightheadedness took him again, as if Amy's twirls from before had displaced their dizziness upon him a second time. His breath was shallow around the ache of a pounding heart. Everyone married. There was no reason the idea of doing so promptly should be so alarming, and yet he still could not breathe.

He thought, briefly and inexplicably, of Claire Dalton's green eyes, and finally began to hear Mrs Fairburn's discussion of his future again. "...can only recommend, therefore, that you find a bride of some means, Benedict. It's the only way to be certain. After all, you have two brothers and two sisters, and while

William's commission is paid for, there are always expenses to being the eldest."

"I'm sorry, Mother. I missed that. Could you repeat it?"

With a more gentle look than he expected, his mother repeated, "If you are not married suitably by the time Aunt Nancy dies, she intends to leave her fortune to the..." She paused, looking at the papers again, although Benedict could hardly imagine that she did not already have the words committed to memory. "The Institute of Saint Sophia. It is a workhouse and school for orphans. I must recommend, then, that you—"

"Yes," Benedict said faintly. "I got that part. Thank you. A school for orphans, why—?"

"It's that vicar of hers," Mrs Fairburn said with some asperity. "He's of gentle enough birth, but his father died young and his mother had no means of support. He was taken in by a school and given an education that let him climb to the rank of vicar, and now he has convinced her that it's a more noble use of her fortune than leaving it to family."

"And she would prefer to leave her fortune to the children of reprobates than her own flesh and blood if I should not marry in time or well enough?" Offense was beginning to claw the emptiness out of Benedict's chest: he had imagined there might be caveats to the inheritance, but not like this. "I thought I was—"

Suddenly aware of the conceit of his words,

he silenced himself, but Amelia, feeling no such compunction, finished what he had chosen not to say: "But Benedict is her favorite!"

"Which is, I believe, why he is being given time to find a bride and convince her that his offspring will have more need of her fortune than a scattering of unfortunate orphans," Mrs Fairburn announced. "Had William the misfortune to be born first—" She performed a delicate shudder that did her second-born no justice; he was an eminently suitable young gentleman in all ways save for lacking an inborn ability to flatter old, wealthy aunts.

A heartbeat later her refined theatrics were set aside for practicalities. "We must waste no time, Benedict. There is a highly fashionable ball tomorrow night. You shall be presented there and it will be made known that you are eligible and intend to wed soon."

"Mother," Benedict said faintly. "You speak of me as if I was a young lady."

Delores Fairburn fixed him with a gimlet eye. "And in every respect except your God-given sex, you are, my dear boy. What is Aunt Nancy's fortune but the dowry promised you upon your marriage? I will have a tailor sent to you first thing in the morning. It will be too soon to have a new suit for tomorrow night, but surely clever hands can turn one of your more unfortunate outfits into something new."

"My clothes are not unfortunate—!" That, of all things, was what he chose to seize on. Even he saw it as the measure of a desperate man.

Mrs Fairburn ignored his outburst, as was only to be expected, and turned the same unrelenting eye on her youngest daughter. "You, on the other hand, have no need of new clothes. I will expect you to behave decorously in the background, Amelia. Soon enough it will be your turn, and mothers who remember you as a pleasant and supportive sister will stand you well when your Season comes."

"Excellent," Amelia said in short tones. "Perhaps if you burnish my hair and put it in a tail you'll be able to sell me at the next horse auction for a fancy price."

"Oh, Amelia," sighed Mrs Fairburn, and although that was the end of the conversation, it was not, Benedict thought, the end of the conversation. Stiff with discomfort, not all of it on his own behalf—though enough of it was—Benedict stood and with mumbled apologies, took his leave of the female Fairburns.

Charles, he hoped, would know what to do.

Charles did not know what to do.

Charles, indeed, stood within the confines of the Dalton's drawing room and swayed, aghast. Visibly swayed: he might have allowed himself to imagine it was only a heady dismay, save for the fine, large mirror his mother had chosen for the drawing room while he was at war. In it, he rocked, and in it, he watched hope drain from Benedict's face with every moment that Charles did not speak.

He ought, he knew, to offer congratulations and voice enthusiasm for Benedict's prospects. He ought to have a good chuckle, clap Fairburn's shoulder, and take him out for an evening of Cyprians and drink. He ought, amidst all that revelry, to discuss the least probable and most inappropriate choices for a bride, so that when it came to the serious business of actually deciding whom to marry, all of that nonsense was behind them. He ought to dredge up a name or two, girls Benny had been sweet on in their school days, and suggest them, to see if any of them made Benedict blush and therefore remained likely candidates.

He ought to do all of those things and more, and in the heat of worry flooding him, thought he had said at least one or two of the more polite or jesting articles that had crossed his mind. Not until a queer ache in his chest burst and faded when he took a breath did he realize he had not said *any* of those things, and that Fairburn's expression now bordered on panic.

Determined to reassure, even if the marriage meant the end of the Lads and all the rough, gentle protection from Society that they offered, Charles stepped forward, clasped Benedict's shoulders, and proclaimed, "Demme, sir, this is terrible news indeed!"

He became aware that Worthington was nearby, and though the valet was far too discreet to show any outward sign of emotion,

Charles recognized the particular brand of indifference Worthington suddenly displayed as being one of utmost disapproval. Cursing himself, Charles tried again, this time blurting, "That is to say, what a dreadful mess this will make of the Lads! We cannot do without you, Benny, it will ruin our harmony! Dear God. I need a drink."

The last was not in response to Fairburn's shattering announcement but rather a frantic attempt to silence his own entirely unseemly responses. Charles turned hastily and found Worthington there, a snifter of brandy already to hand. The valet offered a second snifter to Benny, who took it purposefully, like a drowning man determined to finish himself before the sea did. Both men drank before Charles threw himself into an overstuffed sofa and gazed upon his friend in genuine apology and dismay. "Forgive me, Ben. I have no idea what came over me."

Benedict sat more gingerly, his smile pained. "Amelia did say you would be heartbroken. No, you only have the courage of your convictions, Charles. I feel each of the things you've voiced, and yet..."

"And yet what choice do you have," Charles finished grimly. "*Tomorrow*, Benny? She intends to put you on the market tomorrow?"

"Great-Aunt Nancy is poorly and there is no time to waste." Fairburn drew a hand over his face. "I feel certain Mother will have decided the date by which I must be married by morning, and have arranged a church by afternoon. It's November, Charles, and Great-Aunt Nancy isn't expected to last the Season. Married! In five months' time, unless the old bird hangs on! I suppose I expected to marry sometime, but so suddenly! How am I to find someone both rich and beautiful with whom I can share affection in so short a time?"

"Women do it all the time," Charles said with a thoughtful shrug of one shoulder. "Or at least find someone with whom they can bear to share a bed long enough to produce heirs. Perhaps you should ask your sister."

"Amelia is certainly not sharing her bed with anyone!" Benedict looked rather like he might call Dalton out, though the latter stopped his outrage with a laugh and lifted hand.

"Mrs Durrell, Benedict. Your sister Linda, not Amelia. Dear God, what do you take me for, man?"

"A gentleman and a soldier," responded a deep, soft voice from the doorway, though the accolades were lost beneath a host of other, less flattering descriptions as not one, not two, but five young men jostled, elbowed, edged and poured their way through the drawing room door in a manner that implied an unsuccessful attempt at each of them gaining a certain pride of place as the first.

Charles, surprised, said, "Vincent," to the first voice, then stood as the rest of the Lads filled the drawing room almost beyond capacity. "Are we meant to go out tonight? I had forgotten. And all of us at once? No, I could not forget!" Delight chased away his dismay at Benedict Fairburn's news as he gestured for Worthington to pour more drink and greeted each of the Lads individually. Ronald Vincent, the one to have a kind word as they'd entered, looked faintly uncomfortable, as he always did in the confines of a fine house, but Charles thumped one of his massive shoulders and murmured, "Don't think I didn't notice you were the gentleman among them, Vincent. Have some brandy and a seat. Take the couch; it's big enough for you."

"Almost," Vincent agreed, but took Charles's seat and, in settling, reduced the full-sized couch to the appearance of having been made for women, or even children. He was simply that big, in height and breadth alike. Charles had never met a man Ronald Vincent couldn't tower over, even after the man had lost most of one arm to cannon fire. A black haze of fearful memory rose at the thought, recalling too much of the battles that had returned him to England's bonny shores. Charles closed his eyes, drawing a breath to steady himself, and was almost grateful to receive a punch much like the one Charles had delivered to Vincent, only harder, to his own shoulder.

As Charles opened his eyes, Evander drew his hand back, shaking it as if he'd encountered more resistance than expected. "Your mother invited us, Charles. Didn't she tell you?" He snaked past Charles and plucked a snifter from Worthington's hand, deliberately oblivious to Vincent as the intended recipient.

Worthington's light brown gaze flickered from Hewitt to Vincent and back again, but the valet's hesitation was so brief that Charles might have imagined it. Before he could decide if he had indeed seen the flicker of disapproval in Worthington's gaze, the valet had another drink for Vincent, as if the slight had not happened. More drinks were handed around: to Ackerman, so fair of hair and face that he might have been a woman; to O'Brien, whose roughshod Irish birthright ought to have had him as uncomfortable as Vincent in this company, but never did, and finally to Cringlewood, who, as the only peer amongst the Lads, should have been served first and who had, as always, waved ceremony away. Worthington, Charles knew, liked Cringlewood intensely, not only for his lack of affectation but because against all likelihood, the young noble had formed a close bond with Vincent, whose Scottish heritage was nearly as raw as O'Brien's.

For a moment or two, *why* they had gathered hardly mattered as Charles smiled 'round at them. These were his friends, his Lads, companions born of battlefields and schoolyards and the chance encounters that made up a life. They were his buffer against and his connection to a world changed beyond measure by the report of a rifle. He could not, in truth, imagine his days without them.

His mother, however, could and most fervently did, and so as Hewitt's words settled in, Charles peered at him in surprised curiosity. "My mother invited you? Worthington?"

"Not two hours since," Worthington agreed. "I was asked to dispatch letters stating the urgency of the matter, and all save Master Fairburn were immediately available. He, of course, had already made his own way here." With this observation Worthington offered Benedict a nod, as if congratulating him for not requiring a summons.

"I stood up my father to respond," said Cringlewood. "I hope it's good, Dalton, or I'll have hell to pay."

"It is impossible that an invitation from Mrs Dalton could be anything less than good." Samuel Ackerman's voice was as light as his complexion, a tenor so pure it was a pity he never raised it in song. "She does not, after all, particularly care for us Lads, whom she sees as interfering with Dalton's duties in marrying and producing grandchildren for her, so she cannot have requested our presence for anything short of thunderous dramatics."

"Mr Ackerman has the right of it," said Mrs Dalton from the door. As one, the seated Lads came to their feet, arranging themselves into some semblance of order and decorum.

Charles's mother, looking resplendent in a rich blue suitable for a woman her age, examined them all from the doorway, then smiled with satisfaction. "Splendid. Gentlemen, I require your assistance. I have a young lady new to London here, and I should hate to see her embarrassed tomorrow evening at her debut. If it is no hardship, I would ask you to befriend her, offer your solicitous support, and, of course, make her widely regarded as desirable by filling enough of her dance card that the other young gentlemen are forced to fight for the remaining spaces.

"Claire," she said, and withdrew to allow a vision to appear.

There were so *many* of them. Seven Lads and Worthington; together they entirely filled the drawing room. Claire, embraced by the doorway, felt small, shy, and in desperate need of a friend. Were it not for Aunt Elizabeth's fist in her spine she would likely have retreated, but instead, entirely against her will, she stepped forward to perform a small and tentative curtsy.

Somehow she did not expect every man in the room, even Worthington, to bow in return. It gave her a whisper of confidence. With confidence came the ability to draw a breath, and with breath came a clarity that let her look from one man to another.

One was impossible to overlook: he stood

head and shoulders taller than the rest and at least half again as wide, though the breadth was predominantly in his shoulders; the cut of his coat, nipping at his waist, told her that. One sleeve was pinned up neatly, suggesting a grievous injury taken in the war. He had curling brown hair, light eyes, a long face, and a sense of quietness that pervaded even the boisterous good nature of the gathered Lads.

Charles, following her gaze, had the good sense to offer, "Sergeant Ronald Vincent," as introduction. Claire nodded once, then looked at the man beside him, who wore a better cut of clothing than Claire had ever laid eyes on. He was otherwise unremarkable: handsome enough, with brown hair that looked as though he couldn't be troubled to maintain its order, and a mild gaze that turned surprisingly attractive as thin lips twitched in a smile. "Nathaniel Cringlewood."

"Your honor," Claire whispered, appalled. She knew the Cringlewood name, of course; one *did* know the names of the peerage, and it horrified her that she had decided one of their ilk was nothing remarkable. He, though, could not hear her thoughts, and his smile lingered as she wrenched her gaze to the next of the Lads.

This one and the one beside him she knew: Evander Hewitt and Benedict Fairburn, both of whom looked upon her without a shred of recognition. Charles offered their names as well, bent, it seemed, on introducing each of the Lads whether they needed it or not, and said, "Samuel Ackerman," next.

Had it not been for Vincent's extraordinary size, Claire supposed she would have looked first and longest — perhaps forever — at Samuel Ackerman, whose visage might easily have graced one of heaven's angels. Like Cringlewood, he had thin lips, but unlike the young lord, he barely smiled. Nor did he need to: his eyes, shockingly green, offered all the warmth of expression necessary. She did not *want* him to smile at her: she did not think she could bear the beauty of it, and was relieved when Charles spoke the final name and allowed her to look to the last Lad.

Subaltern Gareth O'Brien was black of hair, black of eye, warmly swarthy of skin, and sported a shadow along a strong square jaw, as if his beard could not be kept back for even a day without multiple interventions by a razor. Or perhaps the short beard was purposeful: a deadly scar ran down his jaw and throat, visible mostly in the way the hairs grew against the grain there. He did not smile at her: he grinned, an open expression of charm and invitation. Claire rather thought he might ask her to dance right there in the drawing room, given less than half an excuse. She tried not to smile too widely in return, afraid it might offer the excuse he sought, but could not help herself, and responded to the infectious pleasantry of his expression in kind.

Charles did not introduce himself, of course, or Worthington, but Claire couldn't help but look on both of them as well, feeling as though she settled them into their proper place by doing so, as part and parcel, each in their own way, of the Lads. Charles was shorter than *all* of them, even Worthington, and where so many of them met her gaze with vivid liveliness, Charles's eyes were half-lidded, almost desultory. He was one of the least handsome of them, she realized; Charles, whom she had thought so attractive when they were children.

But if Charles was ordinary, and these Lads merely his collection of friends, not even the best of London's best, Claire thought faintly, then it was as well that Aunt Elizabeth had chosen to introduce her to them tonight. It offered some thin thread upon which to prepare herself for what would no doubt be an overwhelmingly admirable crowd at tomorrow night's ball — and a crowd for which she could not imagine herself suited, despite her new clothes and beautifully coiffed hair.

"Gentlemen," Charles said in a clear and ringing voice, "may I present my cousin, Miss Claire Dalton."

To Claire's immense satisfaction, Benedict Fairburn's jaw fell open in stupefaction.

Benedict had known, he supposed, that Charles's cousin was coming to Town. Had even known, he supposed, that she had arrived. Should, then, have deduced from the moment Mrs Dalton stepped aside that the young woman presented was necessarily Miss Dalton.

It had simply not occurred to him. The lady in the doorway was an altogether different creature than the one he had last seen in the country. A figure that had been so hidden as to be presumed dowdy in her country dresses was now revealed as delectable. Her small size was now dainty, not sturdy, and her gown's bodice was scooped enticingly low. Her face — he wrenched his gaze upward from the lovely swell of bosom to fix it on her face, trying to appear at least moderately gentlemanly through his amazement. Her face, now that it was no longer hidden in the depths of a bonnet or by hair that overwhelmed delicate features, was fresh and sweet and her full lips deliciously kissable. There was, he discovered to his delight, the faintest scattering of freckles across her pert nose, and he wondered how he had failed to notice them before.

Her eyes, now the shade of cool jade, flickered over him with disinterest, then warmed considerably to emerald fire as O'Brien — because O'Brien had no expectation of propriety, being from a Dublin gutter — stepped forward to bow over her hand and entirely block her from Benedict's view. He did not hear what O'Brien said, but he heard Miss Dalton's laughter, and felt a flush of heat wash over his cheeks. Then it was Nathaniel, and he *did* hear the Earl-in-waiting ask for the first dance at tomorrow evening's ball, which would set Miss Dalton up enviably for the entirety of her Season. Cringlewood lingered in his discussion with her long enough that Ackerman, the only other Lad to come anywhere near Nathaniel in riches, was finally obliged to intercede for fear none of the others would have a chance to speak with her.

By then Benedict had retreated to the hearth, where Worthington, all-knowing as usual, had a brandy already awaiting him. Benedict muttered his thanks and told himself he was only biding his time, though in truth there was an instant before Vincent paid his compliments during which Benedict could easily have brought himself to Miss Dalton's attention. But the moment was gone, dashed to bits by Vincent and then Hewitt, whose damnable lack of caring what she thought made Miss Dalton laugh again.

She moved amongst them comfortably, smiling, exchanging stories, *telling* stories on Charles that made them all laugh, while Benny watched from his post of shame, until the hour had grown late enough for a light supper to be taken. As soup was brought around, Benedict realized, with a start of horror, that his opportunity was about to be lost. He gestured for his soup to be put on a table and set aside his snifter, hoping it had not been refilled as often as he thought. Gathering courage in both hands, he stepped forward to greet her. "Miss Dalton. I confess, I did not know it was you when you arrived."

Claire Dalton looked up at him — quite some distance up; she was of a perfect size to be gathered into his arms and adored, he decided — and offered the most delightful smile he could ever remember being the lucky recipient of. "A shame, Mr Fairburn," she murmured so sweetly that it only emphasized the meaning of her words, "for I certainly knew it was you."

Still smiling, she turned to the rest of the Lads. "Forgive me, gentlemen," she said in suddenly sleepy-sounding contentment, "but I fear that tomorrow will be a long day, and that I must retire. It has been an utter pleasure to meet so many of Charles's delightful friends, and," she added with carefully chosen precision, "to renew my acquaintance with Misters Hewitt and Fairburn. Good night."

Worthington left a ribald party of Lads later with the teasing laughter that Hewitt and Fairburn were rightfully subject to ringing in his ears. He was not, certainly, pursuing Miss Dalton. There were beds to turn down, perhaps several, should any of the Lads decide to stay the night. It could not, though, be said that he was displeased when, far enough beyond the drawing room to show a shred of discretion, he discovered Miss Dalton pressed against a wall, a hand against her chest as she shook with near-silent laughs of satisfaction.

When she saw him she straightened, trying hard to turn her expression to something more suitable for a young woman, and utterly failing. Then she gave in and let herself laugh again. Indeed, she gave in so far as to dart forward and seize Worthington's hands in her own. "I cut him, didn't I? I cut him as deeply as a mouse might," she said with a sudden flash of anger. "The other one, Hewitt, is so awful I cannot even remain angry at him because I cannot care that deeply, but Mr Fairburn has the makings of a gentleman beneath his dreadful first presentation, which makes his initial rudeness all the more unforgivable, and from such a handsome man. But I cut him," she said again, with anger still flushing her cheeks, "and he felt it. Did he not?"

"I believe he did, Miss." Worthington extracted his hands from Miss Dalton's grip so gently that she didn't notice it being done and could therefore be allowed to believe *she* had released *him*. "If you continue with this presentation of indifference and disdain, I believe you will have him quite thoroughly captured before the Season is much started."

"What?" Startled laughter escaped the young woman, who looked at her hands and seemed relieved that they no longer held Worthington's. "Heavens, no, Worthington, I have no such interest in or designs upon Mr

Fairburn. I do not wish a husband with only the makings of a gentleman. He must already be one. A woman's job is to raise her children, not her husband; that is his mother's duty."

Worthington bowed. "Of course, Miss. My mistake. Forgive me for speaking so openly."

"Not at all. You have already been a fount of great advice to me, and I cannot think that you are inappropriate for having been so." Miss Dalton cast a quick glance at the drawing room door. "I must go before they begin to leave and find me here laughing like a child. Good night, Worthington."

She fled before he had time to speak. Even so, he waited until she was out of sight and her footsteps were fading before he allowed amusement to touch his lips, and a murmured, "Good night, Miss," to follow her up the stairs.

Chapter Four

Claire had been to balls and soirées before. Indeed, as the daughter of one of the wealthier families in her home town of Bodton, she had helped to host some fine fêtes, or what had seemed to her at the time to be fine fêtes. Now, however, she gazed in astonishment at a crowd so large that every soul from Bodton could be placed in it and lost to one another's sight.

She could not, in the first moments, decide which was more impressive: the house and hall itself, or the sumptuously dressed, too-warm bodies within it. The entry hall swept some twenty feet upward, with cornices enriching the ceiling where chandeliers did not drip. The floors were marble. The walls were set with marvelous paintings of seasides and warfare and draped with velvet that could protect them when they were not on ostentatious display. Vast archways and doors led into other rooms. Claire could see no more than the swish of gowns through them, but the entry hall alone seemed as impressive as any endless country manor could be.

Gowns ranging in every shade from purest

white to deepest mourning purple were visible, so that a scattered rainbow seemed to sway across the floors. Claire clutched the skirt of her own creamy, green-trimmed gown as if to reassure herself of its suitability, took a deep, steadying breath, and swayed.

The smell was, frankly, appalling. Even the finest perfumes and colognes could not overcome the number of overheated people and the astringent scent that rose from them. Claire suffered a brief impulse to flee. It was not to be; she had been announced, people had politely clapped a greeting, and somewhere in the crush was Nathaniel Cringlewood, who would dance with her. She could not, despite the smell, retreat from a promised dance to one of the peerage, and so into chaos she descended.

But it wasn't chaos after all. There was a flow and ebb to the movement, surges that swept the Dalton cousins along, then slowed to allow them to greet other attendees. Charles knew an astonishing number of people. Claire met, smiled at, and mostly forgot them as new names and faces were introduced. A few stood out, primarily a young woman upon whose shimmering white and silver gown Charles accidentally trod. She, accepted his gracious apology with a nod and a gesture of rueful exasperation toward the crowd, as though to say, *what else is to be expected?* before turning away. Claire breathed, "Who was that?"

Charles, mystified, replied, "I have no idea,"

before introducing Claire to a dowager duchess so resplendent in a deep purple gown thirty years out of fashion that even in the crush, she was afforded room to move. "Cousin to the Regent on his mother's side," Charles informed her after they'd offered the duchess their greetings. "The peak of society. Here at Cringlewood's request, probably. I'd certainly never have met her if I lacked his friendship."

The duchess and the rueful young woman were followed by a general whose curly white muttonchops extended a full five inches from either side of his face and gave the impression he was of one exact width from his pate to his pointed shoes. Shortly thereafter, a young man approached and introduced himself to Charles with the clear purpose of then being introduced to Claire. Out of the dozens she met, those four were the ones she remembered.

Of all of them, the last—a dashing youth with sandy gold hair and soulful brown eyes— bowed over her hand as a slightly bemused and wary Charles said, "Claire, may I present Mr Jack Graham. Mr Graham, my cousin, Miss Dalton."

"Forgive me my boldness, Miss Dalton, but I saw you arrive and knew that if I did not make your acquaintance before you reached the ballroom I would have no chance at all to request a dance. I confess to lurking here while you crossed the room in hopes of encountering you. May I have the honor?"

Claire looked at Charles, whose modestly elevated eyebrows left the decision to her. She returned her gaze to Mr Jack Graham. "Are you always so bold, Mr Graham?"

"Only in the presence of beauty, Miss Dalton," Graham said with such sincerity that Claire laughed.

"I'm afraid you've mistaken me for another, then. I will accept platitudes of prettiness, but beauty is beyond me. I haven't the nose for it."

Charles, to her utter surprise, murmured, "I think you do yourself a disservice, Claire," but Graham, the corner of his mouth rising in contained humor, replied, "I assure you that I am only being agreeable when I say you may be right. Still, I was moved to remain—" his eyes sparkled at the contradictory words, making Claire smile again, "—here by the ballroom door in hopes of making your acquaintance, whether moved by beauty or tremendous prettiness. I *am* forward, I know it, but will you dance with me?"

An absolute gentleman ought to have insisted on her beauty; that was the way it was done. But a man who conceded that a woman's perception of her own attractiveness was appropriate was intriguing. Before she knew it, Claire had said, "I would be pleased to dance with you, Mr Graham, although I have already promised the first two dances and then the first of the second set and—pardon, I must check my card."

She did, deliberately tilting it so that Graham could see it was already nearly half full. It would have been half full, she was certain, had Charles's large friend Mr Vincent not, the evening before, stepped upon the foot of the ruthlessly charming Mr O'Brien when he was about to claim a second dance for himself. Or, indeed, if Mr Fairburn had roused himself to arrange a dance this evening ahead of time, but he had not. Charles, however, had, and the result was that she looked quite popular before even setting foot in the ballroom.

"My word," Graham exclaimed at the sight of the card. "I am vindicated, Miss Dalton, in my brashness. Had I waited I would have been lost. Perhaps the third dance?"

"The third dance it shall be." Claire smiled as he wrote his name on the card and curtsied when he bowed and took his leave. He was very handsome, she decided, and didn't realize she'd spoken aloud until Charles said, in slightly gruff agreement, "I suppose that he is. Not very tall, though, Claire."

"He's as tall as you are, Charles!"

Charles gave her an acknowledging smile. "As I said. Now, the dancing will be starting soon, and I must deliver you to Cringlewood. Don't promise all your dances before you get to him, Claire. He will have friends of his own here, all more noble than Jack Graham."

"Wait. Do you know Mr Graham? Is there something of which I should be warned?"

"Know him? No, not at all, which is how I know there are nobler men awaiting you." Charles offered his arm once more, and together they slipped into the ballroom.

Rumor ran ahead of Benedict Fairburn like a flood-swelled stream, informing all of Society of his forthcoming fortune. He could no more pick out the words than he might have from a stream's babble, but he could see it clearly enough. Feathered and bejeweled heads dipped together, murmurs were exchanged, and then those glittering blonds and brunettes lifted their gazes to look upon him with critical, calculating interest. On the mothers, that calculation never faded, though on most of the daughters it softened to comeliness and charm. He was politely pleased to make the acquaintance of daughter after daughter, bowing and smiling and all the while suffering a terrifying constriction of breath in his throat.

No doubt it was the heat. So many people made for veritable waves of rising warmth, and the air he breathed felt as though it had been thinned by other lungs before it reached him. Perhaps that was also why his hands, despite the heat, seemed so cold: his humors were off from too-thin air and the overwhelming number of young ladies being presented to him. He had always supposed it would be splendid to be in such demand, and had upon occasion joined throngs of admiring

young men in pursuit of a particular new
Society beauty. Now, faced with the same
degree of pursuit, he had the sharp desire to
find every single one of those young ladies and
offer his devout apologies.

Here and there he requested a dance of an
especially pretty daughter. Once he regretted it
before the question was even finished, as a
small, well-rounded young woman changed
from politely intriguing to simperingly cloy
and clung to his arm as if already wed to him.
It was all Benedict could do to stop himself
from actually shaking her off, and indeed he
only managed to disengage when a striking
strawberry blonde said, "Ah, there you are, Mr
Fairburn," and nimbly inserted herself between
Benedict and the round girl. "Do forgive me,"
she said to the other girl, but rather than offer
any excuse beyond that she simply walked
Benedict toward the dance floor.

"Do forgive me," she repeated, this time to
Benedict. "You looked in need of rescue. Miss
Priscilla Hurst, and we had best behave as if
we were previously acquainted."

"Miss Hurst, it is my great pleasure to renew
our acquaintance," Benedict said quietly but
heartily. "I'm sure we met at the park recently.
Would you care to dance so we might continue
its renewal? But no," he said almost instantly
as his companion's beauty began to make itself
known to him, "I'm sure this dance must
already be promised."

Miss Hurst, who was tall and slim with skin the color of skimmed milk, a long neck, and eyes so pale he might have been looking into thin ice, barely changed expression as she lifted a dance card only lightly scattered with names. "I am disinclined to fill every slot, Mr Fairburn. My coloring is ill-suited to the flush that exercise flatters many young ladies with. But having taken you from your companion, I expect it would be rude to refuse a dance now."

With utter self-possession she allowed him to guide her.—and there was no mistake that she *allowed* it—onto the dance floor, where the strains of one of the more sedate music sets swirled around them. "How fortunate," she said with no evidence of humor. "I shall not flush."

"And I shall try not to flatter too much, that you retain your milk-like tones," Benedict offered gallantly. Miss Hurst gave him a faint smile—her lips were thin, but very red against such pale skin—and curtsied to his bow as the set began. Her gown was as icy blue as her eyes, color in it shifting as she glided from one step to another, until Benedict felt he looked into the heart of a winter storm. Intrigued, he said, "You knew my name," and thought, though didn't say, that she had also hanged convention to introduce herself, rather than await an introduction.

"Mr Fairburn, I'm afraid nearly everyone knows your name tonight. You will be known henceforth as one of the Season's most eligible bachelors, and there will be many women who cry themselves to sleep when your engagement is announced."

Curiosity piqued, Benedict asked, "And will you be among them, Miss Hurst?"

One beautifully thin eyebrow lifted. "That remains to be seen, does it not, Mr Fairburn?"

Perhaps, Benedict thought, being pursued was not as dreadful as he had imagined. It was with a certain regret that he was denied a second dance—"My complexion," Miss Hurst said mildly—and with a certain pleasure that he departed the elegant lady in search of a cooling drink for her. He would have to learn about her circumstances, but his mother couldn't fault her for her beauty, at the very least; Mother was a redhead too.

His pleasure lasted all the way to seeing Miss Dalton laughing on the dance floor with O'Brien. They looked offensively well together, though it was difficult for O'Brien to look poorly with anyone; his was a beauty exceeded amongst the Lads only by Ackerman. And Miss Dalton's transformation was completed by her laughter, for it brought great warmth to her prettiness, a warmth complimented by the copper-and-green-trimmed gown she wore. She was an earthly angel, and he was suddenly determined to put his past mistakes behind him. He could charm; all of the Lads could, save perhaps Vincent, who chose quietness over flattery.

O'Brien saw him as they left the dance floor and steered Miss Dalton his way before she could object. The men clasped hands briefly, but Benedict bowed to Miss Dalton with absolute sincerity. "You are a joy to watch, Miss Dalton. May I offer you a drink, and perhaps be honored with a dance?" He offered the drink he'd fetched for Miss Hurst, and halfway to claiming it, Miss Dalton hesitated.

"Oh! I'm afraid my card is full this evening, Mr Fairburn." Her uplifted wrist, whence the card dangled, proved her words to be true. "I had no notion of such popularity, but Charles's Lads have been very kind to me, and I have been introduced to a wonderful array of young men who have obliged the Lads by asking me to dance."

A pang shot through Benedict's heart, sharp enough to tingle down to his fingers, though he kept a careful hold of the drink. *He* was one of the Lads, by gum, not some outsider to be shooed away. And yet the others had begged a dance each the night before, while he had sulked and hidden in his cups at the hearth. It was no wonder Miss Dalton felt more warmly toward them than himself, even to the point of excluding him in her own mind from the Lads' numbers. "Then I am a perfect fool for not asking earlier," he said truthfully. "I shall act with more alacrity in the future. Please, do take the drink, Miss Dalton; you must have little time to rest and refresh yourself with a card so full. Take it and do enjoy your evening."

"Thank you." Miss Dalton accepted the drink with genuine gratitude, and bestowed a winning smile upon Benedict after she sipped. "Just what I needed. Oh!" she said again as an older gentleman with a wife and daughter appeared to renew an acquaintance with O'Brien, then to introduce all of them to Miss Dalton.

Her early dance with Cringlewood was a topic of much discussion and cause for an invitation to the newcomers' home. Benedict found himself put thoroughly into the background, and with a mumbled, "O'Brien," excused himself to find another drink for Miss Hurst, who, unlike certain other young women, showed an interest in and had time for him.

Jack Graham danced exquisitely; that, Charles allowed. More, he would be a fool to imagine that Graham was less than handsome: he had something of the summer sun about him, from the soft sand of his well-cut hair to the golden tint of his skin. He dressed beautifully, too. Better, arguably, than Charles: he wore a bottle green coat that nipped his waist to narrowness; beneath it lay a complementary waistcoat and flawlessly white shirt with a ballroom cravat. Fawn trousers clung to his calves, and every item fitted perfectly. Only his shoes seemed cause for concern.

They were of excellent make, but there were

marks of wear at the seams where the leather had stretched thin. A young gentleman of means ought to have had the uppers replaced before wear became visible. Charles was thus forced to deduce that Graham lacked means, and was, therefore, a poor choice for his cousin Claire's pursuits of romance.

It was a pity, then, that Graham requested and received a second dance with her. After discharging his own dancing duties, Charles released Claire into Graham's willing arms and deliberately failed to meet the eye of a ravishing brunette who clearly hoped to be his own next dance partner. Instead, he made his way through the press, seeking out Evander Hewitt.

Hewitt stood at a gaming table with a bit of his own coin laid down against the cards; Charles briefly examined his hand, then tapped his shoulder. "I need to speak with you, Evan."

"Demme, Charles, I'm about to take the whole table!" Hewitt protested with fine conviction.

Charles twitched an eyebrow. The upstage one, visible only to Hewitt, so that if he insisted on not joining Charles at least his bluff wouldn't be known to the whole table, but Evan muttered, "All right," sullenly and folded. "Keep my stakes," he said to the table at large, carelessly, as he stood. "It's only a sovereign or two."

"Good man," said one of the others, and they returned to their game as Charles ushered

Hewitt away to as quiet a corner as could be found within the busy halls. "Do you know Jack Graham, Hewitt?"

"I might, a bit. Sandy hair and not so ta— about your height? A bit," Hewitt repeated at Charles's nod. "Why?"

"How are you acquainted?"

Evander Hewitt paused in the act of reaching for a drink from a passing servant, then withdrew his hand to look hard at Charles. Color suffused his face, more suddenly than the room's heat could account for, and he spoke stiffly. "There a reason you're asking me instead of one of the other Lads, Charles?"

"There is." Charles spoke gently, aware as always of Hewitt's sensibility. "Cringlewood and Ackerman are too high, O'Brien and Vincent, too low. And Benny is beset upon by fortune hunters just now."

Every word was true, though they did not make up the whole truth. Still, they made up enough of it that Hewitt's color slowly subsided. "He's not the gambling sort, if that's what you're asking. Alone in the world, though, if I remember, and a bit of a hanger-on because of that."

"A fortune hunter himself?" Charles asked, and received a bitterly scathing look in return.

"Aren't we all when it comes to marriage, Dalton? How rich do you have to be to marry for love? And if you're that rich, they won't let you anyway. I'll look into him, if you want.

After Miss Dalton, is he?"

"He asked for a second dance."

"On an evening's acquaintance? Cheeky. Now if it were O'Brien I wouldn't be surprised, but he has the manners of a—"

"Evan," Charles said, gently again, and Hewitt subsided.

Subsided on that topic, at least, and this time did snare a drink from a passing servant before speaking. "Did you see the girl Benny's paying court to? Her grandfather came up in trade, they say, but the family is rich as Midas and she's a beauty. Looks like his mother thirty years ago, if a bit icier."

"No!" Charles spun in curiosity, following the wavering line of Hewitt's pointing finger to pick Fairburn and a statuesque redhead from the crowd. "Demmed if she doesn't! Do you think he sees it?"

"Would any man?" Hewitt smiled slyly. "Shall I tell him?"

Charles caught his arm. "No."

Hewitt shook him off. "The war took the fun out of you, Dalton. I'm back to the tables. Don't lose me another hand."

Charles, softly, said, "Of course not, Evan. Let me make up what I lost you," and wondered if he would offend or relieve with the offer.

Both: Hewitt's blue eyes darkened, but a light, jovial smile played across his mouth, and if his voice was forced, even Charles, listening for it, couldn't tell. "As well you should, man. As well you should!" Accepting the coin Charles slipped him, he hurried away, unaware that Dalton watched him until he was lost to the crowd.

"May I confess something to you, Miss Dalton?" Jack Graham accompanied Claire to a table no longer groaning with delicacies; it had been too-well picked over in the course of the evening for that. But enough remained to stave off the worst of hunger, and Claire was determined to eat before having any more champagne. She already felt dizzy and light from the evening's activities, and did not wish to embarrass herself in any way.

Graham had graciously departed after their second dance, leaving her to meet both Ackerman and Vincent for their promised sets. She had been so dazzled by Ackerman that she had barely been able to look at him, incapable of speech. Nor did he seem to expect it, relinquishing her, with a barely visible smile, to Vincent, who had seemed very large and sturdy and plain in comparison. He was shockingly graceful, though, for a man of his size, particularly for one who was missing an arm and couldn't be expected to complete certain aspects of the dance. Claire fancied she enjoyed her dance with the huge Scotsman more than the one with the beautiful English boy. But after that was her single empty slot of the evening and, perishing of hunger, she sought the dining tables where Graham had tentatively approached her again.

With food to fortify herself, she felt generous and happy. "You may confess anything you like, Mr Graham," she had said, "particularly if you can locate us some seating."

"I believe I can do that." He roused two young men well into their cups from a sofa and gestured grandly for Claire to take a seat. Groaning with pleasure, she sat and wiggled her aching feet. Then, with a sigh around a small bite of bread pudding, she nodded her permission for Graham's confession.

"Miss Dalton, I have enjoyed my evening far more than might have been expected. I would like to ask you to go driving on the morrow, but —no," he insisted as Claire straightened with what she knew to be far too much eagerness to accept. "No, please, let me finish, Miss Dalton. We none of us pretend that these great social gatherings are either more or less than what they are: a chance to make and renew acquaintances, of course, and to perhaps begin to build friendships, but their thrust, especially as the Season approaches, is toward marriage."

A cough clogged Claire's throat. She, too, had enjoyed the evening immensely, but could simply not imagine that Graham intended on proposing after two dances and a glass of champagne. He brought that champagne to hand, giving her the sip she dearly needed to clear her throat, and looked apologetic as she brushed eyes glittering with cough-induced tears. "I'm sorry," he said. "I approached that badly. What I meant to say, Miss Dalton, is that I enjoy your company tremendously, and I feel you should know from the start that I am not the man your family would wish you to marry."

Cold water dashed over her could not have been more surprising. Claire took another, rather larger, swallow of champagne before daring to say, "Are you not, Mr Graham? Are you a dangerous man? A boundless rake? Do you break hearts and leave women bereft?"

If he was a rake, his smile, wide and open, accounted for it: Claire could see any woman falling in love with that smile. But he shook his head even as he smiled. "Not at all. I believe I'm very bad at making women fall in love with me, in fact. But neither am I wealthy, Miss Dalton. I have seen already the company you keep. I can in no way put myself forth with the likes of Mr Cringlewood or even Benedict Fairburn."

"Oh," Claire began, flustered, but Graham interrupted her again with a wry smile.

"It is my aim to make, in time, a modest and sensible marriage to a woman of some means. I suspect you may be a woman of such means, Miss Dalton, but I could not in conscience permit myself to imagine that such an arrangement would be suitable for you. The best I can hope for, I fear, is a deep and abiding friendship with a woman of your status. So I wonder if you might consider a drive with me with no other pretensions than friendship at stake."

Claire decided in that instant that there could certainly be no other gentleman as frank and disarmingly honest as Jack Graham. In absolute sincerity, she placed her hand on his arm. "You do yourself too little credit, Mr Graham, but neither — of course! — am I prepared at this moment to consider marriage to anyone! I have, after all, only been in London for a few days, and the Season is yet hardly begun. And it would be my most genuine pleasure to go for a drive with you tomorrow with, as you say, nothing other than what I am sure will be a beautiful friendship at stake. At two o'clock, shall we say, or would another hour suit you?"

Graham's long lashes shuttered over brown eyes before he opened them again to full and charming effect. "Two o'clock is perfect, Miss Dalton. I look forward to seeing you then."

Miss Dalton had danced every set of the evening save one, and in that one she sat with a strikingly handsome young man who was in every way Benedict's opposite. Where he was dark, the youth was fair; where he was slim, the man was sturdy; where he was tall, the other man was of middling height. He was impeccably dressed in fashionable green and fawn that made Benedict feel drab, and Miss

Dalton had gazed upon him with adoration visible even across a crowded ballroom. All of this, while Benedict had spied on her from a distance in hopes of finding her looking his way even once.

And not once had she glanced at him. Not on the dance floor with any of the Lads, suggesting that nary a one of them had bothered to tell her a friendly story about him. There was no reason for this to be of consequence to him, and he could hardly allow even to himself that it somehow rankled. The thing to do was clearly to press his suit with Miss Hurst, and so he had: not to an indelicate degree, but certainly with as much attention as the sandy-haired gentleman paid to Miss Dalton.

The hour was now late, with the last set about to be played, and though Miss Dalton had danced twice with the blond man, Benedict had danced only once with Miss Hurst. He approached her and received a wary look for his troubles, a look he dispelled at once with a smile. "Fear not, Miss Hurst, I am not here to ruddy your complexion. I wondered if I might sit with you for the last set, though, as I find myself suddenly tired and in need of such excellent company as you have offered this evening."

Miss Hurst smiled, though her smile touched only the corners of her lips. "Of course, Mr Fairburn. I would be pleased to have you join me."

"May I be forthright with a question for you, Miss Hurst?" he asked as he sat.

"I hope that you are. It is less tedious that way."

"I shall endeavor not to be tedious, then. Is that—a lack of tedium—why you approached me earlier, under the guise of having at some previous point been introduced?"

"You must admit it worked." Miss Hurst's eyes warmed, blue increasing in depth. "I have been quite properly brought up, Mr Fairburn, despite what you may think thanks to my unorthodox introduction. But there are times, I admit, when I think of my grandfather, whom I knew only a little, for he died when I was a child. Memory tells me he was a bold, brash man, unconcerned with convention if he saw no gain in it. I like to imagine myself a little like him, and on the rare occasion where it seems possible to bypass expectation without doing myself or my acquaintances a disservice, I like to try. So, yes, it was to break up the usual tedium of proper form, in a moment when doing so seemed to your advantage. Did you dance with her, the bosomy young lady?"

Benedict, who thought of the girl the same way, still blushed with surprise to hear Miss Hurst describe her so. "I did. She is not as fine a dancer as you, Miss Hurst, though she is passable."

"Her legs are shorter," Miss Hurst said with unexpected charity from a woman of her cool mien. "It's easier to make some of the longer steps at my height."

"I suppose there is that," Benedict said in surprise, and thought briefly of Miss Dalton's diminutive size and the enjoyment she seemed to have on the dance floor despite what must be short legs. Then he thought of her pressing her hand to that unknown gentleman's arm, and quite swiftly said, "Miss Hurst, would you perhaps do me the honor of a drive in the park tomorrow afternoon? I believe I should like to extend my acquaintance with you."

Her considering silence gave him time to reflect and to realize he was not displeased with himself for asking. Moreover, he was delighted when her silence ended with, "Yes, Mr Fairburn, I would do you that honor. It sounds like a very pleasant excursion. Shall we say two o'clock?"

"Two it shall be," Benedict replied, and retired feeling the evening was a triumph.

Chapter Five

"What were you thinking, Claire, to accept an invitation from a man who admitted himself unsuitable for marriage? If you are to go driving it ought to be with someone well known as eligible and suitable, so that you become more sought after by association. I shall have a note sent to inform this young man that you are not available today after all, nor any other day."

Aunt Elizabeth delivered this speech over four-minute eggs and toast with enough lashings of salted butter that Claire forewent the marmalade. She also listened politely to her aunt's proclamation, taking a bite of the very nice egg before saying, "Please don't, Aunt Elizabeth," when she meant *you certainly shall not, Aunt Elizabeth.*

Mrs Dalton paused with a bite of egg suspended halfway to her mouth, then slowly lowered her etched silver spoon to say, "I beg your pardon, Claire?" in a tone that expected her niece to quiver and retreat.

"I said please don't. I am new to London and while I'm sure I'll soon have many friends, at the moment it is yourself and Uncle Charles and Charles Edward and," Claire took care to put on a slightly pained expression, "the Lads." She allowed her face to clear instantly and put all the innocence she could muster into her voice. "Who are lovely, do not mistake me! But they are so many, and so very...laddish. They come and go together, as if regimented, making it positively impossible to become good friends with any of them. So it seems it might be wise to search out my own friends, don't you see? I have no expectations at all of Mr Graham, nor he of me. It is the most suitable first friendship in Town that I could imagine."

"It is not suitable at all," began Aunt Elizabeth, but Claire, determined to be blithe, carried on as if her aunt had not spoken.

"Besides, if he *is* on the fringes of Society due to his lack of wealth, then first it is only charitable to maintain an acquaintance with him, for we who are fortunate enough to be comfortable have a duty to those who are more wretched, do we not? I've spent many a happy day at home visiting with widowers and widows alike, making certain that they feel wanted."

"But those are widowers, Claire," Elizabeth protested, "not men in their prime."

"And," Claire concluded, "if he *is* to make a suitable marriage for himself, why, then, is not being seen with me as useful to him as being seen with Lord Cringlewood might be for me?

It shows that he can be regarded as an acceptable match for someone in the right circumstances. It would be an absolute cruelty, Aunt, to cut him away before our first outing. Think of what people would say."

Elizabeth Dalton, unaccustomed to being thwarted, sat across the table from her niece and thought for the first time that perhaps it was as well that she had borne no daughters. The girl was wrong in every way that mattered, and yet the argument she presented was a pretty one indeed. Worse, as if the matter was settled, Claire said, "I had best go see what Madame Babineaux has arranged for suitable driving ensembles. Thank you so much for your understanding, Aunt Elizabeth." With this, she departed the table with a winning smile that gave no impression that she realized she had won a route.

The girl was either dangerously clever or a fool, and Mrs Dalton, gazing now at her cooling eggs, could not decide which.

Claire sank against the breakfast room door after it closed behind her, and bit a knuckle to keep from giving a shrill laugh. It had been a near thing there with Aunt Elizabeth, and she wasn't absolutely confident of her victory. Never once had Charles Edward described his mother as easily flummoxed, and she would no doubt recover in short order. With that in mind, Claire hurried for her rooms to admire the driving ensemble that Madame Babineaux had assembled amongst her other pieces for Claire. The gown was simple and the overcoat a lovely mustard yellow that Claire would not have imagined to choose for herself, yet which had become an instant favorite as soon as she had tried it on for Madame Babineaux's fittings. She looked forward to wearing it out for the first time, but it was hours before Mr Graham would come calling. The coat must wait. Her hair, though, in order to be perfect, required some attention, particularly so that her charming little hat would nestle nicely in brown curls. Attending to such activities should keep her out of Aunt Elizabeth's way until it was too late; that was all Claire wanted.

Nearly three hours later, with her scalp aching from Marie's ruthless ministrations, Claire conceded to herself (and herself alone) that there might have been more comfortable ways to avoid Aunt Elizabeth for the interim. But the deed—and her hair—was done, and she emerged to the drawing room, where Charles Edward looked at her approvingly and said, "Oh, well done, Claire."

"Thank you. You ought to let Madame Babineaux do something about *your* wardrobe, Charles." She kissed her cousin's cheek and settled herself enough to rise gracefully when Mr Graham was admitted.

He was not, she decided as he bowed over her hand, *quite* as handsome in daylight as he was by candlelight. The warm glow of the flames brought out the sunshine in his hair and skin, whereas actual sunlight diminished it. That was perfectly fine: they were, after all, to be bosom friends, not lovers. And he was still impeccably attired both in clothes and by an open, honest smile that made her instantly glad she had stood up to Aunt Elizabeth.

The thought of her aunt made Claire glance nervously toward the door as Charles and Graham exchanged pleasantries. It was well and right that they should, but she didn't want to add Mrs Dalton's presence to the mix, and so with a smile suggested they depart to catch the best of the afternoon light.

"As you command," Graham said cheerfully. "A pleasure, Dalton. I hope we'll see each other again. Miss Dalton?" He offered his arm, and to Claire's relief they departed the house unmolested.

A pretty little cabriolet pulled by a sturdy grey awaited them, though Graham, disarmingly, admitted, "I've hired it, I'm afraid. Can't afford to keep a carriage this fine. We'll look well, though, won't we? And I'm trusting the weather to hold and brought a picnic."

"Then hold it shall," Claire proclaimed as she stepped into the cab. "This is lovely, Mr Graham. Thank you. I haven't gone for a drive in the park since I was a child, I think. Last time I visited London, it was snowing!"

"That must have been three years ago, then.

Last winter there wasn't enough snow to stop the young folk from driving in it."

"Ah, but I was with my aunt and uncle, who are old enough to avoid the cold when they can. But you're right; it was three years ago." Claire smiled toward the sky. "But now it's only a little chilly, and I'm glad for the sun. London can seem so…colorless, without sunshine. Not like the country, where it's always green or gold or white. Or mud," she added after a moment of prosaic thoughtfulness.

Graham laughed. "We have our share of mud too. Do you miss it? The country, not the mud."

"I've hardly had time to," Claire admitted. "I miss my friends, but I've been writing to them, and that makes them seem near. And I shall soon make more friends here in Town. It does my heart good to be your friend now, Mr Graham."

"And mine, Miss Dalton. Now, see, I always find a bit of color in London. Look there, the yellow brick standing out against the black. Or —" He brought the horse about in a deft turn, and the empty black branches in the near distance suddenly became whole trees lining the still-green walkways of the park. "Or a stretch of green," he said in triumph, and Claire clapped her hands in delight. "Shall we try a bit of speed?" Graham asked.

"Oh, let's! Not too fast, we wouldn't want to look like mad things, but yes, please!"

She laughed aloud again as Graham clucked the grey into a trot, bouncing speed enough for the cold wind to pull tears from the corners of her eyes. A whole circuit of the park, both of them waving gaily to passers-by, many of whom smiled and some few who looked so disapproving it heightened their joy even more. As they reached the gates they had first entered, Graham reined in the team to a walk again, though the smile never left his face. "Too mad?"

"Perfect!" Claire exclaimed. "Once more around to cool the horse, and then our picnic, perhaps?"

"Perfect," Graham agreed, and took the cab around in a much more sedate turn that earned them no further ill looks. "Pleasant," Graham whispered as he helped Claire out of the carriage afterward, "but less fun, wouldn't you say?"

"A different kind of fun," Claire suggested. "Here, will I lay the picnic out while you hitch the horse?"

"An excellent thought, although I'm afraid the basket is rather heavy. Let me at least settle it in the grass." Graham did so, and laid out an oilskin beneath a double thickness of blankets, so damp wouldn't rise to stain their clothes.

A second carriage nearby drew up as well, and two young people disembarked. Claire glanced up to smile without truly seeing them, then returned to arranging the picnic to her liking. They had been fortunate in the weather, she thought; the oilskin beneath the blankets kept away any dew, and it hadn't rained to soak the ground thoroughly. Satisfied with all things, including the arrangement she had made for the picnic lunch, Claire sat on her heels to look for Graham, and discovered the woman of the other couple preparing their picnic blanket as well.

She was extraordinary, Claire decided at once: her strawberry blonde hair was neatly pinned beneath a splendid hat of blue and white pinstripes that matched her overcoat perfectly. Her gown's skirt beneath the coat's gores was yellow, but such a pale yellow as to make Claire think of the most delicate spring roses. The impression was increased by the woman's slender build. Claire had not yet stopped gazing in admiration when the woman's picnic partner approached, and for a critical moment Claire examined them together as a couple, seeing if they suited one another.

He was dark of hair and warmer of skin tone, well dressed, and as proportionately slim and tall as she, making them a handsome pair. Claire reached for wine to pour, still watching them curiously, and accidentally poured wine onto the blanket as the man doffed his hat to reveal himself as Benedict Fairburn.

"Oh, *dash* it!" burst from her lips before she could stop herself, and inevitably, Fairburn and his companion turned her way curiously.

//

Miss Priscilla Hurst was the most suitable driving companion a gentleman could hope for. She spoke willingly about fashion and the weather, and knowledgeably about topics not generally considered suitable for a lady, such as politics and the war. Benedict found himself murmuring, "I believe your grandfather should be commended, Miss Hurst, for engendering a woman able to engage in such conversation."

"Have you any brothers at war, Mr Fairburn?"

"One," Benedict replied in surprise. "Why?"

"And have you any sisters?"

"Two."

"Ask them sometime what they think of the politics of war, sir. You might be surprised what we women think and talk about when men are not on hand to worry that we could harm ourselves with too much intellect."

Maybe she was too unconcerned with convention to be suitable after all, Benedict thought, but demmed if she wasn't interesting. And interest*ed*, or surely she would never have dared such frank statements on so little acquaintance. Unless that was why such a beauty was still unmarried: perhaps her opinions were too readily voiced. Well, no matter. Benedict was sure that by the time he had returned from his picnic, his mother would know all there was to know about Miss Hurst. Her suitability would be determined then.

Rather than dwell on it, Benedict drew the

horses off the track and helped Miss Hurst from the carriage. "Let me post them and then I'll take the basket out."

"Nonsense," said Miss Hurst, and with a long snaking arm, seized the basket and took it to lay their lunch out. Trying not to whistle with pleasure, Benedict put the horses to post and sauntered back to Miss Hurst's side.

There were other picnickers: a young woman in a magnificent mustard coat and a hat that swept becomingly over her face as she set her own food out, and another young man a small distance away hitching a handsome grey with the careful actions of one not well-practiced at the art. Pleased at the idea that others were out to enjoy the unusually fine November afternoon, Benedict was smiling as he approached Miss Hurst and removed his hat.

A most unladylike outburst emanated from the picnicker nearby. Miss Hurst and Benedict both turned in surprise, only for Benedict to meet Claire Dalton's startled green gaze.

The cause of her distress was obvious: she had poured wine not into the glasses set out, but onto the blanket. But she looked not at the wine or glasses, but rather at Benedict, as if he was the cause of her surprise. He cleared his throat and looked around to meet Miss Hurst's curious eyes. "Are you acquainted with that young lady, Mr Fairburn?"

"The cousin of my closest friend," Benedict said in some despair, because it was abruptly clear to him that—

"Mr Fairburn," Miss Dalton said in a tone as grim as the tenor of his own thoughts. "What a surprise to encounter you here this afternoon. I do suppose we really must all join for company, rather than sit so close and pretend we don't know each other."

Were he slightly less well-bred, Benedict would have allowed his shoulders to slump. As it was, he could permit himself no more than a smile, as if the proposition was the most natural and pleasant in the world rather than the wretched thing he, too, had concluded must be done out of politeness. "Yes, of course. Please, allow me to move our blankets together. The work of a moment." He could not manage any note of enthusiasm in the recitation, but then, neither had Miss Dalton.

Miss Hurst had not yet opened the wine, so it was their blanket he moved, judging the risk of spillage to be lesser. After tucking the two blankets together he offered a strained version of his best smile. "Miss Hurst, may I present Miss Claire Dalton. Miss Dalton, Miss Priscilla Hurst."

Discernible conversation was momentarily lost in a blur of greetings and mutual admiration, every nuance of which sounded sincere to Benedict's ear. Then the other gentleman approached and Claire, sounding more lighthearted than she had issuing the invitation to join them, called, "Ah, Mr Graham,

I have found friends! Please, come meet them!"

Claire's companion was the sandy-haired fellow from the night before. His gaze skittered over the newly arrived pair and he slowed considerably between one step and the next, casting a quick, almost desperate glance at Miss Dalton. She, in turn, smiled with fixed determination and said, still lightly, "Of course I insisted they join us. Mr Jack Graham, may I present Miss Priscilla Hurst and Mr Benedict Fairburn."

Miss Hurst's attention, Benedict realized, was entirely on Graham: on the handsome, strong-jawed face and the loose, easy sand-gold curls and the dark doe eyes. It was the very same way Miss Dalton had looked at Graham the night before. Without further thought, Benedict concluded he loathed the man, although he took pains to hide it with an overly pleased greeting. Graham exuded the same enthusiasm for him, effused over Miss Hurst to a degree that made Miss Dalton grow chilly and Miss Hurst, cool by nature, veritably icy. Finally, he seemed to realize he had overplayed his hand and trailed into an uncomfortable silence that lasted an untoward amount of time.

Well, they could not stand there silently all afternoon. Benedict, through a smile meant to hide clenched teeth, said, "Perhaps we should sit. Do be careful, Miss Dalton, you spilled wine there."

He thought she would cut him for the reminder, but even as he thought it, she relented. "So I did. Thank you, Mr Fairburn; it would have been difficult to get out of this dress."

"We have lemonade," Miss Hurst offered. "Less dangerous to the fabrics."

"But so bitter," Graham said almost beneath his breath. A momentary pause broke the conversation while all three of the others tried to decide if they should behave as if they had heard that, or not. Better not, Benedict thought, and in the same instant it seemed the women had drawn the same conclusion, as Miss Dalton said, "Lemonade would be splendid, thank you. Perhaps the wine can be saved for later, and poured by someone with steadier hands."

"That would no doubt be myself," said Miss Hurst. "I'm told I have ice in my veins, which surely means I cannot tremble with emotion."

"One of our wines is white," Graham said smoothly. "Perhaps you might hold it in those icy hands to chill it."

"Oh, but everyone's hands must be icy!" Miss Dalton blurted. "Is it not very cold suddenly?" It was not; the sun shone as warmly as it could in November, and what little wind there was hardly stirred the hair, but Benedict, having been about to say something similar, felt a sharp pang of sympathy lance him. Miss Dalton's pulse was quick in her throat, and her eyes were round with dismay as Graham and Miss Hurst broke their tête-à-tête to look at her.

She went on a little wildly, as if having not thought through what she planned to say. "The wind is very chill, is it not? I hope you've packed something to warm the humors with, Mr Graham!"

Graham seemed to remember himself and procured a broken smile for her. "Yes, of course. The wind is quite bad, Miss Dalton."

Soon, Benedict thought, they would have convinced themselves of a veritable storm with thunderous clouds and lashing rain rather than the mild afternoon they were actually experiencing. Claire's attempt at a polite fiction had already gone too far, and the situation only grew worse as Graham blundered on. "Perhaps we ought to have chosen a gazebo for our picnic. But I have brought fish pasties, bundled well enough to still be warm, and that should help to ward off the chill!"

"I don't care for fish pasties," said Miss Hurst.

Graham's smile went rigid. "It is as well I did not pack it for you, then, Miss Hurst."

Miss Hurst said, "No, you would not have," with such icy precision that Benedict cast a stricken glance toward Claire, as if she might somehow provide an explanation for their companions' peculiar behavior. She met his eyes with her own rounded by dismay. The slightest twitch of one furrowed eyebrow conveyed a world of questions so clearly that it was as if she had spoken aloud: *What*, that minute motion asked, *is going on? Do they know one another? Of course they know one another; how do they know one another? Did you know of any of this?* and finally, *How could you have let me invite you to sit, if you knew?!*

Benedict responded in equally eloquent silence, the cords of his throat tightening and his head jerking an infinitesimal amount to the side in what amounted to violent denial. *No!* He said with those tiny actions. *I know nothing of their previous acquaintance! I am as horrified as you are!*

Miss Dalton could not quite be said to droop, but there was an unquestionable release of tension that moved her closer to Benedict's side. She believed him, then, which gladdened Benedict's heart more than was sensible. He found the sensation that she was perhaps sheltering from the storm by huddling closer to him to be pleasant.

And a storm there was: Miss Hurst and Mr Graham were now laying out foodstuffs as if they were weapons, each of them trying to move more swiftly and more beautifully than the other. Benedict had lost track of their intercourse, and considered trying to insert calm into their swift exchanges, but at that moment Miss Dalton looked up at him.

Her evident and sensible horror of their companions' behavior was starting to flee: he saw a terrible urge to laugh shining in her green eyes and in the barely-controlled tremble at the corner of her mouth. She bit her lower lip to contain it, and he was suddenly taken with the fullness of her lips, the flush of color where her teeth held back laughter, and the smile still fighting to break through. The impulse to kiss her was nearly impossible to resist. To stop himself Benedict clapped three fingers over his own mouth, and in so doing discovered he, too, was holding back laughter.

Miss Dalton's entire lower lip was now in her teeth, and her eyes were so large he was convinced he might fall and drown in their laughing green loveliness. She folded her knuckles at her mouth and slid a look toward Graham and Miss Hurst, then returned her gaze to Benedict's. *Whatever are we going to do about them?* her eyes asked.

Benedict took his hand from his mouth and captured Miss Dalton's fingers, smiling openly now, though it was a small and intensely private smile for Miss Dalton alone. Without taking his eyes from hers, he answered with a slow blink that let him gaze at her through his lashes. *Forget about them,* that look suggested, and suddenly Miss Dalton was not smiling anymore, but rather pink-cheeked and wetting her lips with unconscious anticipation. Benedict moved his head toward hers a fraction of an inch, no more.

Benedict Fairburn was going to kiss her. Claire, who had never been kissed, was more certain of this than she had ever been of anything in her entire twenty years. He was going to kiss her, and she could think of nothing she would rather have happen.

It was therefore with tremendous guilt that she leaped from him when Mr Graham let forth a roar that would have best suited a caged lion, and it was with no pleasure at all that she saw Benedict flinch with equal guilt and, immediately upon that emotion, horror.

Horrified at what he had nearly done, no doubt. Claire had never blushed so hard in all her years, either, color burning her face so brilliantly that tears stood in her eyes. Desperate not to let them fall, she stared without seeing at Graham, who was on his feet and...dripping. Dripping with lemonade, his cravat stained with it, his collar losing its starch with its acid wetness. He stood with breast heaving, an outraged gaze locked on Miss Priscilla Hurst, who sat placidly on the picnic blankets, examining her lemonade glass as if curious as to how it had come to be empty.

"What...?" Claire's pleasure at the prospect of being kissed and her conviction of Mr Fairburn's horror both faded into her *own* horror at how badly she had nearly behaved. She had come driving with Mr Graham and had all but forgotten him by gazing into Mr Fairburn's astonishingly blue eyes. Had he kissed her she could have been no more than a hussy, and worse, one who had acted out her passions in front of another couple.

That the other couple had been entirely involved in their own passions, that their behavior had opened the window for her momentary interest in Mr Fairburn, and that if anyone was at fault it could not with any degree of logic be considered to be Claire, were all thoughts she thrust aside with zealous determination. She had been dreadfully weak and could certainly not afford to be again if she wished to make a good marriage.

"Forgive me," Miss Hurst said, her voice as placid as her pose, "my lemonade seems to have slipped."

"*Slipped*?" Benedict asked incredulously, no longer paying any attention to Claire at all.

Graham, in a strained voice, echoed, "Slipped. I am sure it was entirely my fault, I was..." His imagination failed as to what he had been doing. Claire, who had been so possessed by Fairburn's gaze she genuinely had no idea what had prompted the—slip—swallowed hard and suggested, "...so involved in your story that a careless gesture struck Miss Hurst's glass?"

All three of the others turned their attention to her. Claire, looking between them, felt mortified, young, and very plain. Miss Hurst was a genuine beauty, her excellent features all the more striking for the cool hardness in her eyes. Graham was sunlight to her ice, and Claire had thought Mr Fairburn terribly handsome all along. They were all quite perfect, even with Graham dripping lemonade, and Claire, embarrassed, looked away to see that she had knelt in the spilled wine after all, and that a raspberry-colored stain was encroaching upon her cream-and-brown skirts. Tears filled her eyes a second time and she dared not look up again for fear they would fall.

"Yes," Miss Hurst said slowly, "I believe you have the right of it, Miss Dalton. A careless gesture is all. And oh, no, my dear girl, your skirt!" Her iciness fled and she surged forward to push Claire aside so that she no longer sat in the spilled wine. "Hot water and salt," Miss Hurst said fiercely. "If we're quick enough we'll get that out before it sets. Come, Graham, snap to it. Have you got anything useful in that basket of yours?"

"Em, a well-packed pot of water for tea if the weather turned inclement—"

"Well, get it! Now, on your feet, Miss Dalton, over to the grass. Mr Fairburn, this is an extraordinary request, but you will have to be polite about it and look away. Hold Miss Dalton's skirt out straight from her body so that the hot water doesn't splash on her as I pour it through. Move, man!" Delivering orders like a seasoned general, Miss Hurst bustled Claire to the grass and arranged her skirt so that Fairburn could hold it without risking her modesty. "Fortunately," Miss Hurst said to Claire, "it is only at your knee. If it had been your hip Mr Fairburn would have to marry you as soon as we got the stain out."

"Oh," Claire said faintly, and held still as Miss Hurst took Graham's teapot—made of thick clay and warm to the touch—to carefully pour still-steaming water through the stain.

In seconds it had faded to a faint splotch that Miss Hurst examined critically. "Have we a salt shaker?"

"Yes," Fairburn said, "but I fear that if I release Miss Dalton's dress she will end up burned by the heat or chilled from the damp."

Miss Hurst snapped, "Well, look for it, Graham," and for the second time he leaped to her command, finding the salt in Benedict's picnic basket. He brought it to Miss Hurst, who stripped her gloves away, removed the shaker's stopper, took a handful of salt in her soft white hands, and proceeded to scrub it into Claire's skirt with an impressive ruthlessness. After a rinse, another scrub and a final rinse, she declared herself satisfied, and Claire, who had watched the entire process with a growing sense of disbelief, embraced the other woman. Forgotten was the ill behavior of before; gratitude took its place.

"Thank you. Thank you so much, Miss Hurst. Priscilla. I may call you Priscilla, mayn't I? And you must call me Claire. You have gone far beyond the call of duty on such little acquaintance. I hope I may also call you my friend."

"Oh." Miss Hurst stiffened in surprise, then

gingerly returned Claire's embrace. They parted and Claire saw uncertainty in the taller woman's pale eyes. Uncertainty and tentative, uncomfortable hope. "Yes, you may call me Priscilla, and friend. Thank you, Miss Da— Claire. I—forgive me, I am awkward. I do not consider myself one to make friends easily, and your generosity overwhelms me."

"Well, we shall be friends," Claire said stoutly. "Surely friendships have been built on less than an expensive dress saved from ruin."

Startled, Miss Hurst smiled openly, an expression which transcended cool beauty and somehow made her more ordinary and approachable. "Surely they have," she agreed. "Now, Miss—Claire—I think we should get you home and in front of a fire before the chill creeps through wet fabric and makes you ill. I should like to see you home myself. Graham, I assume that cabriolet is hired. I will take it and Miss Dalton home, then return the cab and settle the bill. You will make your own way home. Mr Fairburn, I apologize for having to leave you in so unorthodox a fashion. I hope we will see each other again."

With this, she tucked her arm through Claire's and led her to Graham's cab, only slowing as they reached it. She helped Claire up, then accepted Claire's hand in return, admitting, "I have not thought this through," quietly as they settled into the seats. "I am not a good driver, Miss—Claire."

Claire smiled in sudden, pleased conspiracy. "Fortunately, I am. I'll drive it home, have one of my aunt's servants drive *you* home, and then have the cab returned to its hiring place. The Daltons will settle the bill, in thanks for your services to me. I insist."

"You are the soul of generosity, Claire." Priscilla Hurst pressed her hand against Claire's arm, and, together in sisterly camaraderie, they drove away.

Jack Graham, watching the young ladies drive away, looked as though he didn't know what had hit him. Benedict dearly wanted to disdain him for that, but feared his own expression was far too similar. He had come to the park with one woman, been entirely transfixed by another, and was now left alone as the both of them departed together in evident solidarity. It had in no way been the afternoon he had expected, and he could not help but feel he had been somehow routed. The women could not conceivably have planned the events that had transpired, but they seemed to have come out to the female advantage.

As he mused over this, Graham began packing up the remains of his picnic. Benedict had questions for the sandy-haired man, but the crisis over Miss Dalton's dress had put the lemonade incident so thoroughly behind them that it seemed callous to bring it up again. Worse, just as he decided to be callous and ask anyway, Graham said, "I would like to apologize for my earlier behavior, Mr Fairburn. You must think very poorly of me. All I can hope is that you will not allow that ill perception to reflect upon Miss Hurst, who I am certain is a lady of flawless qualities," which made it impossible for Benedict to say anything except, "Of course I accept your apology, and assure you that I think no less of Miss Hurst."

"I am relieved. Thank you, Mr Fairburn." Graham collected the last of his picnic materials and, with a short bow, abandoned Benedict to the park.

Chapter Six

An inquisition lay in wait for Benedict at home in the guise of his sister, who seized his arm as he stepped through the front door. "Well? Did you thaw Miss Hurst, Benny? Mother has been speaking to her friends—"

"To her own friends, or to Miss Hurst's?" Either seemed likely, knowing their mother's skill in extracting Society gossip.

Amelia did not have dimples: her beauty was too refined for that. Benedict had always thought it a pity, though, because her smile was so warm and infectious it could only be made more so with dimples. "Mother's friends, silly goose. Come, I have Abigail bringing tea and biscuits to the drawing room, and Mother is having her afternoon lie-down, so I can tell you all her gossip and you can tell me all of yours."

"Thus making you the foremost expert on all things Hurst," Benedict said, amused, as Amelia dragged him toward the drawing room. Tea would be welcome, though, and if the price was relating the afternoon's encounters, well, he wanted to tell someone anyway. The maid was there before them, straightening doilies and tidying curtains as she awaited the young mistress and master of the house. Once assured that all was well, she was dismissed and Benedict threw himself into a deeply winged chair to take a gulp of too-hot tea. "Did she learn whether Miss Hurst has ever been engaged?"

"What?" Amelia asked in real astonishment. "No, not a word of it, why?"

"We had a most peculiar interaction with Miss Dalton—Charles's cousin—and her escort for the afternoon, a Mr Jack Graham." Benedict told the story of the afternoon's adventures, leaving out his moment of intense attraction to Miss Dalton, and concluded with, "I thought they must know one another, but perhaps it is only that he is choleric and she, phlegmatic."

"If she was ever engaged to him it was so discreetly that not even Mother could unearth it, so I can't imagine that it's true," Amelia proclaimed. "Now, her grandfather was in trade, so she's not from a long line of money—"

"Yes, she told me that."

Amelia paused, clearly reassessing the order in which to offer information. "She has a brother inclined to gambling, but Mother is given to understand he was cut off some years ago, forced to make his own way so that the family would not be ruined."

"Cold," Benedict said, and thought of Miss Hurst's pale, icy gaze. Another image intruded, though: the rich summer green of Miss Dalton's eyes. He shook his head, trying to clear it away. She had seemed so kissable, and then so remote and uninterested the moment after. Women were confounding. Wrenching his mind back to the matter at hand, he concluded: "Cold but practical. I suppose one does not make a fortune in trade through sentimentality."

"I suppose not. Now, to the details. Her parents are both still alive and *very* proper, Mother hears. She is, of course, arranging an opportunity to meet them by coincidence so she can form her own opinion, but so far, Benny, I think she sees no impediments to your engagement. And I understand that Miss Hurst is a great beauty."

"Almost as beautiful as you are," Benedict said in one part perfunctory flattery and in one part utter truth. If Miss Hurst was ice with her light eyes and strawberry blonde hair and skim milk skin, his sister was fire with auburn locks and flashing brown eyes and the warm coloring suited to exercise that Miss Hurst had freely admitted to not possessing.

"You've been spending too much time with Mr O'Brien," Amy said, clearly pleased. "He flatters as easily as he breathes."

"The thing is, I think he means every word of it," said Benedict absently, then heard himself and smiled at Amy. "As do I, in fact. My expectations of womanly beauty are preposterously high, Amelia, with you and Mother as my standards."

Miss Dalton did not, Benedict reminded himself, compare, although she was much improved by Town. That was no doubt important to remember, even if her general pleasantry made up for what was not strictly beauty. She was, he had to admit, a friendly soul. Or she was, at least, to everyone but himself. Look how quickly and easily she had forgiven Miss Hurst's astonishing behavior, and how eagerly she had begun a friendship there. Perhaps she missed her country girlfriends. Benedict remembered that one or two had visited Claire during the Lads' holiday there. They had all been introduced, of course, but he hadn't thought of them again during the holiday, much less since.

Beneath those ruminations a thought formed. Benedict said, "Amy," before it was fully considered, and she looked up curiously. "Amy, I believe you should make Miss Dalton's acquaintance. She seems a creature fond of her female friends, and being so new to London she can have very few as of yet."

Amelia gave him a measuring look. "And the fact that she has struck up a friendship with Miss Hurst has no bearing on this suggestion, am I right?"

"Of course not! Only in that it occurs to me that if she can make friends with as aloof and reserved a woman as Miss Hurst that a lady of your own charm and openness would soon become a bosom companion."

"To whom she would spill out all sorts of details about what she's learned from her friendship with Miss Hurst," Amelia said in amusement. "Oh, stop making that sour face, Benny, of course I'll call on her. I love to make new friends and don't care a whit for your ulterior motives."

Under no circumstances was Claire prepared to admit the near-fiasco of her afternoon drive with Mr Graham to her aunt. Fortunately, Aunt Elizabeth was out calling on friends when Claire and Miss Hurst arrived home, and if Uncle Charles, who *was* home, even noticed she'd gone out with a gentleman and come back with a lady, he didn't mention it to her and would not, she trusted, mention it to his wife.

Charles Edward, to whom she might have confessed the whole story, appeared in the drawing room door with two of his Lads in tow, thus negating any possibility of sharing gossip. "Claire, there you are," he said in evident self-satisfaction as his Lads—the youthful noble, Cringlewood, and tremendous Scotsman, Vincent, an odd pairing to Claire's mind—bowed and greeted her curtsies with smiles.

"Cringlewood here has finagled invitations to the Thornbury House party tomorrow night, invitations for all of us Lads and, at my behest, yourself and another. Do you know the Thornburys, Claire? Well, you shall. Very much the high set. The house has been in their keeping since the Great Fire, and they're keen on being seen only with the best of the best. No sad crush, this, it will be a much smaller to-do than the ball last night, no more than a few hundred people there, quite exclusive. The Regent may attend. Send a note to that Graham chap of yours and invite him along. It'll be a fine opportunity for you to see and be seen. Now, we're going out, so I beg you to tell Mother that I've come down with the pox so she shan't expect to see me for days."

"The pox, really," Claire said, mildly horrified. "Do you really think Aunt Elizabeth would not rush to your side, and quarantine the entire household, in such a dreadful case?"

Charles blinked lazily. "How foresightful of you. Something else ludicrous, then, cousin. Surely you can think of something."

"She's your mother, Charles. I implore you to make your own excuses. I have enough on my hands, making my own."

"Have you?" Charles's gaze sharpened with interest. "What have you been up to, Claire?"

"Nothing I wish to discuss," Claire said with the most asperity she could manage. "Charles, Mr Graham is not part of the highest set. Will the Thornburys not be gravely insulted if I should bring him?"

"I think they should hardly even notice him," Nathaniel Cringlewood put in. "I would offer to escort you myself, save I must squire my sister."

A swirl of dismayed amusement churned Claire's heart. "The offer is generous, sir, and I thank you." She worried her lower lip, thinking of Graham's extraordinary behavior at the park that afternoon, and wondering whom else she might turn to for an escort. "Are you certain I should not go with *you*, Charles? I should not like to be misfit amongst such company."

Charles gave a dismissive huff. Cringlewood, charmingly, promised, "Not a chance of it, Miss Dalton. Bring Graham along, though I do ask that you save me a dance. I won't be so bold as to ask for the first again, though."

As Cringlewood spoke, Ronald Vincent gave her a careful, questioning look that she was not sure how to answer. He was so very large, Claire thought, that he could not also be sensitive enough to see through to the heart of her predicament. His unasked question retreated judiciously when he did not see whatever it was he looked for in her face, though, and he said, "I might beg a dance as well, Miss Dalton, if it's not above my place to do so."

Cringlewood hit the huge man on the shoulder in fond exasperation, and Claire, too late, understood the question Vincent had not asked aloud: the hint lay in the phrase *above my place*. She thought of him as one of Charles's Lads; he clearly thought of himself as a soldier and a blacksmith whose station was not high enough to offer himself as her escort to the Thornbury party. Cursing her failure to understand and now bound to attend with Graham, Claire smiled at both men. "I would be delighted to accept both invitations. Thank you, your honor, Mr Vincent."

"Best save a dance for me too," Charles said cheerfully. "You're my favorite dance partner, for you're the only girl in London my mother won't be thinking of marrying me off to. The pox, now, Claire, or some such story for my mother, please?"

"I have no intention of saving a dance for a poxy man." Claire spoke with as much severity as she could, which wasn't much, and laughed as the gentlemen bowed themselves out. As they exited, her maid Lucy came in bearing a platter upon which sat an attractive, lightly scented calling card. Curious, Claire accepted it and sat to read it while Lucy waited.

In handsome script, the card read *Miss Amelia Fairburn requests the honor of calling upon Miss Claire Dalton at the eleven o'clock hour on the morrow,* and lit a flame of interest in Claire's breast. She hadn't even known Fairburn *had* sisters, though clearly this must be one. She gestured for a pen and ink and responded in the affirmative immediately, sending Lucy away to have the card delivered. Then, pleased and full of anticipation, she settled in to think up a suitable excuse for Charles's absence from the evening meal.

ff

It could, Charles thought gloomily, be the last time all the Lads were gathered together as bachelors. Benedict would be bound to matrimony desperately soon, and while Miss Hurst was a beauty, there was no hint of anything about her that suggested she could possibly understand the bonds that held the Lads together. She was not the sort of wifely material who would respect their camaraderie enough to allow her husband the freedom he needed to spend evenings with his friends.

Of course, many husbands eschewed wifely companionship for male friendship, whether in the dining room for a smoke and port or in a carousing dance hall like the one in which the Lads were now gathered. Perhaps that would be the saving grace of Benny's marriage, and perhaps not much would change, after all. Content with this thought, Charles allowed himself to consider the ribald hall with a more cheerful air.

There was little in the way of formal wear to be seen: it was all buckskins and breeches, with loosened collars and untied cravats. Smoke and the scent of alcohol filled the air, and the noise occasionally rose to such fervor as to become palpable. Wantons danced or climbed into mens' laps. O'Brien pushed one such off with a laugh. Perhaps they *could* carry on like this once Fairburn was married. Then again, Benedict was a decent sort, and likely to acquiesce to his wife's wishes. Charles's momentary good mood faded with the fear that in no time the Lads would be—well, not decimated, since there were only seven of them to begin with. Septuginated, if such a thing existed.

"You're moping, Dalton." O'Brien, having sent the bird off, slid into the low-backed stool beside him and demanded whiskey for them both. "Is it as bad as all that, then?"

"Stop that," Charles said with utterly ineffective sternness. O'Brien looked at him with such cow-like innocence as to render the possibility of coherent thought behind the brown eyes impossible. Despite himself, Charles snorted laughter and accepted the drink O'Brien had ordered.

"Stop what, now?" O'Brien asked. "Sure and all I've done is sit and order a drink with a friend so."

"The brogue, Gar. Lay it on any thicker and I won't understand a word you're saying."

"Acht! That's a dreadful thing to say to a mate, mocking me for me own words spoken from the heart. Can I help it if me heart's voice is as Irish as the day is long?"

"I fancy you can," Charles said dryly, and finally O'Brien laughed.

"Maybe so, but it cracks that sour face of yours, Major, and that's worth it."

"No. Not Major. Not anymore, O'Brien. Please."

O'Brien shook his head. "You'll always be my major, Dalton," but he ended it with

Dalton's name and not his rank, and that was enough. "Is it bad tonight, then?"

"No. Not the nerves." Charles gritted the word out through his teeth, hating that saying it admitted his failure of courage. O'Brien made a sound hardly audible in the din, but it was enough. They had had the conversation a hundred times; a thousand times, and it needed no more repeating. O'Brien would never agree about Dalton's weaknesses, and for that, Charles was grateful. "Not tonight," Charles went on. "Anticipation of things changing, perhaps. You lads steady me."

"My Nan would tell you not to borrow trouble, God rest her. Benny's not married yet and six are nearly as good as seven anyway."

"Ah, but what about when it's five, and then three, and then myself all alone? What then, Gar? Or do you intend never to abandon me?" Charles smiled, but Gareth O'Brien straightened his strong back and met his eyes with a forthright gaze.

"Nor will I, Dalton, though I'd be nothing as fair in your service as your man Worthington. But I'll never take a wife who'd stop me from coming when you called, either. Not me and not Vincent, not ever. Nor that bastard Hewitt, either, I'd wager."

"What did you call me?" Hewitt swung past, already more drunk than was sensible, with a well-rounded blonde hanging off him and laughing uproariously. They crashed into

Dalton, who braced to avoid spilling his whiskey. O'Brien clapped a hand to his shoulder.

"Good man, saving the drink. That's another sip ye won't drown in, in hell."

"Had hell been intent on drowning me, I'd have died in Spain," Dalton said, then, disgusted at his own moroseness, shook off the languor and shoved back to crash against Hewitt in return. "Put the bird down, Evan. We've got some serious drinking to do. Tonight we'll drink our sorrows for Benny so we may celebrate with clear hearts when he weds. Fairburn!" he roared, and as if waiting for the call, the crowd ejected Benedict Fairburn with forceful deliberation.

The crowd may have somehow been waiting for it; Fairburn had not been. Possessed of a tall tankard foaming with beer and a look of surprise, he lost his footing and upended the beer over a burly, red-faced fellow who might have—by size—been Vincent's brother.

The burly fellow bellowed and swung an affronted elbow without so much as looking, catching Benedict in the eye. Fairburn howled in pain, bringing Lads from all around the hall. As they gathered, so too did the burly man's friends. Charles came to his feet slowly, tension clenching his jaw. He knew himself well enough by now to recognize that a blind fear or a blind rage could rise in a heartbeat, when trouble came knocking. Gut tight, judging the potential for carnage, he spoke to — *shouted* to — the burly man, whose shoulders were sufficiently broad that his head looked like a small and poorly considered afterthought. "It was an accident, sir, nothing more. There's no need for trouble."

"Demmed if there isn't," Hewitt snarled from Charles's side. "There was no call for him to throw an elbow."

Vincent, too large to move so smoothly, none-the-less inserted himself in front of Hewitt, more than half-blocking him from the burly man's view. Like a bear protecting an unruly cub, Charles thought tightly, though in the end it was Charles, not Hewitt, whom Vincent was trying to save from a scrape.

Fairburn, who had by this time regained his feet and some degree of speech, prodded gingerly at his bruised eye before attempting to tender an apology to the increasingly-florid brute. His, "Forgive me, sir. I was clumsy," was a statement which, to Charles's mind, bordered on outright fabrication, but might keep the peace. Fairburn went on, "Perhaps I could buy you and your friends a round of drinks, and accept the bill for the cleaning of your clothes," in his best attempt to make amends.

The burly man, who had begun to look appeased, reversed his attitude with Fairburn's last words. He swept his hat off to reveal the bristly remains of hair on a balding head, not fashionable at all. Even given the general lowliness of the dance hall, Charles wondered what sort of ruffian they were letting through the doors. Then the pin-headed man spoke in an accent so clipped and refined that Charles could only compare it to that of Cringlewood's grandmother, the duchess. It in no way belonged to a man with the face of a longboat-worker, and yet that face issued forth a cultivated, "Are you saying that I *smell*, boy?!"

Alarmed, Charles sought Cringlewood's gaze, desperate for some indication of who this velvet-voiced dockworker could be. Cringle-wood, to Vincent's right now, with Ackerman looking on from beside him, lifted one shoulder and let it fall. He clearly didn't know the man either, which was curious; the peerage tended to recognize one another on sight.

Benedict, taken aback, blurted, "Er, what? No! Only that I poured beer all over you — !"

"And now you hide behind half a dozen men! Are you a coward?"

A deadly silence rolled out from that query, broken only by the soft sound of shuffling feet as the establishment's patrons cleared a circle around the pending fight so they could observe without becoming embroiled. Whispers followed the shuffling, and the bets were on.

Benedict had not yet recovered enough from insulted astonishment to respond. Charles slipped past Hewitt and Vincent both until he stood in front of them all save Benedict himself.

"In point of fact," he said with his own best vowels, and in as quiet a voice as he could manage through a haze of rising anger, "Mr Fairburn is standing in *front* of half a dozen men, which is more than I can say for you, sir. As for your accusation, I should not say such things."

Behind him, Ronald Vincent drew in a slow, careful breath of recognition, and Charles felt the tenor of the Lads change. They had gathered to defend one of their own; now they were preparing to fight. The one was not the same as the other.

"Should I not," sneered Vowels, as Charles abruptly thought of him. "Do you think you can scare me, you crass piece of—"

"I should not," Charles repeated, with more heat, "say such things if I were you. Retreat, sir; I will not have my friends insulted and I am not unfamiliar with battle."

"You?" Vowels said incredulously. "You, you little pipsqueak, hardly tall enough to lick my boot? You, with the lazy eyes and quivering thin mouth? I doubt you know what end of a sword to hold, much less have ever fired a weapon in battle. You could not—"

Even fine accents, it seemed, could be silenced with a fist to the mouth. Vowels howled as Benedict, shaking his fist and glancing at Charles in pained apology, muttered, "Forgive me, I—" Anything else he intended to say was lost in a rush of action as Vowels's men swarmed Charles's Lads.

It was not, from the start, a fair fight. O'Brien had come around to Charles's left while Vowels postured; together with Vincent, the three of them surged forward. It required no discussion for Vincent and O'Brien to attend to the men at Vowels's sides while Charles dealt with Vowels directly.

Vowels was right, of course: Charles was small by comparison, but large men rarely thought that small ones had any advantage in a fight. Vowels swung; Charles stepped inside the blow and drove his fist deep into the bigger man's gut, doubling him. He seized the man's ears, lifted his head a few inches, then slammed it down again toward his own swiftly-rising knee; a crunch sounded and blood flew around adenoidal screams in the aftermath of a broken nose. Charles cast him aside, kicked his jaw to silence him, and looked up to see that the fight was, for all purposes, already over.

Vincent held an unconscious man by his scruff, with a second one at their feet. Spreading red marks on their foreheads suggested the one Vincent held had been used as a battering ram against the one on the floor. Vincent dropped the one he still held, and glanced up to shrug apologetically at Charles. Samuel Ackerman, some feet beyond Vincent at the fringe of the circle, stood with his foot on a man's throat and an expression of mild disdain on his flawless features. Between them

Cringlewood had taken a blow to the corner of his mouth and throttled the offender in return. The man was, Charles trusted, still breathing, though if Cringlewood wished it, there was no doubt that the law would see to it that he shortly ceased to do so — or look the other way if Cringlewood took care of it himself.

O'Brien, on Charles's left, had struck one man down and chased another into the edges of the watching crowd; they faced off now, though there was little doubt the other man had lost his will to fight. A few steps behind O'Brien, Hewitt sat astride a doughty-looking fellow, still raining blows upon him. Charles shuddered from his bones out, trying to settle the fighting rage and confoundedly grateful that it was anger, and not bowel-watering fear, that had come on him this time. After a few seconds, hoping he could trust his voice, Charles said, "Evander," mildly, and Hewitt stopped with visible reluctance.

Fairburn, standing a few steps behind Charles, murmured, "I believe I could have acquitted myself more handsomely, but there was no one left to hit. Dalton, I am sorry, but I was afraid if that fellow kept on it would be pistols at dawn. A bar fight seemed wiser."

"Probably wise. I'm concerned about this one, though, Fairburn," Charles said, nudging Vowels with one foot. "If his voice is any indication, then despite his face he's Quality — "

Charles's thought was cut off by the arrival

of a dandified man of considerably too great an age to wear the foppish fashion he had chosen. His voice, however, matched the outrage of his outfit, and his whiskers quivered as he shrieked, "That was our *theatrical troupe!*"

Relief swept Charles so thoroughly he nearly laughed, and the merriment of his expression spurred the fop to greater fury. "You have spoiled a night's entertainment! A month's entertainment, for I'm sure they won't play the hall now, not after such rude treatment. My God, the cancellation fees I'll have to pay! The word on the street—" His eyes lit with a sudden fervorous greed, as if realizing word on the street of a fight in his dance hall would no doubt bring in dozens, even hundreds, hoping to see another such disruptive show of ill behavior, but he couldn't allow that to stop his tirade. "—will be ruinous! I shall have to close the hall! Out! Out! Get them out of my hall!"

Like the Red Sea, the hall patrons parted, allowing the Lads to be manhandled and thrust toward the doors. Manhandled, but not, Charles noted, too roughly; they had done themselves proud, and the proprietor's enforcers clearly weren't certain of their ability to quell the Lads, should it come to it. Still, they were flung with a certain dramatic flair onto the streets. All of them—save Vincent, who was simply too large to unfoot—landed on their backsides or backs on muddy, cold cobblestones.

The doors behind them were slammed shut as a final statement, though they were opened again seconds later to allow curious passers-by to rush inside and hear all about the commotion. Some of them even stepped over the Lads, no one offering assistance.

Charles found himself smiling beatifically at the foggy night sky. "Well. I suppose we won't be welcome *there* for a while."

"Oh dear, sir," was Worthington's only comment upon the arrival home of what he often thought of as his charge, although he had no specific compulsion to care for Charles Edward's well-being, only his clothes.

The young Mr Dalton gave him a positively brilliant grin, promising, "Ah, but you should see the other blokes, Worthington," as the valet helped him out of his coat. "We're only dirty from being thrown out. Well, a bruise or two here or there. Cringlewood's sporting a bruise that's swollen his lip up like a girl's and Fairburn's got a mouse that makes him look twice as mean as he is. Three times," he decided, "Benny's not a mean man. We've got to keep them out of Mother's sight until they're healed up or she'll want to know what's what."

"That may be difficult, sir," Worthington murmured. "You have the Thornbury party to attend tomorrow evening. Even if she doesn't see them, word will certainly come back to her."

"Blast!" Charles fell backward onto his bed, splayed out like an infant in a cot. He was not injured, Worthington surmised, but he was certainly inebriated. A restorative would be necessary in the morning. In the *later* morning; it was already well into the early morning hours, and only dark due to the time of year. A toot like this in June would have seen the young sir home with the dawn.

The young sir was not, however, so inebriated as to be unable to think, as was evidenced by his eventual, "Perhaps you can run a bit of interference, Worthington. Find a way to distract her from the topic until bruises are faded and gossip is dust."

Worthington replied, "Gossip is never dust," but also — inevitably — promised, "I will do my best, sir. Now, Mr Dalton, please, we really must do something about your trousers before there is an indelible mud stain on the bed. Your mother," he added as he set about dealing with the trousers, "did not believe Miss Dalton's claim that you were suffering the headache, and expects you to be at breakfast at nine, Mr Dalton."

"The headache," Charles echoed. "Just as well she didn't try to claim the pox. Mother would have been in here fussing over me for days. I believe I may die if you force me to arise at such an unforgivable hour, Worthington. You would not be so cruel." With that, Charles rolled over and drew a pillow onto his head, asleep almost before the action was complete, for he well knew that Worthington would, indeed, be every bit that cruel.

Quietly and efficiently, Worthington went about setting the rest of Dalton's clothes and room to rights, even pausing to draw a duvet over the gently snoring youth before pausing at the door to look at his young master in fond concern.

Charles would not have begun the fight; Worthington knew that. He would, though, have ended it, in hopes of proving something to himself, if not to the world. It had happened before. The worry was that it would happen again, and again, until the stakes were raised so high than only death would settle them.

On that distressing thought he left Charles to sleep, and went to seek his own few hours of rest before duty called once more.

Chapter Seven

Breakfast was a stilted affair, marked by Aunt Elizabeth's stern look and alleviated by Charles Edward's occasional groans, which caused Uncle Charles to peer over the edge of his papers each time as if surprised anyone could make such a sound. For her own part, Claire tried not to fidget on the edge of her seat until the meal had been taken, and fled at the earliest opportunity to dress for Miss Amelia Fairburn's arrival.

Miss Fairburn was splendidly timely, arriving at the stroke of the eleven o'clock hour, and had such exquisite manners and bearing that at first Claire was afraid her hopes of female companionship would be dashed. She bore a superficial resemblance to Miss Hurst—Priscilla, Claire reminded herself warmly—in that they both had red hair and pale skin and were both indisputable beauties, but it was as if they had been created as differently as could be within the same palate. Miss Fairburn's hair was the deep auburn of cooling embers and her skin inclined to a golden undertone. She wore orange shot with cream, tones that complemented her coloring perfectly and caused Claire to glance at her own modest white dress with uncertainty. It had been much easier to dress in the country, she thought in despair. There, she had never worried that she might be lacking in fashion, always trusting her mother's guidance. Now, though, it was clear her mother had—to be generous—questionable taste, and that Claire had been dreadfully *un*fashionable. She could hardly imagine going back to the dresses she had once worn.

While Claire despaired, Aunt Elizabeth greeted Miss Fairburn with the pleasure of long familiarity, then left the young women to themselves. Steeling herself for the no doubt tremendously proper conversation about to take place, Claire lifted a tentative smile to Miss Fairburn and was nearly knocked over as she rushed forward to seize Claire's hands. "Oh, do tell me," she pleaded breathlessly. "Is Charles in as dreadful a state this morning as Benny? The butler had to get a cold cut for his eye, it's so swollen and blackened! And he won't speak a word of what happened, so I'm desperate to know, Miss Dalton, absolutely desperate!"

Claire, startled, laughed aloud. Miss Fairburn, looking abject, withdrew her hands and twisted them in her skirt apologetically. "Oh dear. That was awful of me, wasn't it? I should have been much more reserved, but oh,

Mother is in such a state and I can see that Mrs Dalton hasn't any idea of what went on, so I must know, Miss Dalton! I simply must know what condition Charles is in!"

"You are perfect," Claire assured her happily, and took the other girl's hand to lead her toward one of the sofas. "I'm entirely relieved to find that you're not determined to be absolutely proper. It is so much easier to make friends if we can be forthright with one another. Charles is alarmingly thick of head this morning. I believe he actually could not prevent himself from whimpering each time the sun pierced his eyes at breakfast. But what is this about Mr Fairburn? Certainly, Charles is uninjured, at least beyond that damage he has done to himself by drinking."

"Oh—!" So sharp was Miss Fairburn's disappointment that for a scandalous moment Claire thought she might actually curse. She did not, leaving Claire strangely dissatisfied, but she did, after recovering herself, say, "Then I must corner one of the Lads and hear the whole story, as Benny won't let a word of it past his lips. He was in some manner of fight, Miss Dalton, at, I suspect, some low-class dance hall or—" She silenced herself again, but Claire was able to follow her line of thought, and blushed terribly at the near-mention of a house of ill repute.

"You think I am shocking," Miss Fairburn deduced with an air of satisfaction and sorrow.

"Perhaps I am. I apologize, Miss Dalton. I ought to know better, but at times with three older brothers and only one sister it is easier to think in masculine manners."

Before she knew it, "Well, your brother's manners are certainly ill enough to provide a bad example," had escaped Claire's lips. She clapped her hands over her mouth, utterly horrified as Miss Fairburn's lashes parted in gossip-hungry astonishment.

"What on *earth* has Benedict done now? Oh, never fear, Miss Dalton, I am most inclined to believe the worst of my brother, and never to defend him." Although the words were spoken with utmost sincerity, they were also said with tremendous fondness, more as if Miss Fairburn imagined her older brother to be a somewhat ill-behaved puppy rather than a grown man.

Her own remark now seemed entirely out of proportion, but Claire, embarrassed, related Mr Fairburn's mouse comment in the country, and conveniently forgot the appealing blueness of his eyes in the park the day before.

"Oh my," Miss Fairburn said with real surprise. "That *was* badly behaved of him. Oh, don't judge him too harshly, please, Miss Dalton? I know that I tease and poke at him myself, but I am, after all, his sister, and cannot be expected to take him seriously. I'm sure his apology was in all candor; Benedict does not like to offer insult, and will have been losing sleep over it, I'm sure."

Claire pursed her lips and had a sudden wish for a fan so she might hide her thoughtful expression behind it. But a fan was not at hand, and Miss Fairburn's canny eye read the hint of relenting that slipped across Claire's face. "He has tried hard to make up for it," Claire said with a curious combination of reluctance and pleasure. "Perhaps I have been too unforgiving. It is only—" Goodness, she thought: Miss Fairburn seemed to bring out an impulse to speak frankly, which could be dangerous indeed.

"It is only what?" Miss Fairburn pounced, cat-like, on the phrase, and Claire, sorrowfully, thought of herself as a mouse after all.

That, in fact, lay at the heart of Claire's troubles. Hesitantly, not daring to look straight into Miss Fairburn's deeply colored eyes, Claire confessed, "I fear that I *am* little more than a mouse, Miss Fairburn. They were all so splendidly handsome, and I..." She cringed, now unable to take her gaze away from the rose-patterned carpet stretching across Aunt Elizabeth's oak floors. "I thought myself quite fashionable in the country," she whispered, "modestly fashionable, but still quite...I suppose Mama had it firmly fixed in her mind and my own that fashion plates were... *excessive*, showing the most dramatic sorts of fashion, rather than what one might truly wear. And...and perhaps Mama clucked her tongue a bit over the gowns some of my friends wore, but I hardly imagined myself *so* differently bedecked from them. It is only with having come to Town that I realize how…how like a sad country mouse I was. The Lads have been very kind since I arrived, and there is Mr Graham, of course—"

"Wait," Miss Fairburn commanded. "We shall discuss this Mr Graham, but let us first address this mouseish nonsense. Stand up and let me have a look at you, Miss Dalton. I'm sure to have an opinion. Yes, stand. Your posture is excellent and your skin perfectly clear and unblemished by the sun. You can have no doubt, of course, that your wardrobe is of impeccable style, and I dare say that shade of yellow trim would make me look jaundiced but makes you a spring flower in bloom. Now turn."

Flustered, embarrassed, and delighted, Claire turned, casting a shy and hopeful look over her shoulder at Miss Fairburn, who stood as well to examine Claire with an increasingly critical eye. "Well, my dear," the red-haired girl announced, "you *are* very small, there is nothing to be done about it. Even the tallest of shoes would only make you slightly less short. Nor are you beautiful, Miss Dalton, not when regarded with a clear eye. You may have the cheekbones for beauty, but your nose is too snubbed and your smile perhaps slightly too large. You do, however, have a very becoming way about you, and I dare say many's the man who could not tell the difference between a pretty woman and a beautiful one, *and*," she said with sudden emphasis, "as a pretty woman instead of a beautiful one, you may find yourself pursued by young men who are interested in *you*, rather than called upon by those primarily interested in breeding their family line to an attractive one, as if with horses."

Claire could turn no more under this barrage of assessments, and indeed found herself obliged to sit before she swooned from so much direct opinion. She knew she was short; nothing *could* be done about that. She also regarded herself as pretty, not beautiful, and so to hear herself described so did not—precisely—sting. Nor was it exactly comfortable, though, and it took some little while before her breathing became steady again, or the heat faded from her cheeks. When she trusted her voice again, it was to murmur a bold question: "Have you such ruthless suitors, then, Miss Fairburn? Because you *are* very beautiful."

"Thank you." Miss Fairburn accepted the compliment not as if it was her due, but with a real smile and downward glance, as if she was unaccustomed to being flattered. Or to being told the truth, Claire thought, which was odd, given how readily she had dispensed truth to Claire. "My mother has sheltered me," she answered after a moment. "Deliberately, I believe, because she herself was so sought after by those desiring to claim a beauty—and my mother is, even still, considerably more beautiful than I, Miss Dalton. Please do not think me as one who claims false modesty when I say this, but Mother truly is exquisite. So I have had very few suitors, in truth, and I am only not quite twenty. Mother has made some reluctant overtures toward bringing me out—I have the wardrobe, and we are generally invited to all the right sorts of balls and parties—but I have been spared the full press of it all so far, and now Benedict has become the priority. I am primarily there to observe, not be observed. Mother was very young when she was brought out," Miss Fairburn added even more softly. "I believe she is tolerably satisfied with her lot, but she has made some effort to protect me, and if that means not coming out until I'm twenty-one-or-two, then…" She sighed suddenly. "Then I shall have had what freedom I am to be allotted, and will expect to be married shortly thereafter. This is a very complicated game we play, is it not, Miss Dalton? This game of Seasons and marriages, all the plotting and hoping, and my, I do go on, don't I? And I am sure I've said things I ought not have. But they were said in the strictest confidence, Miss Dalton! You would not betray me?"

"Never!" cried Claire, agog at the depth of confidence offered on a mere few minutes' acquaintance. "I shall take your most private thoughts to my grave, Miss Fairburn! I must say that I feel now that I know you quite well, and hope that you will soon be able to say the same about me."

"I will," Miss Fairburn proclaimed, "as soon as you have told me everything about this Mr Graham!"

Mr Jack Graham, Benedict thought, looked irritatingly well in a dashingly dark blue coat and trousers that fit perfectly to below the knee, where stockinged calves were shown off to excellent accord. Miss Dalton, at his side, wore pale pink silk trimmed with forget-me-not blue, though the flowers were no doubt an artifice, rather than plucked from the autumnal garden. Still, the blooms in her hair were lively and cunningly wound about her head. She and Graham made an altogether fine-looking couple.

Not that Benedict looked poorly in well-fitted black, and it was nigh unto impossible for the divine Miss Hurst to look anything other than striking. Even so, Graham had had to *hire* a carriage yesterday. By those lights he ought not be at the Thornbury House at all, much less there and daring to look so dashing.

Of course, if Benedict were to cast those same lights nearer to home, he would be obliged to admit that neither Ronald Vincent nor Gareth O'Brien should be at this party and looking well, either. But *they*, by gum, were at least of the Lads! *They* knew well enough that it was Cringlewood's station that had gotten them in! They, like Benedict, were dressed much more soberly and appropriately than Graham. Graham, the peacock, who attended the party on Cringlewood's invitation as well, through a kindness offered to Miss Dalton! It was somehow intolerable, and Benedict could not quite put his finger on why.

It should not eat at him as it was doing. The party was of an entirely more rarefied air than he and most of the Lads were accustomed to, and the decor of the house so fashionable as to be uncomfortable to Benedict's eye. Motifs of Egypt and China should not, perhaps, mix. The Thornburys were clearly comfortable with the dramatic lines and clashing colors, and the other first *ton* attending the party looked on approvingly, their own houses no doubt reflecting these latest extravagances of architecture and color. But the less extravagant and expensive pieces that would follow had not yet reached the parlors and dining halls of Benedict's set. And his family was not unfashionable by any means. They were just not...*this*...fashionable.

"I find myself a trifle overwhelmed," Miss Hurst breathed beside him.

Benedict's heart suddenly warmed toward the lady. He put his hand over hers at his elbow and dipped his head toward hers, murmuring, "*You* are overwhelmed, Miss Hurst? You at least were invited of your own accord. But let us keep our chins up and let no one see that we quake in our shoes, shall we?"

Miss Hurst favored him with a smile. "We shall." Bolstered by one another, they swept through the halls, occasionally greeting an acquaintance known to Benedict by way of Cringlewood.

Benedict was quite proud of the looks they garnered, for they made a handsome couple, until he remembered the purpled bruise around his left eye. It had faded since the night before, but it was not yet of a hue that only the rude could comment upon. Only the rude *would* comment on it—Miss Hurst's own pale eyes had widened, but she had spoken not a word—but none-the-less, it was of sufficient color as to gain attention, and Benedict wondered, not for the first time, if he perhaps should not have come.

That, however, would have forced him to spend the evening with his mother and her scathing comments, which was worse than the curiosity and murmured commentary of the *ton*. He ought to have put a few rumors about, he realized: stories delineating how he had acquired the bruise. Perhaps rushing into traffic to save a child from carriage wheels, or, more prosaically, perhaps a fencing bout with button-tipped weapons.

"—gust of wind caught the carriage door," one passer-by murmured to another as Benedict escorted Miss Hurst toward the dance floor. "Footman didn't catch it and it caught the gent square in the eye. Footman's been sacked, I hear, though Cringlewood's such a soft-hearted fool he'll likely find the boy work in the kitchens. I hear Cringlewood invited him here as an apology."

"No, they're thick as thieves," the other replied. "That's one of the beneath-my-touch lads that Cringlewood runs with to irritate the Earl."

Benedict couldn't allow himself to respond, or even to look as though he'd heard, though he equally brindled on Cringlewood's behalf. The nobility did, it was true, keep to their own, but Samuel's friendship with Dalton went back too far to be merely pretense. Hearing the accusation spoken aloud and in earshot, though, Benedict was ever-more grateful to Cringlewood, who had no doubt put about the footman story in order to explain Benedict's blackened eye. And perhaps to explain his own swollen lip, though Benedict hadn't seen him yet this evening and supposed his bruising might not be as visible as Benny's own.

As soon as they were far enough out of earshot to dare it, Miss Hurst whispered, "Is that really what happened?"

"It is precisely what happened," Benedict whispered back, "if you change the word 'door' to 'fist' and 'footman' to 'ill-tempered stage player'." No sooner than the admission left his lips did he consider it intemperate, but Miss Hurst let go a startled, bell-like laugh and squeezed his arm.

"We must find some time alone this evening so you might tell me the whole story. I believe that Thornbury has very fine gardens, excellent for uninterrupted...conversations." She cleared her throat lightly as a hint of color flushed her cheeks.

Benedict was obliged to breathe rather deeply himself as his thoughts followed hers, and saved himself from blushing only by observing—silently, of course—that she was entirely correct, and heightened color did her complexion no favors. A subtle blush along the cheeks was one thing; a blotch of high color centered on the cheekbone was something else, especially when it left patches of deathly whiteness in the surrounding skin. "A walk would be lovely," he said swiftly. "And—if I may be so bold, Miss Hurst—two dances? The first, perhaps, and the second entirely at your discretion? And I shall be at your call should you at any moment require an excuse to rest for a set."

"A walk, two dances, and a set for conversation? People will talk, Mr Fairburn." Miss Hurst did not sound displeased at the prospect.

Benedict turned to her, uncaring that they might interrupt the flow of bodies moving through the halls, and lifted her hand to his lips. "Is that not the purpose of the evening, Miss Hurst? I look forward to being the cause of much speculation."

"As do I. And I believe the music is beginning, Mr Fairburn, so if we're to dance the first set, we had best make haste."

"They'll wait on your beauty," Benedict replied, feeling rather pleased with himself, and Miss Hurst laughed again as they did, in fact, hasten to the dance floor.

She was an excellent dancer, he discovered again. Better than he, though he considered himself a reasonably graceful man. Perhaps it was her height, or the elegant sweep of her ice-green gown, or that the cotillion suited her particular demands of exercise, but as they stepped around one another, bowing and curtsying, gloved fingertips brushing, Benedict began to think he could become reasonably fond of the chilly Miss Hurst. It would not be one of those nonsensically romantic arrangements, but romance was always secondary to practicality within their station anyway. It was crass, he supposed, to wonder what Miss Hurst's dowry was, but marriage was commerce, as Great-Aunt Nancy's pending bequest had made painfully clear to him. He supposed that his mother would discover the details of her dowry, and once she had approved them, he would find the opportune moment and propose to —

"Miss Dalton!" The lines of the dance had shifted, putting him in the middle of the dance floor instead of on its margin where they had begun. Miss Claire Dalton was suddenly and briefly his partner as the dance's steps exchanged their positions again.

"Mr Fairburn," she replied with less obvious surprise, and that was the total of their conversation. He saw her again, petite and pretty, over Miss Hurst's shoulder, and then the complicated shifting patterns of the set took her away entirely.

Miss Hurst's face had, in the moments Benedict had been away from her, gone rigid and white. By this he deduced that, as he had met Miss Dalton, she had most likely met Jack Graham, who no doubt squired Miss Dalton again tonight. Unable to ask so directly, he murmured, "Are you well, Miss Hurst?" and watched her shake off her rigidity as a bird might ruffle snow away from its feathers.

"I am. Forgive me. I twisted my ankle and the pain was quite sharp, but I am well now."

This was a blatant untruth, but there was no polite way to press the matter. Instead, Benedict asked, "Shall I escort you from the floor, then? I would hate to give you a limp in the first set of the evening."

"That might be for the best," Miss Hurst agreed quietly, and so without delay Benedict helped her through the ranks of dancers and found seating. Drinks were procured from a passing servant and Benedict, solicitously, enquired as to whether he ought to call a doctor to look at Miss Hurst's ankle. He thought, but couldn't be certain, that he detected the faintest hint of exasperation at the charade that, having begun, Miss Hurst could not easily extract herself from. "No, I'm sure that won't be necessary. Some rest is all I need. Thank you for your thoughtfulness."

"Miss Hurst! I mean, my dear Priscilla!" Claire Dalton appeared from the dance floor, her eyes large with concern. Benedict jolted to his feet and bowed. The curtsy Miss Dalton gave in return was exceedingly perfunctory, all her attention for Miss Hurst. "I couldn't help but see that you retreated from the dance, and I had the most terrible fear for you! Are you well?"

"I am. A foolish little turn of my ankle, nothing more. I shall be right as rain in a few minutes." Miss Hurst's gaze wandered beyond Claire. "You've abandoned your dance partner?"

"Oh, only momentarily. I shall return to him straightaway, but I had to see for myself that you were not in distress. Take care of her, Mr Fairburn, for she is my friend, you know."

"Yes, of course," Benedict said automatically before blurting, "Perhaps you would do me the honor of a dance later, Miss Dalton?"

"Oh." Miss Dalton blinked at him as if only seeing him for the first time. She glanced at Miss Hurst, at her card, and finally to Benedict. "Yes, I suppose so. The second of the second set, if that's suitable to you. I am obliged to, oh, most of the other Lads before then." He perceived the faintest chiding in the observation, as if he had been lax in failing to ask earlier. "Thank you, Mr Fairburn. Priscilla, do save me a set in which we might sit and talk. I should like that so much."

"The third of the second," Miss Hurst promised. "After your dance with Mr Fairburn."

"Splendid! I shall see you then. And now I had best go find Mr Graham again before he's entirely lost on the dance floor." With no further ado Miss Dalton hurried back to the dancing, leaving both Benedict and Miss Hurst looking after her.

"She's a sweet creature, isn't she?" asked Miss Hurst. "A little countrified, perhaps, with that willingness to make friends quickly, but sweet."

"Surely it's better to make friends too easily than not make them at all."

Benedict had not meant the words to cut, but Miss Hurst's pale face grew paler yet. Very softly, she said, "Perhaps you might find a physician to examine my ankle after all, Mr Fairburn. I think I should sit a while longer. For my health."

Cursing himself, Benedict did as he was bidden.

Cousin Charles was too circumspect, Mr Vincent too reserved, and Mr Ackerman still too beautiful for Claire to even dare speak to him as they danced, and so from them, Claire learned not a single word of the Lads' adventures in the dance hall the night before. Nor would the young Earl-in-waiting Nathaniel Cringlewood engage with the topic beyond the obvious falsehood regarding a carriage door and a clumsy footman, and while Mr O'Brien was clearly inclined by nature to tell a woman whatever she wanted to hear, Vincent had given him a surprisingly effective quelling look as he escorted her onto the dance floor. Under the burden of that look, even O'Brien would say nothing of interest.

Fortunately, Mr Evander Hewitt had no compunctions at all against spreading gossip about his own friends. Over the course of their dance together, he told a rather embellished version of the previous night's events. By the time the dance ended, the Lads, with their fists alone, had vanquished a battalion of thirty, all of them armed to the teeth, and had themselves escaped grievous bodily injury largely thanks to Hewitt's own battle prowess. The story, growing more outrageous with each spin and turn, was told with such bland insincerity that twice Claire clung to his arm for support, giggling helplessly when she ought to have been sedately stepping away. By the time she was delivered to her escort she could barely stand from contained laughter, and had to beg for a seat before she swooned.

"Mr Hewitt amuses you," Jack Graham said with a touch of priggishness that sent Claire into shoulder-shaking silent laughter again.

"Mr Hewitt is a dreadful man," she whispered when she had control of herself again. "He tells awful lies all the time, and doesn't care a whit for anyone's feelings. He should be ashamed of himself and he's not, and while I know I should loathe him, he's so outrageously duplicitous that I cannot help but be, yes, amused by him. Thank goodness that you are a gentleman, Mr Graham. I could not bear a man like Mr Hewitt for longer than the space of a single dance. But there is something refreshing about a dreadful companion, is there not? At least it isn't dull."

"Speaking of which," Graham said softly.

Claire looked up to see Mr Fairburn approaching to claim his dance. Miss Hurst was at his elbow, her expression unreadable, and Claire wondered whether Mr Graham had meant Fairburn or Hurst by his comment. There was no time to ask: the other couple was there, pleasantries were being exchanged, and then Claire was on Fairburn's arm and floating out to the dance floor.

They took their places within the lines and, as one, both looked toward Miss Hurst and Mr Graham, who stood close enough to look intimate were it not for the intensely upright carriages of them both. "I wonder," Claire began, but then so too did the music begin, and her thoughts were lost to the steps of the dance.

"You appeared to be enjoying your dance with Hewitt," Benedict said when the opportunity arose, and Claire, in the spaces available, replied, "He told me—with some adornment—how you came by that bruised eye, Mr Fairburn. I am in awe of the Lads now. I had no idea you were so formidable."

It might well hurt to blush when one's eye was so swollen, she decided as Mr Fairburn's expression grew briefly and distinctly pained. "I would like to assure you that I do not usually embroil myself in common fisticuffs, Miss Dalton."

"Any more than you usually insult young women before you have met them?" Claire asked archly. "Miss Fairburn believes I should forgive you, Mr Fairburn."

"You seem to have forgiven Hewitt." Mr Fairburn appeared to be struggling with, and defeating—if only just—petulance. A silent beat in the music brought the sounds of the party to them with startling clarity: laughter and someone's shrill, angry voice cut above the general roar of the music and the dance began again.

"I believe I shall never forgive Hewitt," Claire said thoughtfully. "However, it is nearly impossible to retain my anger at a soul who cares so little for my opinion of him. There is no use in retaining anger toward such a creature. But it matters to you, so I find it much easier to stay angry at you. Isn't that silly?"

"Yes," Benedict replied slowly, as if thinking her response through, "but it is also honest. And you are correct: I do care. So I wonder, Miss Dalton, if you might—" The dance took them apart, as it had done throughout. When they came back together, Benedict continued as if his speech had been unbroken. "If you might consider forgiving me, which would do my heart unspeakable good."

His eyes were very blue, searching her face. Claire had the sudden brief fear that she might have sprouted an unseemly blemish, but he seemed to find no fault in what he saw. The sound of the music faded again, but, as the dance didn't stop this time, Claire thought it must be herself fading away from the party, seeing and hearing nothing beyond her partner.

Or very little beyond him, at least: somewhere there was upset happening, a dissonant note in the general good humor of the gathered crowd. Such unpleasantry could have nothing to do with her, though, not when Mr Fairburn's hands and gaze were holding hers. "Yes," she whispered after what felt like the longest time, no longer certain of what she was responding to, only that the answer was, "Yes, of course, Mr Fairburn. Of course, I will."

Relief and delight swept Benedict's face. He lifted her hands to his lips, kissing her glove-clad fingers. "Thank heavens, Miss Dalton. You have made me a happy man. I don't think I could have borne your easy camaraderie with the other Lads a moment longer if you excluded me by your lack of forgiveness. I shall sleep more easily at night now."

Forgiveness. Claire shook herself, trying to put a meaning to the word, then remembered what Mr Fairburn had sought all along. "Forgiveness," she said in a brightly tripping voice. "Yes, of course. I'm glad to put your heart at ease…" The gaiety faded before she had finished speaking, and she thought she saw comprehension flash in Mr Fairburn's eyes. Before it could be pursued, however, a piercing shriek echoed against the high ceilings and the dance crowd parted in time to allow Claire and Benedict to watch Miss Priscilla Hurst deliver a resounding slap across the face of one Mr Jack Graham.

Claire could not possibly be escorted home by Jack Graham: that was Charles's sole thought in the shocked silence that followed Miss Hurst's assault on Mr Graham. It made no difference what Graham's crime was. To have a woman apply violence to him suggested that he had invited it, and was therefore a dangerously inappropriate escort. Unforgivably, Charles abandoned his own dance partner and began pushing his way through the crowd, searching for his cousin.

He found Cringlewood and O'Brien first, both of them shaking their heads without him having to ask: they didn't know where Claire was either. Neither did he have to ask them to help him look. With apologies to their dance partners — more than Charles had offered — they slipped away to look for Claire as well. It was Vincent, though, not only the tallest of the

Lads but easily one of the tallest men at the party, who saw her first, waved Charles down, and mouthed, *Fairburn,* in reassurance.

A fist he had not known clenched released its grip on Charles's heart. Benedict wouldn't be fool enough to let Claire return to Graham, even if he was escorting the other party in the altercation. Following Vincent's gestures, Charles found Fairburn and Claire in the heart of the dance crowd, both of them still shocked and unmoving even as the rest of the dance began to gather itself back into motion around them. Charles stepped up behind them, putting an arm around Claire's waist. She looked up to see who it was, gave a glad gasp of surprise, and buried her face against Charles's chest.

"It's all right," Charles murmured to Fairburn. "I've got her. Go to Miss Hurst. Have O'Brien and Vincent deal with Graham. Not Cringlewood, for God's sake. Don't drag him into this. Bad enough that he's responsible for him being here."

"No," Claire said in a shaking voice, "I'm responsible. I must know, Charles. I must know why—"

"You," Charles said with a sharp clarity, "did all you could to avoid Mr Graham as an escort to this party, and I brushed your every argument away without hearing a word of it. The fault could well be considered mine. As to what has happened, we shall learn that soon

enough. Go, Fairburn. Claire, come with me."
He knew the authority in his voice was
difficult to resist. It had stood him well at the
front and did no less good in the confines of a
house party.

Fairburn, whose compliance had never been
in doubt, cast an agonized glance at Claire,
then went. Claire, trembling, chose not to look
up as Charles escorted her off the dance floor.
"I don't want to stay," she whispered. "Is it
cowardly of me to leave?"

A knife twisted in Charles's gut. "It's only
men who are cowards if they retreat, cousin.
Women are considered wise to do so,
especially if their reputations are at stake."

"But so is a man's, if he retreats. His
reputation is ruined. How terrible it must be,
Charles! How dreadful to face guns and
cannons and to know that running will destroy
his reputation, when I dare not even stay and
face the curious eyes of Society! How unfair!"

She could not know, Charles told himself;
none of them save Vincent and O'Brien really
knew, though there was plenty of talk. Men his
age did not come back from the front, pale,
withdrawn, but without visible injury, and *not*
cause talk, but that talk would never have
reached his cousin's ears. Not, at least, in the
little time she had been in London. So all he
said was, "It may be unfair, but it at least
allows you to retreat, Claire, and right now
that's the best thing to do. Come. Come,

Worthington will have our coats and the carriage ready by the time we reach the door. Now stand tall, Claire. We're out of the dancing hall now and no one in these rooms saw the altercation. They don't know it was your escort involved, and so if you look proud and confident no one will have a word to say against you. Can you do that? Can you do that, Claire? Good girl," he said as she straightened, and if there had been tears on her face, they were now no more than drying smudges on his coat. "There we go. There we are. A few more moments, cousin, and all will be well."

All would *not* be well, not until he had the truth of Jack Graham's story, but that was hardly the thing to say to Claire just now. True to his expectations, Worthington awaited them at the door with cloaks and coats alike, and without comment escorted them to the Daltons' waiting carriage.

Within it, Claire collapsed against Charles's side again, not crying, but shaking with nerves. Charles pressed his hand against her hair, and wished for a way to confess his empathy without betraying his secrets.

Chapter Eight

"Mr Jack Graham to see you, Miss. Are you at home?" Worthington veritably bristled with disapproval and for once chose not to hide it. No one in the Dalton household could approve of Graham's visit after the previous night's fiasco. Not that anyone save himself, young Master Dalton, and Miss Dalton—as yet—knew about it, but it was inevitable that before the day was out, Mrs Dalton would be aware of the dreadful behavior displayed by her niece's escort.

The hour was so early that Miss Dalton still wore morning clothes, though the simple cream gown needed only a smart overcoat to be suitable for going out in. This was important to Worthington; had she been entirely unsuitably attired he would have told Graham that Miss Dalton was not at home at all.

As it was, she, pale already, paled further at the sound of his name, but straightened with impeccable poise. "I am home," she announced softly, "but I would appreciate it, Worthington, if you might remain in the drawing room with us. I should not like to be alone with Mr

Graham, under the circumstances."

Worthington would not have left them alone together in any case, but was decidedly glad to reply, "Of course, Miss," to her very sensible request. Miss Dalton smiled wanly, stood, and nodded for him to fetch Graham.

The young man entered like a guilty puppy, hands wringing together. His abject brown gaze would soften the hearts of harder women than Miss Dalton, but had no effect on Worthington, who positioned himself by the hearth, glowered, and did not offer Graham refreshment. The air itself seemed weighted by Graham's arrival. Worthington glanced at the hearth to make certain the flues were open and that the heaviness was in his imagination only.

Miss Dalton performed precisely as much curtsy as necessary. Graham bowed far more deeply than convention required but not nearly as much as his ill behavior demanded, in Worthington's opinion. "Miss Dalton," Graham quavered. "I won't take much of your time, as I have business to attend to, but I felt I had to apologize for last night's...outburst."

"What happened last night, Mr Graham?" Miss Dalton's tones were wonderfully cool. Had he been, say, Evander Hewitt, Worthington would have applauded her for them. Being only a manservant, he merely retained every degree of stiff disapproval at his disposal.

Graham, glancing Worthington's way, appeared to feel appropriately quelled, and swallowed several times before speaking again to Miss Dalton. "You must have guessed by now that I am...previously acquainted...with Miss Hurst."

"I had," Miss Dalton said frostily, "deduced that, yes."

"Yes. Well." Another nervous gulp slid down Graham's throat. "We didn't part on the best of terms, and have not—had not—seen each other in..." He cleared his throat. "In some time. It is indelicate to mention the number of years, given that it might put an age to Miss Hurst."

Miss Dalton, slowly and with careful precision, said, "I believe at this late date her age may be immaterial, Mr Graham, although I will not press you on the number. What, exactly, was said last night that your... reunion...ended in a scream and a slap?"

"I confessed that I—" Graham gathered himself, glanced at Worthington, and deflated as if a pig's bladder suddenly emptied of air. He was not an accomplished liar: his voice became listless and dull as he spoke slowly, looking for the right words to say. "I confessed that I had never been as wealthy as she imagined me to be, a statement which only sealed my apparent betrayal of her all those years ago. Miss Hurst is a woman of high passions and could not contain herself in the face of such news. I hope that you will still call her friend, Miss Dalton, for I once admired her greatly and would hate to be the cause of a rift betwixt you. And now I have said all I came to say, and business calls; I shall leave you in peace."

So abruptly that Miss Dalton had no time to respond, Graham turned on his heel and hurried out. The heavy air lingered in his wake, Miss Dalton breathing shallowly as the door drifted shut. Without taking her gaze from it, she said, "Worthington, did it seem to you that his confession of finances seemed... insufficient? That he was perhaps deliberately misleading me?"

She had been quick-witted and clever enough that he had felt something had to be done to take her from the country to the city. Now, Worthington thought ruefully, it might have been better if she had been just a little less insightful. He might have lied, even so, but it went against his grain to do so. "Yes, Miss."

He might have cracked a buggy whip over her, so swiftly did she respond. "I thought so. Worthington, please fetch my coat. I shall be going out directly. You may tell my aunt I am visiting Miss Fairburn and may be some time."

Worthington cleared his throat. "And where will you actually be, Miss?"

Miss Dalton gave him a sharp, smiling look. "Discovering why I am being lied to."

"That," Worthington said, though not loudly enough to be heard, "is what I feared, Miss," and went to fetch her coat.

ff

Claire had not expected Worthington to acquiesce so easily, and did not think to look over her shoulder as, barely two minutes after Jack Graham had left, she hurried out of her aunt's house and scouted the street until she saw his sandy-headed form climb into a carriage. She ran to her uncle's waiting carriage, gasped, "Follow that cab!" to the driver, and didn't notice Worthington step quietly from the curb to the rumble at the back of the carriage, and from there, signal the driver to pursue Miss Dalton's quarry. To her mind she commanded the entire escapade, though as Graham's carriage drove into a darker and danker part of London than she had ever seen, she began to question her wisdom.

And yet, having come so far, she was determined not to stop now, even as the streets broke from cobble into mud and houses became hovels, standing only because they leaned too closely against one another to fall. Hither and thither in the decay were great swaths of land that stood empty of buildings but held cattle, horses, graves, or rough-sleeping men whose clothes were the faded shades of old and forgotten uniforms. Claire pressed knuckles against her lips and stared through the carriage's gauze-shielded windows with the horror of one born to comfort and never truly appreciating the degradation of the poor.

Not that she had neglected her duties to the

poor of Bodton, but in truth, while often wretched, they were also often still encased in the leaking but solid stone walls of a country farmer's home. She had been inside houses that stank of animals kept inside for warmth and she had made garments by the dozens for the parish's poorest children, but they had never been gathered in such numbers, or under such bleak London skies. Everything seemed grey to her, as if rising soot had turned the sky to charcoal and it had leaked onto the world below. Ubiquitous shadows ranged from dull blue to coal black. From within them peered pale, filthy faces who judged her carriage as dangerous but rich pickings.

She could imagine no possible business for Jack Graham to have here, not even when his carriage drew up to a ramshackle but forbidding building of huge, soot-dark stones. By comparison to nearby shanties, it had an aura of permanence. It stood three stories in height, with small windows and an enormous black oak front door that opened onto a rough cobblestone courtyard. The courtyard was unlike anything in the previous half-dozen streets: no one had built into it, encroaching into its space. Claire wondered what manner of person or people lived within to retain such sovereignty over the courtyard when there were clearly so many desperate people nearby. Her question was answered nearly before it was formed.

The tremendous oak door opened ponderously. Through it came a narrow and hard-faced woman whose iron grey hair showed the remains of once-lustrous walnut brown at its loose ends. No fewer than a dozen children, and perhaps as many as twenty, spilled out around her. They ranged in all sizes, from infants barely able to walk up to boys and girls of twelve or thirteen years, nearly all of them as grim as the woman who fronted them.

Two of the children, a boy and a girl of perhaps four, broke from the group and ran toward Graham, who bent and caught them into a long embrace. He kissed each of them atop the head, then stood again and strode toward the woman, offering a small purse which she dumped into one palm.

The glitter of coin was clear even in the distance. Claire fell into her carriage seat, dizzy with shock. She had not known what to expect in following Graham, and yet had unquestionably *not* expected to find him the — the *father?* she wondered in abject horror — of two small children. He had said nothing of being married, which left only one answer as to the children's parentage. They could be nothing other than illegitimate, their mother some poor creature abused by Graham. Had he taken the children and delivered them to this — this caretaker? Was the mother out there in the world somewhere, wondering what had happened to her babies? Or had she been relieved not to have the mouths to feed, having perhaps already chosen to sell her own body to survive? But if Graham could offer support to this hard-faced caretaker, surely he might have done the same for the mother of his children — !

With a roiling belly and trembling hands, Claire worked the carriage curtain out of the way so she could peer forth again. Both children clung to Graham's legs, and he smiled at them often, touching their hair as he spoke with the woman. She pointed at the children, lip curling, and the girl hid her face against Graham's leg. Claire's heart twisted in sympathy, and without thinking, when Graham suddenly shook the children off and stalked away, Claire leaped from her carriage to approach the woman caretaker.

She was not five steps out of the carriage before she knew she had made a dreadful mistake. Lean, calculating shadows detached themselves from the blue and grey hues of buildings, observing her. She was not *haut ton*, perhaps, but she was of better quality than anyone in sight, and worse, a woman alone. In palpitations, she cast a single look at the carriage and was purely astonished to find Worthington a mere step behind her, his expression as absolutely mild as it had ever been.

Still, he startled her so badly she clutched her heart and gave a high, soft laugh. The corner of Worthington's mouth turned up and kindness softened his eyes as he said, "This way, I think, Miss," while gesturing to allow her to lead the way.

Had she been moving at any rate of speed, Claire would have tripped over her own feet. Words escaped her lips on a whispered gasp: "You're not going to stop me?"

"You've come this far, Miss," Worthington said placidly. "It wouldn't be my place to delay a woman with a purpose."

Charles would never forgive her if she somehow managed to steal Worthington away from him, but just then Claire was convinced she would do nearly anything to keep the stalwart valet at her side. Not that it would be appropriate for a man to do the work of a lady's maid, but perhaps as butler to her own household when it was established....

These unlikely thoughts carried her forward, and Worthington's silent presence at her back bolstered Claire's courage immeasurably as she approached the iron-haired woman, who looked on them both with disfavor. "What is it you toffs want?"

"The gentleman you were speaking with." Claire cleared her throat, trying to put strength into her voice. Her heart beat wildly, bringing heat to her face and icy tingles to her fingers, but she was committed; she couldn't stop now. "Mr Jack Graham."

"What about him?"

"What business has he with you?"

A sneer that revealed snaggled teeth where

any existed at all appeared on the woman's face as she looked Claire up and down. "Not what he'd want with you, missy. Can't remember."

"You can't—! He was just—!" Partway through her outburst, Claire realized what kind of forgetfulness this was, and, faintly, said, "Worthington?"

As if it was a rehearsed expectation, the valet stepped forward with a glitter of coins at the ready. Two were deposited into the woman's hand—pounds, Claire saw with some surprise; a considerable sum—and the rest remained between Worthington's fingers, waiting for information deemed worth of them before they fell.

The woman tested one of the coins in her teeth, eying both young lady and valet suspiciously before shrugging a thin shoulder. "Them two nips are his to care for."

It was the only possible answer, and yet its cold confirmation struck Claire as surely as a blow. She did not—quite—step backward with the shock, though she was for long seconds unable to act beyond making sure she still breathed. She had not often been conscious of the act of breathing before; it seemed strange and awkward now. "And you..." The question faded because she had no clear idea what she should ask, but when Worthington, beside her, drew breath to press the woman, Claire suddenly rallied. "And you are their caretaker," she said with an unfelt briskness. "The caretaker of all these children?"

Another unpleasant smile revealed more missing teeth. "You hope so, don't you? Hope I'm not the mother, don't you?" The ugly smile faded and the woman glanced toward the children, all gathered a safe distance away and staring at Claire with a lack of expectation she found worse than hope. Unable to bear it, she returned her regard to the woman, who, in the moment Claire had looked away, had entirely changed her mien.

She was still iron-haired, too thin, lined with age and her cheeks hollow with toothlessness, but her carriage was that of a gentlewoman. Her eyes were still unforgivingly angry, but her voice was shocking in its culture. "I am not the mother of any of them," she said with soft rage. "My own child was taken from me and died in a workhouse after I shamed my family by bearing him out of wedlock. They cast me out, but I would never have gone back to them if they had begged. I called in every favor, every guilty conscience and every drab of sympathy I could twist from those who had once been my friends, and I began this place, St Sophia's Institute for Wayward Children. It is a house for unwanted children, and here I do my best for them. They are fed. They are housed. They are educated, and if they work hard and are lucky they can find themselves a position as a governess or a tutor, or perhaps a decent lad or lass to marry."

Claire, trembling, asked, "How often are they lucky?"

"Not very."

This, too, came as a blow. Claire let her eyes close and swayed before finding the strength to ask, "And what happens to those who aren't?"

The woman's bitter shrug answered as fully as words. Claire pressed her lips together until they hurt, then spoke as carefully as she could. "I admire your efforts. All of Society should, though it is, of course, more comfortable for Society to pretend such duties as yours are not necessary. Madam, I do not wish to offer insult, but I wonder if I might somehow be of assistance to you. Food, clothing…"

"You'll ruin yourself," the woman said flatly. "If you got found out, it'd be a moment's leap in the gossip rags to conclude you were caring for a child of your own and your prospects would end."

Claire's face crumpled with agreement, but she rallied and said, "Worthington," in a tone both sharper and more pleading.

"Miss," he said gently, and Claire knew that every coin he had on him went into the woman's hand.

Her hand, nails blunted with work, age spotted and with thick veins marring them, closed around the coins. Claire, gazing at those long fingers, could imagine them gracefully at needlework once upon a time. "It won't hurt," the woman said begrudgingly. "I thank you for it. The children do, too."

Claire nodded once, then spun away as tears rose and sentiment threatened to embarrass them both. Half-blinded, she bolted for the carriage, and instead blundered directly into Jack Graham's well-tailored chest.

Jack Graham blurted, "Miss Dalton!" and visibly swallowed a curse all at once as their abrupt encounter sent a shower of fruit and hot pasties tumbling from his grip. Miss Dalton seized her skirts and made a basket of them so quickly that not one of the apples hit the ground, and Graham rescued two of the tumbling pasties before they could stain her skirt.

Worthington had not imagined the young woman had such quick reflexes, particularly as he saw the sudden pallor of her face as she recognized and was identified by Graham. Still, not a single precious bite of food fell to the earth, and rather than respond to Graham in any way she simply turned toward the children and shook her skirt a little, offering them the bounty she had caught.

Like little ponies they raced forward to seize apples and pasties alike, the youngest burning their mouths on the latter while the older ones were wise enough to taste the fruit first. When Claire's skirts were emptied and settled down, Graham stepped around her to offer the caretaker another satchel of apples and, judging from the scent wafting up, pasties alike. Discreetly, the sandy-haired man slipped more coins into the woman's hand, then turned from her to kneel.

The two children he had embraced before ran to him. They were both pretty in the way of youth and innocence: large eyes, hair that had not yet darkened to a mature hue, dirt everywhere, making them indistinguishable in gender save for one wore trousers and the other a dress. Both showed their work-roughened little knees. The girl swallowed a bite of her pastie and peeked over Graham's arm at Miss Dalton, then, in a stentorian whisper, asked, "Shall she be our Mama, Uncle Jack?"

Miss Dalton went white, then red, and settled out at a shade close to her normal complexion, as if her emotions were in such turmoil that neither cold nor warm humors could dominate. *Graham*, to Worthington's satisfaction, turned equally crimson with appropriate mortification, glanced once at Miss Dalton, then kissed the girl on top of her head. "That isn't a proper question to ask, Emma. She is a friend, and I must go and speak with her now."

Children of their age — no more than four or five, Worthington surmised — ought to express dismay when their only family, having just arrived, announced he must now leave. Neither child did. Together they stepped back, hollowness beneath their eyes, and with very pretty manners bowed and curtsied before chorusing, "Good-bye, Uncle Jack."

"Good-bye, Emma. Good-bye, John. I'll come visit again as soon as I may." Jack straightened and turned toward Miss Dalton with both face and voice strained. "Miss Dalton. Perhaps you would allow me to escort you home so I can…explain."

"I would like that," Miss Dalton said unwisely but not unexpectedly.

Worthington cleared his throat. "There's no need for you to return in a public conveyance, Mr Graham. Miss Dalton's carriage awaits. Perhaps she could escort *you* home."

"Perhaps she could," Graham murmured. "She has been a surprise in every other way."

Indeed she had been, Worthington thought, and assisted them both into the waiting coach.

"'Uncle' Jack," Claire said quietly, once within the confines of the carriage. It seemed much more luxurious and rich than it had on her journey out; the ebony inlays around the windows now an extravagance, the soft blue velvet covering well-padded seats a touch of the divine that defied the harder, colder reality she had just encountered. It was difficult to look at Jack Graham, whose face was a twist of torment and guilt. "Are you really their uncle?"

"Oh, Miss Dalton!" Graham burst out. "Forgive me for embroiling you in this unfortunate situation! I admit I have longed to have a confidante, but it should never have been one as delicate and refined as yourself—!"

Claire, with a hint of exasperation warming her, said, "I have seen a little of poverty, Mr Graham, and I certainly know what fate befalls women and children both when they fail Society's expectations. *Are* you their uncle?"

"I am." Graham fell back in his seat, pale and wan against the rich blue velvet. For long minutes they rattled along in silence, Graham lost in thought as he gazed out the window. Claire, burgeoning with curiosity, was not so desperate as to intrude. His look was one of sorrow and regret, and whatever the story, it could not be an easy one to tell.

"I had a sister," Graham said suddenly, as if finally committing himself to the tale. "Juliet. She was five years my younger and we all doted on her. She was hardly more than a girl when a..." Here he cast a brief look at Claire and nearly strangled himself on his choicest words, replacing them instead with an understated, "...bad man. A cruel, beautiful man, seduced her. She was very young and very foolish, and very certain he would marry her. He did not," Graham said with such simplicity as to make Claire's heart ache. "He abandoned her. My parents cast her out. And I —I abandoned all, to care for her. I had— nearly—been engaged to be married, and I abandoned my beloved as well, without explanation."

An ache of comprehension clogged Claire's

throat. It was a few seconds before she was able to whisper, "Miss Hurst," a deduction for which she received a sad smile.

"Yes, Miss Hurst. I hadn't seen her again until our afternoon in the park. I must apologize again, Miss Dalton—"

"Not at all," Claire said with such resolution that she was surprised by it. She had imagined a falling out between Miss Hurst and Mr Graham, but not a tragedy. "Please, will you tell me the rest?"

Graham shrugged. "My parents cut me off when it became clear I wouldn't abandon Juliet. They put it about that she had contracted consumption and that I blamed them, had abandoned *them*. They died a year later, and I learned then that they had almost nothing to their names. Their lavish lifestyles had been propped up on nothing. Evidently, my marriage to Miss Hurst had been expected to be the saving of us all." He shook his head, putting that away. "I had a little money of my own, but Juliet's pregnancy was difficult. I spent most of what I had on her, and gambled to replace it. I'm a fair gambler," he admitted. "Not stricken with the urge for it, which makes it easier to walk away when the cards are against you. So we managed, until—"

He wet his lips and returned his regard to the window, finding, Claire thought, safety in speaking to it rather than herself. "The birth was hard. She died and the doctor cut the second child out of her. I had...no manner of caring for them. No prospects, no family, no fortune. I found Miss Beacham and put the children into her care, with all the support I could offer. I've spent the greater part of the past four years at one kind of trade or another, making what coin I could, and seeing them as often as possible. I have finally put a little — a little! — away, from gaming. I've made enough to dress well, enough to remind old friends that I still live. I hoped enough time had passed that people would have forgotten. You know how they do," he said more softly. "One departs in shame for some time, then returns without speaking of it, and all is, if not precisely forgotten, at least bypassed. And perhaps they might allow the past to rest, were it not for Miss Hurst."

"You can hardly blame her, Mr Graham."

Surprise darkened the color of his eyes. "No. No, of course not. But it seems the old passions still run high. Pris — Miss Hurst was never shy about showing emotion."

Claire thought of the other woman's cool reserve and thought she must have been much changed, at least on the surface, by Graham's departure, though it did seem he brought out a tendency toward high emotion in her. "So why did you return, Mr Graham?"

"I was perfectly frank with you the night we met, Miss Dalton. I hope for nothing more than to make a modest marriage. I only left out that

I also hope to be able to take my sister's children from that wretched school and raise them in a caring home."

"So you hope to marry a woman who could agree to that," Claire murmured.

Graham's expression collapsed. "It's too much to ask, I know, but I do hope. I dream of marriage to a woman of such stature that she can ignore convention and do as she likes, but such ladies are beyond my reach. What am I to do?"

"I don't know." Claire leaned forward to press her hand on top of his. "I don't know, Mr Graham, but I admire you deeply for your commitment to your sister's children. You are a man of integrity and honor and I dearly hope that this may all be resolved in a suitable fashion. I will do everything I can to help you, I promise. The children must be looked after."

"You are entirely too kind, Miss Dalton. I think I should disengage from our friendship, for fear of contaminating you with my own woes." Graham glanced out the window and, following his gaze, Claire saw that they were nearly at the Daltons' residence. "I believe this should be our last encounter."

"Oh, no! Not when we have agreed already to be fast friends! No, Mr Graham, that would not do at all." The carriage rolled to a stop and Worthington himself opened the door for them. Graham disembarked first, then offered a hand to Claire, who stepped out with a smile for him. "Thank you, Mr Graham. I insist that we must see one another again. I cannot abide not knowing the end of this story. I am positive it will turn out well."

"Miss Dalton," Graham said, which was neither an agreement nor a disagreement, and on that note, departed.

Chapter Nine

Benedict had, as was suitable and proper, escorted Miss Hurst home the evening before, but even as he had done so, Miss Dalton's emerald eyes haunted him. Miss Hurst had offered no explanation for her behavior at the party; Benedict had not pressed for one, his natural curiosity consumed by thoughts of Miss Dalton's grace and her smile as they danced together. She had forgiven him. That was a prize beyond measure.

He arrived home late, having completely forgotten about his blackened eye, and withstood his mother's questions on the matter with unusual good will, proposing increasingly unlikely scenarios as to how he had gained the bruise—one of which was even the truth!—before confessing with apologetic solemnity the story that Cringlewood had put about at the party. She chose to be satisfied with that, not only because she preferred it to the more likely truth, but because upon confession, Benedict also sat and asked with due intent whether she had learned anything of interest regarding Miss Priscilla Hurst.

Hurst was not, his mother informed him, an especially sociable creature. This, he had the impression, suited his mother nicely, as it would help to divorce him from the Lads. Neither were her parents particularly sociable either, but that, Mrs Fairburn felt, was directly because they felt the sting of the Hurst fortune having been made in trade so recently. Another generation or two and they would be comfortably removed from the inglorious working men who were their predecessors. In the meantime, Mrs Fairburn had laid eyes upon Miss Hurst and deemed her beautiful, which was a pleasant addition to the fortune she was expected to inherit.

Benedict listened with half an ear, feeling it was all interminably dull when there were dances and laughter to be had with Miss Dalton, but to Mrs Fairburn's eye he seemed attentive and thoughtful. She went to bed satisfied and was even more so when he arrived at breakfast the next day alert and engaging, neither of which were typical morning postures for her eldest son. When, in early afternoon, he announced his intention of dropping in on Dalton, she supposed that he intended to get Dalton's approval — not that it was needed, save for Dalton's group of friends did seem to lean heavily upon his opinion — for marriage to Miss Hurst, and from thence he would have few dealings with the so-called Lads.

It would have come as considerable surprise

to her to learn that her son had not thought of Miss Hurst once since the evening before, and that it was not, in fact, *Charles* Dalton whom he hoped to see, but rather Miss Claire Dalton. Even Benedict was not entirely certain what his purpose in seeing Miss Dalton was, save that he very much wanted to, and that he hoped the afternoon would be a fine one so he might take her for a drive in the park. Perhaps the southern end of the park, as the northern was somewhat laden with the memory of recent disaster, and he had no interest in reminding her of Jack Graham.

It was therefore a shock to him when, just as he was disembarking from his carriage, he saw in front of him an open carriage door from which first Graham, then Miss Dalton, were disgorged. They stood together hand in hand, with Miss Dalton's gaze sweet and gentle on Graham's. Heart pounding, Benedict saw that the carriage wheels and base were marked with signs of travel, as if they had been gone for some time and even more distance. He couldn't spur his legs into action and instead stood suspended, half out of his carriage, as he waited for a chaperone to step free of their carriage.

None emerged. As the footman closed their carriage door, Benedict threw himself into his own carriage and barked, "Drive!"

The carriage lurched forward. Benedict sank into his seat, making certain he couldn't be seen by anyone at the Dalton household as he glared in futile rage at the carriage wall.

It was no business of *his* if Miss Dalton wished to continue carrying on with the cad who had so deeply insulted Miss Hurst that she felt obliged to strike him. It was no concern of *his* if she was so brazen as to ride out all day with a man of questionable character. It was outrageous, appalling and distressing behavior, but she was *Charles's* cousin, not his own; his own family would be in no way besmirched by her terrible choices. It would be an embarrassment for the entire Dalton family, of course, likely bringing them to ruin, and it probably was best to break with both Charles in particular and the Lads in general before the Daltons' taint could spread. Thank heavens he had singled out Miss Hurst! Benedict thought. Thank heavens his mother's attention had been set upon her and not a hussy like Claire Dalton! He would have shamed his entire family and ruined Amelia's chances, had he been seduced by emerald eyes!

"Take me to see Miss Priscilla Hurst," he commanded the driver, and stared furiously out the window all the way.

Miss Priscilla Hurst no more expected to see Benedict Fairburn in her parlor than Miss Claire Dalton had expected to find Jack Graham embroiled in a sticky matter of avuncular responsibility. Indeed, she had no notion he was at her home at all until a maid arrived in her room, pink of cheek and breathless, to whisper, "Mr Benedict Fairburn has asked if he might see you alone, Miss Hurst!"

There was only one reason a gentleman asked for such leave, but rather than the thrill of excitement she supposed she might be expected to feel, a terrible chill filled Miss Hurst's breast. She rose, thanked the maid politely, and went to her mirror as if to make certain she was presentably attired to receive a gentleman caller.

She was, of course. She always was. Appearance was everything in a family that had come so recently from trade, and Priscilla was not one to be caught unprepared. Nor was she unaware of her reputation as cold, though her childhood friends would have been surprised to hear her described so. She had chosen years ago—after Jack Graham's disappearance—to play to it, embracing her coloring where other young women might have despaired of it. She never wore warm colors, although the truth was that they suited her as well as the icy blues and greens she favored. It was too early for those solid shades, though, so for now she wore white trimmed with lace that enhanced her excellent bosom, and her hair up in a simple but fetching design that drew the eye to her height.

The woman in the mirror regarded her so expressionlessly she could not even be said to seem determined or grim. She was not pretty:

Miss Dalton was pretty and approachable and, Priscilla thought, far more lovable than she. She *was* beautiful, which she knew without taking particular pleasure in it. The square but delicate jaw; the thin but well-shaped lips; the straight nose, the strong cheekbones; the light eyes, not large or darkly lashed but well-proportioned to her face. Her forehead was neither too broad nor too high, and her strawberry blonde hair did not require a hot iron to tease it into curls. Twenty-four years had not yet etched lines around her eyes or mouth, and her porcelain skin was as flawless as it had been in childhood.

There ought, Priscilla thought, to be color in her cheeks, knowing Mr Fairburn was in the drawing room waiting to propose. Color of either dread or delight, but there was neither. Mr Fairburn was a pleasant young man of good standing and, as everyone knew, set to inherit his aunt's enormous estate. It was a highly suitable match, especially under the circumstances.

Her grandfather, Priscilla thought, would be disappointed in her, and with that troubling idea, went to see Mr Fairburn.

Miss Hurst was perfection, Benedict told himself firmly as she entered the drawing room. She was as flawless as a sculpture hewn out of ice, and ice, he reminded himself, thawed. He would no doubt find her warm and accommodating once they were married.

For a moment, though, his courage quavered. The Hursts' drawing room had, it seemed, been decorated to suit Miss Hurst particularly. It was papered with green above the chair rail; green that had the cant of marble to it, and the darkness of which lent an especial bright radiance to Miss Hurst's pale gown and complexion. Benedict, in perfectly suitable black and a highly starched collar, felt rather like a dark hole burned into the walls, as if he was a misplaced element soon to be repaired. But that was nonsense, and the lady was waiting.

"Miss Hurst," he began, and then, daring, approached her to take both hands and say, "Priscilla," as if testing it out. It felt strange on his tongue.

"Mr Fairburn," she said, and then, obligingly, "Benedict."

Confidence bloomed in Benedict's chest. She was pleasant and accommodating after all. "Priscilla, I would—that is to say—we have spent—I have grown—oh, forgive me, Miss Hurst, it seems I'm not very good at this. I've never done it before."

Amusement suddenly lit Miss Hurst's face. "I should hope you weren't in the habit of it, at least, Mr Fa—Benedict."

"We get on well, don't we?" Benedict blurted, and then, although desperately aware that he was making a mess of it, went on in the same vein. "Despite it all, we get on well enough? And I've become quite fond of you, as I hope you've become of me. I'd be honored, Miss Hurst, if you would do me the, er, honor, of becoming my wife."

No woman on earth could possibly accept such a poorly offered proposal. Only pride kept Benedict's entire posture from collapsing into embarrassed defeat, and pride became a thin rope to hang on as Miss Hurst considered him with visibly increasing humor. When she spoke, though, it was with caution. "I am surprised. I had feared my...outburst...at the party might have caused you to reconsider your affections."

This was ground upon which Benedict felt he could firmly stand, and he responded boldly. "Not at all, Miss Hurst. I would never press you for the details of your exchange with Mr Graham, but I cannot believe a woman of such gentle mind and spirit as yourself," a phrase he reconsidered even as he spoke it, thinking of how she had also dashed lemonade into Graham's face. But that way lay shakier ground, so Benedict reconsidered his reconsiderations and barreled on, "could be moved to strike any man did he not deserve it in the fullest part. I have every confidence that you were in the right, and he the wrong. More, although startling, I must confess that such actions place a new light on your notoriously cool demeanor—"

For the second time in a single speech

Benedict became convinced he ought not to be saying what he was, but the words tripped on, unstoppable as the ocean current, "—and tell me that as fiery a passion as any man could desire in a wife burns beneath. Miss Hurst, I beg of you, say yes! Tell me I might stir those passions, and we will be happy together!"

Miss Hurst's light blue eyes had widened considerably during his plea, as well they might have: a more indelicate proposal could never have passed the lips of any gentleman. Benedict might as well have asked her to act out carnal desires on the drawing room sofa, so crass had he become. He braced himself for the inevitable and entirely deserved slap, and thus was entirely startled when Miss Hurst drew a deep breath and said, "I would be very pleased to accept your proposal, Mr Fairburn. Yes. I will marry you."

"Really? I mean, that's wonderful. You will?" Benedict narrowly stopped himself from actually cursing in front of his intended, instead biting his tongue and wondering why astonishment instead of unfettered delight spilled from his lips. "Are you sure?"

A twitch bothered the corner of Miss Hurst's mouth. "Yes, Mr Fairburn, I am sure. If you are."

"Of course I am! Yes. Yes, excellent." Benedict gazed at his bride-to-be with a knot of worry churning his stomach. He had not heard in several days how his great-aunt's health was, and now that the proposal was made, a certain urgency was upon him. No one knew how long the old lady might last, but it was important she should at least know of his engagement as soon as possible. "Will we tell our parents and have the banns called from this coming Sunday?"

"I believe the very best of families might regard the banns as common," Miss Hurst replied slowly. "Perhaps we might be coy and wait a short while before purchasing a license instead?"

"Ah. Yes, of course. And enjoy our engagement without public scrutiny for a time. A fine idea, my dear. I can see why your family did so well in trade. Always thinking ahead." Dear God, Benedict thought, someone should stopper his mouth with a cork. Miss Hurst's finely rounded eyebrows pushed together, making an almost indiscernible wrinkle between them, and he smiled weakly, lifting a hand to smooth that wrinkle away. "Forgive me. I am...appalling. Nervous," he offered, though it hardly seemed excuse enough for his unbearable manners. Miss Dalton, he thought incongruously, had been right to forgive him only reluctantly.

Miss Hurst smiled. "No need to be nervous now, Mr Fairburn. We have come through the negotiations and the deal is made. All that remains is the signing of the contract."

"...indeed. Well then." Benedict put a smile on, uncertain as to why it felt like a mask, and bowed over Miss Hurst's hand. "Shall we tell our parents, then, and begin our private festivities?"

For the second time, Amelia Fairburn burst into the relative order of Claire Dalton's life with the demand of, "Oh, *do* tell me what has happened, Claire! Benedict has only just arrived home with news of his engagement and a positive state of agitation over his visit here! I flew, I absolutely flew here as soon as I could escape, because I simply must know!"

Claire, who had spent something of a pensive afternoon gazing out the window at the busy London street below, thinking on Jack Graham's predicament with sorrow and sympathy, was in no way prepared for this enthusiastic outburst, and sat gazing at Amelia in genuine astonishment for a long while indeed.

Amelia, seeing that she had perhaps overstepped the bounds of propriety, struggled with it, then flung herself into the window seat with Claire and seized Claire's hands. "I'm sorry, I have struck you dumb. Forgive me, Miss Dalton. What on earth was I thinking? Let me—let me begin again!" She leaped up and hurried to the door, where this time Claire's maid Lucy, trying not to laugh, was allowed to announce Miss Fairburn and then retire to a chair in a socially permissible fashion. At the door, Miss Fairburn performed an excruciatingly correct curtsy that Claire stood and returned with less precision, still stunned by the news that Miss Fairburn had swept in with.

"Claire," Amelia said warmly. "You're looking well. I hope you don't mind me calling unannounced, but I felt such a kinship with you after our visit the other day—"

"Mr Fairburn is engaged?" Claire interrupted faintly. Such information was of no particular importance to her, of course, although given that it was unimportant, she couldn't fully understand why the whole world had narrowed to a single spot of distant brightness, leaving Claire herself bereft in a cold and dark place. "He did not visit here this afternoon. How can he therefore be engaged?"

No sooner than the words escaped her than did she hear their implication, and forced a light laugh. "Oh dear, that came out entirely wrong. Of course he—" She swallowed. Explanations were beyond her. "My dear Amelia, you had better come here and tell me everything. Lucy, we will need tea. Immediately, please."

Amelia swept down upon her again, seizing her hands a second time, though this time she looked down at their joined fingers in surprise. "Claire, your fingers are numbing to the touch. Come, we mustn't sit in the window, you'll catch your death of the cold. Now, it's simply impossible that Benny wasn't here this afternoon, he came home fuming about it, so angry he forgot to tell us for an entire half hour that he had become engaged to Miss Hurst."

"To Miss *Hurst*?" Claire's voice rose like a fishwife's and she turned scarlet, pulling her hands from Amelia's to clap them to her cheeks. Her fingers *were* icy and felt wonderful against the heat of her face, but Amelia took her hands a third time and this time drew her to a cozy sofa hardly large enough for two. They settled there together, foreheads nearly touching in the way of confidantes, and Claire whispered, "Perhaps you had better start at the beginning."

"Benny was in a perfectly splendid mood this morning," Amelia said promptly, "and he's never in any mood in the morning, he always sleeps until noon. About one o'clock he said he was going to visit Mr Dalton and by half two he had returned engaged to Miss Hurst."

Claire shook her head. "At one I was returning from a most enlightening excursion with Mr Graham. I never saw Mr Fairburn, nor heard his voice. I could ask Worthington, but I don't believe he ever came in."

"An encounter with Mr Graham? After what happened at the Thornbury House?"

"He came to apologize and did, but offered no explanation, then departed on business. I had a sudden conviction that his business had to do with the dreadful encounter at the party and—" Claire faltered, realizing what a light she might be painted in by confessing the next truth. "—and followed him. Worthington came with me!" she added defensively, as if Amelia might know that Worthington had come of his own accord, and not Claire's command.

Amelia, enthralled, said, "And? Did his business relate?"

"Oh, Amelia!" Claire cried. "It did!" The entire story of Graham's ruin-by-proxy spilled from her lips as quickly as tears spilled from her eyes. Amelia never released her hands, listening in dread fascination up until the moment Claire whispered, "and so we drove him back here, where he helped me from the carriage and then himself departed."

A certain confidence suddenly infused Amelia's voice. "Tell me, Claire. Might you and he have appeared intimate as he helped you from the carriage?"

Claire wiped her tears away and sniffled. "I suppose we might have seemed to be so, yes. I feel such a bond to him now, Amelia! Knowing his tragic story and all! The poor children!"

"I suppose it was then that Benny arrived," Amelia announced. "And upon seeing you, concluded he was unwanted here. What a dreadful shame, Claire, especially—what did you say the name of that institution was?"

"The—what?" Claire frowned, not following the other girl's thoughts regarding Benedict at all, then sighed and pulled the institute's name to mind. "St Sophia's Institute for Wayward Children, I think."

"The very same one that Great-Aunt

Nancy's fortune will be going to if Benny doesn't marry soon," Amelia reported with a kind of grim satisfaction. "How awful."

All thoughts of Benedict Fairburn's purposes in visiting the Dalton household fled Claire's mind as she gazed in astonishment at Amelia. "I beg your pardon?"

"Oh!" A hint of pleasing color teased Amelia's cheekbones. "You must know— everyone does!—that Benny is due to inherit our aunt's fortune. It's why he's expected to marry soon."

"Yes," Claire said with a note of dread impatience, "but what's this about the institute?"

"Only that if he hasn't chosen a suitable bride before Great-Aunt Nancy passes, her fortune will go to the institute for orphaned children rather than the family. You can see why everyone's in such a fuss to get him married off. And Mother is determined he should marry a woman of wealth and stature just in case Great-Aunt Nancy changes her mind at the last moment and leaves the money to the institute instead."

The blankly accepting faces of Graham's niece and nephew, the hopeless eyes of the older children, their squalor, their ragged clothes, the raging pride of the fallen noblewoman who housed and clothed and fed them, appeared in Claire's mind's eye, each of those grim expressions burned in her memory.

She tried to speak and could not; swallowed, wet her lips, and tried again. Even then her voice was nothing more than a hoarse and grating sound; she was finally forced to take up a cup of tea and drink deeply of it before she was able to speak again. The momentary inability to speak had given her time to think; her horror was not now — she hoped — audible.

"Tell me, Miss Fairburn, if it is not too indelicate to ask. Would your brother be... quite bereft financially if he was not to inherit your aunt's estate?"

"Oh no," Amelia Fairburn said cheerfully. "We are more than comfortable, and I dare say there's a generous dowry in my name as well. But one can never be too careful, you know. A brother or son might be inflicted with the gambling disease and whole estates can be lost in an evening. Always better to keep the family fortune held close, and to grow it whenever one may."

"I suppose so," Claire replied, but, entirely lost in the memories of Jack's family and the other wretched children, she hardly heard herself. Indeed, she hardly knew herself: she had been upset over things in the past, as anyone might be, but she had never experienced the cold anger that now held her in its grip. In the past, upset had been accompanied by a churning stomach, cold hands, flushed cheeks, an inability to choose a course of action. In startling contrast she now knew precisely what she wished to do, exactly what she wanted to say. It was only a matter of finding the opportunity, and hoping her anger held until then.

She could not, in truth, imagine that it would not. Amelia spoke; Claire did not catch the words, and looked to the other girl in wordless query. "I said, are you all right, Miss Dalton? I've never seen anyone take such a turn. You are so white and still that I fear for your health. Have I said something distressing?"

"Yes," Claire whispered, "but you could not have known how it would strike me, and I must not let it disturb our afternoon. Do forgive me, Miss Fairburn. I shall be all right in a moment."

Lucy, Miss Dalton's maid, had gone to fetch tea and, with the below-stairs sense of something noteworthy pending, Worthington stationed himself outside the drawing room door. His nominal purpose was to open the door for Lucy when she arrived with the tea. His *actual* purpose was eavesdropping, though he would never regard it in such a light. He listened with interest to the tale of Mr Fairburn's engagement, with greater interest to the story of Fairburn's abortive visit to the Dalton household previous to his engagement, and with outright pleasure as Miss Dalton spoke passionately about the sights she had seen that day.

Before the ladies were finished discussing either Fairburn or orphans, Worthington left his post by the drawing room door to sit at a nearby table and withdraw pen, ink and paper. With the ease of long practice, he applied himself to the writing of several notes: six, in fact, each of them in the hand of Mr Benedict Fairburn, whose quick-scratched penmanship was one of the easiest of the Lads' to emulate. Cringlewood's, with its elaborate swoops and curls, was among the most difficult, as was—strangely enough—the stiff and belabored script used by Ronald Vincent, whom Worthington knew had only barely been able to write when he lost his writing hand, and had had to learn again. The others were all various degrees between, though of course Worthington could write in Master Dalton's hand so exactly that when pressed, Dalton himself couldn't tell the difference.

The notes written, folded and sealed, Worthington passed them along to a footman, who was charged with their immediate delivery to the Lads, including to young Master Dalton, who was upstairs. Another dispatch was sent to the Fairburn household's butler in Worthington's own hand. Upon reading it, the elderly and easily exasperated Fairburn butler sighed, cursed the thoughtlessness of youth, blessed Worthington's thoroughness, and set about preparing the household for the moderate gala that young Benedict hadn't seen fit to mention.

These arrangements attended to, Worthington made a reappearance at the drawing room door, knocking to announce his presence and stepping in with an air of embarrassed intrusion. "Forgive me, Miss Dalton, but it seems that the Lads will shortly be at Miss Fairburn's home for a celebratory dinner, and it will be quite necessary for Miss Fairburn to attend in order to have some hope of balancing the table."

"Oh!" Miss Dalton sprang to her feet with fire in her eyes. "Miss Fairburn, may I be so bold as to invite myself along? I should like very much to help set that table to rights."

Miss Fairburn blinked at Miss Dalton in surprise, but ended on a smile. "I imagine my mother would be grateful for your presence, Miss Dalton. There are so *many* Lads. I would invite you over straightaway, but I fear there's too much difference in our heights to lend you any of my gowns. Might we retire to your rooms immediately so you might dress, after which we will take the carriage back to mine? The fuss of dressing is always more bearable with a bosom companion to talk with."

"I can think of no more splendid course of action," Miss Dalton declared. The two girls hurried, hand in hand, past Worthington, who followed at a sedate pace to assist Master Dalton in dressing for dinner as well.

Chapter Ten

Charles, in an admittedly ungentlemanly fashion, did not wait upon the ladies, but instead left for Benedict's the instant Worthington declared him appropriately bedecked for the evening. Worthington remained at his side, such a constant presence Charles hardly thought anything of it. The valet was, in his way, as much a point of reassurance as any of the Lads, and Charles had long since forgotten that a gentleman's gentleman didn't always go everywhere the gentleman did. With Worthington in tow, Charles was the first of the Lads to arrive, and heartily, if somewhat insincerely, shook Benny's hand, pounded his back, and offered his congratulations.

"Erm," Benedict said, flustered. "Thank you, but how did you kn—oh, curse it, I suppose Amy flew straight over to tell you all. I should have preferred to deliver the news in person."

"Amy, nothing. I had a note from you, Benny. Are you so addlepated as to have forgotten your own correspondence?" Charles clapped him on the back again. "Besides, if you'd only sent a missive insisting we all come over for an announcement we'd have caught on anyway. At least this way we could dress for the occasion."

Benedict took a breath as if preparing a second protest, but—as if responding to a stage cue—Vincent and O'Brien were announced by the Fairburn butler, who looked particularly dour in his well-fitted black and white when compared to the two former soldiers. Worthington, at Charles's side, gave the Fairburn butler a short nod, and the elderly man retreated with a glimmer of satisfaction that caused Charles to briefly consider the possibility that he preferred not to deal with the many and boisterous Lads.

Not that there was an air of rowdiness about these Lads tonight, at least. Both had made a particular effort to look well that evening. Vincent needed no ornamentation to be striking; his height alone assured he could not go unnoticed, but an exceedingly well-made coat of forest green velvet shaped his great size into a downright dashing figure, and his calves, enclosed in finely knitted stockings, were exceedingly well shaped.

Charles encountered the sudden idea that a young lady might easily become quite enamored of such a man. It was a moderately distressing thought. Bad enough that Fairburn was engaged. Worse still that his engagement made Charles see the other Lads in a marrying light. But from another view, if a young woman of sufficient means were to become beguiled by Vincent, then his place in Society could be fixed, and Charles would never lose him entirely to the vagaries of life.

The giant cannon-loader quirked an eyebrow at Charles, who shook off his consideration and smiled. "I was only thinking how well you look, Vincent. The green suits you."

Vincent brushed his hand against his lapel in a combination of pride and embarrassment. "Still feels unnatural, Maj—" He caught himself at Charles's quelling look, inhaled, and corrected the rank to, "Dalton." If a nearly inaudible *sir* finished the sentence, Charles chose not to hear it, and instead smiled.

"It looks as though you were born to it. You, on the other hand, O'Brien...." The words were spoken with laughter as O'Brien performed a small and entirely immodest bow, showing off the midnight blue satin of his coat lining before silencing Charles by placing a fingertip against his own lips in a shushing manner.

Charles, obliging and amused, fell quiet, then let go a shout of laughter as O'Brien, in a flawless upper-class drawl, said, "Don't make me reprimand my tailor, old boy; he promised me I had the coloring to carry it off. Said it matched my eyes."

"It does, and you do," Benedict interjected, as amused as Charles. "And elocution lessons too, it seems. By heaven, O'Brien, is this what you've been up to?"

"You've put me in a marrying mind, Fairburn, what can I say? Best foot forward and all that rot." O'Brien's natural lilt disappeared as though it had never existed, a talent Charles had never suspected the soldier owned. A trifle more seriously, O'Brien came forward to shake Fairburn's hand in congratulations as Hewitt was ushered in.

He had made no especial effort to look well, though in a long-tailed black coat and with his hair in an attractive muss, he couldn't be said to be poorly dressed. Charles, though, saw his face contort in disapproval as he took in O'Brien's flash. To no one in particular—he was not close enough to be speaking to an individual, he said, "If only he had the fortune to go along with it," in a low and nasty voice.

"And what does it matter to you if he did, or does not?" Charles came to his side, near enough to catch the smell of drink on Hewitt's breath, and sought Worthington's gaze instantly. The valet was at hand, as always; he was like the air to Charles, so ubiquitous he was rarely noticed. "Tea, or coffee?" Charles mouthed, and with a nod, Worthington disappeared into the Fairburn household.

"You'll need to sober up, Evan." He received a look as nasty as the earlier words for his warning, but Hewitt didn't actually argue. Satisfied with that, Charles nodded once, then risked the question that needed asking: "Why are you in such straits?"

Hewitt shrugged him off. "Surprised you aren't, mate. Here's one of your own, one of *our* own," he emphasized, clearly intending to remind Charles that he, Benedict and Hewitt had been friends first and earliest, from boyhood on, "getting married off, and you're content to celebrate it?"

Charles studied his childhood friend without letting a frown tug at the corners of his mouth. He expected Evander cared no more about Fairburn's nuptials than he might care for the fate of a dog on the street, but if he was determined that should be his excuse, there was little — especially at Fairburn's party — that Charles could do about it. "Try as I might to keep the world the same around me, Evan, it persists in changing. It would be ill-mannered of me to not at least pretend to be happy for my friend, and it seems to me that an emotion performed often becomes an emotion embraced." Not always; he had too often failed himself in courage to believe that fully, but this was not the time to allow himself, or Hewitt, room for doubt. "Here's Worthington with some tea for you. Congratulate Benedict and then drink up and try to behave yourself."

The other two had arrived while he attended to Hewitt, Cringlewood with a curious eye to their goings-on and Ackerman with the look of a man who'd had other plans:

he wore delicious pink over a silken shirt with a cravat so complex it defied imagination, inexpressibles, and boots of preposterous quality, all of it far beyond what he would have been expected to wear at an informal engagement party. Congratulations and speculations were augmented by libations and soon rose to a dull roar of shared stories, gossip and general good humor. Charles admired the Fairburns's staff, who had met the influx of young men with unflappable aplomb despite what must have been very little notice. Benedict himself seemed a little priggish to Charles, but then, he thought he himself would feel the same way upon finding himself engaged, particularly on what amounted to family command.

Hewitt's voice broke out of the din, tone too sharp to be taken lightly. "Seems like an ice queen, Benny, are you sure you can thaw her? Going to be a cold wedding bed if not—"

Fairburn turned a stiff, insulted look on Hewitt's leer as Charles looked in alarm toward Hewitt's teacup. He still held it, but Charles was dubious as to whether it still contained tea, or whether Hewitt was simply happy to act more deeply in his cups than he really was. Before Charles could step between them, Cringlewood was there with the air of casual authority that he hardly seemed to know he commanded. "Watch yourself, Hewitt. You're dangerously close to impugning a lady's honor. I'd hate to see any unpleasantry come out of Ben's celebration."

Hewitt was taller than Cringlewood to begin with, and drew a breath to make himself taller still. He could not, Charles thought, be fool enough to draw the young lord into a confrontation; it would end too badly for him. Even in the best of circumstances, he would find things brought to light that he wouldn't wish to have exposed. In the worst he could easily end up dead. Before it could be taken any farther, though, Worthington spoke in a clear and ringing voice from the door. "Miss Fairburn and Miss Dalton."

Thank God for Worthington, Charles thought with vivid clarity, and didn't care at all why Worthington, rather than the Fairburn house butler, had announced the young women. As one with all the other Lads, Charles turned toward the drawing room door, and after precisely enough interval to pique their curiosity, the ladies arrived. Hewitt's in-drawn breath exhaled on a whispered, "Demme," and though Charles could not condone the language, he was sympathetic to the sentiment.

Cousin Claire could not have looked more magnificent if a royal crown had been set upon her thick dark hair. She wore a gown of shot silk, green with one breath, blue with the next. If she was not actually crowned, she did at least wear a curve of peacock feathers nestled in her curls. It added to her small height, and gave her a regality far beyond that which Charles would have imagined her to possess.

At her side, Amelia Fairburn was equally commanding. She had the height and the slim figure that were currently so fashionable, and her gown of deep orange brought her auburn hair and brown eyes to life. She *did* wear a tiara, a glittering thing that Charles recognized from a portrait of Mrs Fairburn in her youth. They made a breathtaking pair, and by the faint smiles playing at their mouths, knew it. There was little as attractive as a woman confident of her beauty, Charles decided suddenly, and found himself as one of a rush all trying to pay homage at once.

Claire had been afraid that the Lads in all their finery would cut her courage to bits. She found instead that she was emboldened by it, as much because of the brief, appreciative silence on their arrival as the sheer contrast it provided to the poor children still branded in her mind.

She had been thoroughly distracted throughout Amelia's dressing, providing much poorer company than she ought to have. It was just as well. She was afraid she would earn Amelia's enmity forever in the next few minutes, and perhaps set the Fairburns against the Daltons for all time, but the injustice she had seen seemed to her to require a reckoning.

Nathaniel Cringlewood, as the ranking member of the Lads, took advantage to greet both herself and Amelia with a believable level of flattery. Claire liked him, she decided. She liked most of the Lads, and wished nearly any of them except Fairburn and Hewitt had come visiting to the country four months ago. She wondered if any of them would speak to her later, and said, in a voice that didn't shake at all, "Thank you, sir. You're looking rather handsome yourself."

He was, too, for all that she'd judged him one of the plainest of the Lads. He wore a flawlessly cut coat that looked unexciting beside Mr Ackerman's pink and cream display, but the deep russet of which brought out subtle and pleasing depths of color in his brown eyes. He had gained a little height, too, Claire thought, and cast a glance at his shoes to see a cunning extra bit of heel and sole built in. She needed some of those.

So did Charles, although her cousin's lazy smile and half-lidded eyes suggested he could never be bothered with making himself appear taller. His Hessians were sufficient, it appeared, and the smart military cut of his coat distracted the eye from his unprepossessing size. He bowed over Claire's hand as the other Lads had done, but when he straightened she was surprised to notice an unusual alertness in his hazel gaze, as if his perpetual lackadaisical look was inconvenient just now and he needed to see more clearly.

Benedict Fairburn was the last of the Lads to

greet the girls, and when he bowed over Claire's hand, she caught his fingers with a more steely grip than he expected. He raised startled blue eyes to her, and for a terrible moment Claire was struck again by the fineness of his cheekbones and the excellent shape of his mouth. He was less extravagantly attired than Mr Ackerman, but in red so deep it was nearly black, and cream beneath, he could be considered the best-dressed of the Lads this evening, as was appropriate for his own celebrations. All in all, he made a perfect picture of wealth, health and comfort.

That, in the end, was what allowed Claire to speak. "A word, Mr Fairburn?"

She might have struck him with lightning, such a flash showed in his eyes. He stood, very tall and handsome, and offered his arm. "Of course, Miss Dalton." Leaving the room would be too much, but he escorted her to beside the hearth, where its impressive mantel permitted them to imagine some degree of privacy. Mr Fairburn looked at Claire attentively and they both put some effort into ignoring a room full of Lads who were — mostly — pretending to ignore them as well.

Claire was not tall, and dearly wished Benedict would sit so she could have some advantage of height. But there were no chairs beside the hearth, and she wouldn't be put off on saying what she wanted to due to imperfect staging. "I've heard a troublesome rumor on a somewhat indelicate topic, Mr Fairburn. I was hoping you might tell me the truth of it."

Benedict's eyebrows drew down. "I'll do my best, Miss Dalton. What concerns you?"

"I've heard that the fortune you're set to inherit upon your marriage would otherwise go to St Sophia's, an institute for orphaned and unwanted children."

"Yes, that's right."

Cold filled Claire's belly, and if her chin quivered, it was from indignation, not pending tears. "Have you *visited* this institute, Mr Fairburn? Have you seen the need that this fortune would serve?"

"Of course not," Fairburn said in astonishment. "The inheritance is mine, Miss Dalton, not the provenance of some rag-tag group of unfortunates."

"Mr Fairburn," Claire said, her voice beginning to shake, "are you not a young man of some considerable means already?"

Fairburn's astonishment started to fade into insult. "That is a rude question, Miss Dalton."

"I established at the start that this was to be an indelicate topic! Are you not already a man of some means, Mr Fairburn?"

"Of course I am! Good heavens, Miss Dalton, what is this about?"

"And as a man of means already, are you so determined to have a fortune, a veritable fortune, that you would callously pluck it from the hands of those who need it most of all?

Those who are desperately poor and without resources of their own at all?

"*What*? I take nothing from anyone, Miss Dalton, save that which is my rightful due!"

"If you were so righteous you would refuse your aunt's fortune and show yourself to be a truly noble man!" Claire cried. "I have *seen* those children, Mr Fairburn! You want for nothing and they want for everything! How *could* you! What manner of self-centered, arrogant creature can you be, to steal from the starving?"

"I steal nothing!" Benedict Fairburn roared. "How dare you come into my house and accuse me of such things! *I* am arrogant? *I* am self-centered? *I* am not the one who throws unfounded insults into a man's face when he chooses to do no more and no less than that which is his duty! I am a *gentleman,* Miss Dalton, that is what manner of creature I am, and it is a higher station than I might grant to you!"

Each word struck Claire like a blow: she flinched and flinched and flinched again, her skin heating as if under the impact of a dozen slaps. "Then thank *heavens* I have had the wit to accept Jack Graham's proposal of marriage!" she burst out. "At least *he* has honor and integrity and a concern for those less fortunate than himself! Good *evening*, Mr Fairburn! I wish you all the best with your filthy fortune!"

Claire Dalton swept from the drawing room

as if she were a grand duchess, with her teal skirts aswirl and her head lifted righteously high. Benedict, breathing hard with outrage, could only stare after her. *Everyone* stared after her: Amelia stood with both hands pressed to her mouth, her brown eyes enormous; the Lads gaped at the door, at Benedict, and at the door again. No one spoke for an improbably long time, until Benedict realized it was his place to break the silence.

"Well," he began, then could find little else to say. "Well. I...apologize for subjecting you to such a..." Why, he wondered in spent offense, was *he* apologizing? It had been Claire Dalton who had subjected them all to unspeakable behavior, and Benedict, still reeling, had not yet even begun to understand what her complaint was. "...a display."

"Claire is marrying Jack Graham?" Dalton, alight with unusual vigor even if he had not yet taken his gaze from the door and Claire's departure, put the question to the room at large, as if any one of them might have more idea of what had just transpired than he did.

"She can't possibly be," Amelia said through a cage of fingers. "She said nothing this afternoon, and we spoke of Mr Graham extensively." She did not, however, sound certain.

Charles spun on his heel to examine Amelia with fervor, but it was Hewitt, sounding considerably less inebriated than he had been only minutes earlier, swung to Benedict with curiosity emblazoned across his features. "What was she on about, Fairburn? Orphans?"

"My aunt's fortune," Benedict replied, still staring at the doorway as if Miss Dalton might reappear in it. "My inheritance is contingent on my marrying soon, you know that. I'm sure I told you she's giving it to some lot of wretched orphans if I don't marry."

"Demme, man, if she's that desperate for someone to bequeath it to, I'll get married and she can give it to me!"

"Mr Graham's niece and nephew are dependent on that inheritance." Amelia's whispers remained caged, but every Lad in the room looked her way, Charles and Benedict most particularly.

"What are you talking about? That's nonsense, Amy, I have no responsibility toward Graham's relations what-so-ever. I didn't even know he had any."

"They were orphaned." Amelia slowly lowered her hands, clearly becoming aware she was the center of attention. "The institution which took them in is the one Great-Aunt Nancy intends to leave her fortune to if you don't marry soon."

"How could Claire Dalton, or indeed anyone, imagine that was of relevance to me?"

Ronald Vincent, who was not given to offering opinions in the presence of his betters, said, "I think Miss Dalton *hoped* it would be of relevance to you," unexpectedly.

The words were a stone around Benedict's heart, dragging it inexplicably downward. What Miss Dalton hoped was of no importance to him. He had seen her with Jack Graham—to whom she was engaged to be married!—and he had no reason or desire to care what she wanted. Under those circumstances, it was positively incomprehensible that each heartbeat should now be shooting regret through him, as if he had somehow made an irrevocable error.

Trying to shake the feeling, Benedict scowled at Vincent, who shrugged his broad shoulders and looked elsewhere. To Charles, of course, the leader of their little group. Charles's awakened gaze had not yet left Amelia; indeed, he seemed in danger of devouring her with his attention. "She cannot possibly intend to marry Jack Graham. Not after that horrific public display a few nights ago. At best he can be no better than a ne'er-do-well, and—what was that you said about nieces and nephews, Miss Fairburn?"

When Charles left his sleepy demeanor behind, Benedict reflected, his intensity was frightening. He focused now on Amy as if nothing in the world save her existed, and Amelia, who was well able to stand her ground, faltered beneath Charles's eyes. He took two steps toward her, closing to an intimate distance, though he held her with nothing more than his gaze. Even so, Benedict felt as though he should look elsewhere to grant them privacy, and in doing so, discovered every other Lad save Ackerman had done the same. Ackerman looked on the pair of them with his usual serenity, as if an angel approving of a union.

Charles Dalton, Benedict thought in horror, could not possibly make a match with his sister, and thus spurred, looked back at them.

Amelia didn't look like a woman enthralled by a lover's gaze. Neither did she—quite—look daunted, her voice gathering strength as she spoke. "It would have been a scandal had they not covered it so well. Mr Graham's sister bore twins out of wedlock, and died birthing them. Mr Graham has taken their care upon himself, but has told no one." She swallowed, a hard lump moving slowly down her long throat. "It's possible, Charles, that Mr Graham is a fine match. He seems very noble."

"Nobility of spirit is nothing in the face of family ruin," Charles said flatly. "He'll ruin Claire and besides, I can't believe she loves him, not after his set-to with Miss Hurst the other night. That was ill-mannered of him, and Claire," he said with a sidelong glance at Benedict, "dislikes poor manners."

"She forgave me," Benedict said, offended all over again. Amelia, released from Dalton's gaze, stepped well away from him and frowned at the fire. Her shadow, Benedict saw, was momentarily cast against Vincent, and danced there with the flame's motion.

O'Brien drew Benedict's attention by snorting in a most ungentlemanly fashion. "For insulting her, maybe, but never for this, Fairburn. Of course, that doesn't matter, does it? You're engaged to Miss Hurst," O'Brien said bluntly enough to make Benedict's cheeks heat up. "If it was me," O'Brien went on, "I'd have proposed to Miss Dalton. Your Miss Hurst is a beauty, but Miss Dalton's got fire." He seemed to forget Benedict and spread his hands expansively toward the other Lads, forgetting his fine Society tones for the passion of his own accent. "Have you ever seen a lass go after a lad like that? I've only ever seen it when me ma went after me da for scaring the life out of her when he was after coming out of helping to fight a coal fire. The rage in her eyes was a sign of true love so."

"You have a peculiar idea of love, O'Brien," Ackerman said, almost as unlooked-for a commentary as Vincent's contribution had been. Equally unexpectedly, he cut a brief bow toward Benedict and said, "I'm afraid I must offer my congratulations once more and take my leave, Fairburn. I have other matters to attend to tonight."

"Speaking of true love?" Hewitt asked with a leer, and to everyone's surprise, received such a flat look from Ackerman that even his quick tongue was stifled.

Ackerman, Benedict thought, was never

anything other than pleasant. Presumably a man of his physical beauty simply had to smile or wink to resolve conflict. The idea that he could rise to displeasure was startling. And curious, but Hewitt's crudity had already made it clear that the topic was not to be pursued. They all said a brief good-bye and Ackerman left behind a brief silence into which Benedict said, thoughtlessly, "She has no intention of marrying him anyway, Dalton. She only said it to—"

"Distress *you*?" Cringlewood finished as Benedict bit his tongue on where that sentence would lead him. "Did it work?" the young lord asked. Charles blinked once and looked hard at Benedict, who, having had some time to think, had found somewhere else to take his conclusions.

"It doesn't distress me at all," he said coolly, "nor should it. But I believe she hoped it would. I'm afraid your cousin has perhaps developed an affection for me, Dalton, and seeks to wound where no arrow can pierce."

"You believe Claire has entered an engagement with Graham out of affection for you?" Dalton asked in slow incredulity.

"What else can she do, when I am now engaged to Miss Hurst?" Benedict felt a momentary satisfaction at his interpretation of events, though it faded with his recollection of the disdain—no, the *disgust*—in Miss Dalton's emerald eyes. Her arrival had lit the room, warmed it beyond that which the fire could do, and every Lad there had felt it. With his indignation fading, he thought it seemed colder than ever before.

But his indignation had no reason to fade. He had been wronged. Graham's orphans were no business of his, and Miss Dalton had no right to thrust them at him as if they were.

"Yes," Dalton said thoughtfully, "what else can she do."

"Worthington," Master Dalton said only a moment or two into the carriage ride home, "did it strike you that Fairburn was perhaps more dismayed than he let on about my cousin's unexpected engagement?"

Worthington had anticipated the question, or one like it, because he was not usually invited to ride *in* the carriage, although Master Dalton would never object if Worthington had simply made a habit of it. From time to time, in the worst of weather, Worthington had considered it, but the value of the invitation was too great. Not only did it confer confidence, but an invitation generally served as warning that Master Dalton had something he wished to discuss. There was no quibbling or dancing about the issue as there might have been if Worthington was a regular companion within the carriage's relative warmth, and that, to the valet, was worth more than its occasional comfort.

He did not, for now, judge that Master Dalton required a specific answer, and so simply replied, "Sir?"

"He has been quite possessed by her ever since we visited Uncle George's estate," Dalton went on in out-loud consideration. "Coveting her forgiveness, insulted by her dismissal, enamored, if his gaze has anything to say, by her presence, and positively flummoxed by her bad opinion. Worthington, I believe I've hit upon a capital idea."

"Sir?"

"Well? Don't you want to hear it?"

"Sir."

Dalton gave him a look dour enough to be discernible in the dim light of the carriage, and Worthington allowed a smile to creep across the corner of his mouth. "I can see you're bursting with curiosity, so I will spare you the indignity of having to ask and simply tell you," Dalton said drolly. "I believe Benny should marry *Claire*, not Miss Hurst, and then not only will he be happy but the Lads will be unmarred. Claire is practically a Lad anyway, with her talent for riding and hunting!"

Worthington coughed and Dalton peered at him in the darkness. "Oh, all right, well, don't tell her I said that. I suppose she would be offended. Women get offended at the strangest things. Isn't it a compliment to be thought like a man?"

"Sir," Worthington said, "would you feel it a compliment to be thought like a woman?"

"What? Of course not!"

"And why not, sir?"

"Because a woman is a woman, man! Sensitive and weak and always gossiping about clothes and who is to marry whom."

"Sir," Worthington said again, "is it not fashionable to be considered sensitive? Is it not fashionable to eschew violence unless in an actual state of war, and is eschewing violence not in essence embracing weakness? Is it not true that every gentleman in London can discuss fashion and upcoming marriages, and do?"

"Well, yes, but that's different! We do those things for the ladies!"

"And for which lady did you carefully assess each of the Lads' outfits tonight, sir, because I did not see you discuss them with anyone."

Dalton's eyes narrowed as if he might see through the darkness more clearly that way. "What are you trying to say, Worthington?"

"Only that if you do each of those things and do not consider them feminine, sir, then perhaps Miss Dalton might ride and hunt and shoot without considering them masculine, and that you do her a disservice by regarding her in that light yourself."

A long silence met this exceedingly bold opinion, followed, in time, by Dalton's dry statement. "I believe you are a revolutionary, Worthington. Where do you get these ideas?"

"From observing, sir, nothing more. Forgive

me if I've overstepped my bounds."

"Hnh. I wonder if it would bother you at all if I refused forgiveness. Never mind, Worthington, just take yourself and those observational skills and find out for me if there's any good reason that Fairburn shouldn't marry Miss Hurst so that I can marry him to my cousin instead."

Chapter Eleven

Dawn did not come early on a December morning in London. Claire waited for it an interminably long time, sleeping not a wink after Mr Fairburn's gathering. Her rash announcement of an engagement had been made late in the evening. Hopefully late enough that word of it would not come around to Mr Graham before she had a chance to visit him and explain herself.

It had been a spectacularly foolish thing to say. She knew that now. Had, indeed, known it from the moment she swept out of the Fairburn house. Her rage had cooled in the brisk wind, and a tremble had come into her hands. She had drunk a few sips of water during the night, afraid that anything else would upset her stomach, but with dawn on the horizon and breakfast approaching, a combination of duty and hunger began to hold sway.

Charles would not expose her. Charles was unlikely to even be at breakfast, which meant that she could eat, dress, and with a servant — ideally Worthington, who already knew the trouble she had arranged for herself — visit Mr

Graham early enough in the day to be the one to bear the news.

That these things transpired without incident came as an almost unbearable surprise to Claire. She awaited ruin with every breath, and twice nearly told her aunt the entire story out of desperation and guilt. The second time it was Worthington's presence and the nearly imperceptible shake of his head that kept her from doing so. Smiling with nervousness, she instead asked Aunt Elizabeth if she might borrow Worthington while she did some shopping that morning. Aunt Elizabeth, expecting Charles would not rise until sometime after noon, saw no reason to deny the request. They departed at half past ten and, obliged to go on foot for discretion's purposes, arrived at Jack Graham's home shortly after eleven.

The Graham house was a good, if not extremely good, address, and had modest, visibly maintained front gardens: the grass and hedges were trimmed and rose bushes lined the short drive. The stone stairs leading to the door were in good order, the doorknob polished, and the door itself bore relatively new black paint. Worthington stepped up and knocked twice, smartly, with the heavy, black-painted cast iron knocker, then retreated to stand behind Claire.

A pause ensued. Claire waited patiently, then uncomfortably, and finally nervously. She glanced at Worthington, wondering about the wisdom of knocking again. Before she spoke, the door swung open to reveal Graham performing the duties of his own butler.

Jack Graham was a man in ruins. His hair was unkempt, his eyes shot with red and his jaw unshaven. His cravat was loosened, his collar unstarched and his waistcoat unbuttoned. He wore no coat and his trousers were unbuckled at the knee; one stocking had wrinkled and caught on the buckle, narrowly preventing a length of leg from being exposed. He stood at the door of his own home staring at Claire as if she were a vision, but whether of mercy or damnation she could not tell. "If you have come to do me the kindness of telling me that Miss Hurst is engaged," he croaked, "I already know."

Claire, gazing up at him, wondered what she had gotten herself into, but also found tremendous humor in saying, "No, Mr Graham, I have come to tell you that *we* are engaged."

Graham's dark eyelashes dropped in a slow blink; when they parted again, he looked to Claire, then at Worthington, who stood behind her, and to Claire again. "Well," he said slowly, "then I suppose you had better come in. Forgive..." He waved a hand that Claire was frankly surprised did not still contain a bottle, finished, "...everything," and ushered them in.

From the outside, Graham's house was modestly fashionable. Within, it had clearly once been fashionable, but no longer: the hall boasted old wallpaper, well-kept but beleaguered with *trompe l'oeil* that would not be seen in a modern home, and the rug beneath Claire's feet, though fastidiously clean, showed obvious signs of wear. Neither had the stairs been recently sanded, and that was all Claire had time to glimpse before Graham escorted her into the sitting room. Two chairs huddled up to a hearth which contained no fire, and heavy curtains were drawn despite it being mid-morning. Graham opened them, letting large windows shed light into a room that still had bones of beauty: excellent cornices graced the ceiling and the hearth was of handsome marble. Graham crouched there, striking tinder made of scorched linen to start a fire for warmth: the room was hardly warmer — perhaps no warmer — than the streets outside. Claire sat in one of the chairs, shivering, and didn't remove her coat.

"Sorry," Graham said. "I don't get many visitors. No need to keep the fires burning if no one's going to be here, and this way I keep my bedroom warmer. Can't afford to keep the children here," he said, as if warding off her question. "All I've got is the pretense of decency, not enough to keep them safe or warm or looked after. I bring what I can to the institute after a good night at the tables."

"You told me," Claire said quietly and without judgment, "and yet I had no idea."

"I imagine it would be more difficult if I

were a young woman," Graham said with a shrug. "People seem to expect to visit ladies in their homes more than gentlemen. I can offer you tea, but I'll have to go to the kitchen to make it myself. I haven't had servants for several years."

Worthington murmured, "I insist," and departed, though he left the drawing room door open as a matter of form. As if, Claire thought, servants might pass by to keep an eye on them; as if an open door meant they were not alone in a room together.

Graham sat in the chair across from her and leaned forward, elbows on his knees, fingers laced together. He looked altogether more attentive, if not especially less dissipated, than he had at the door. "Dare I ask how we came to be engaged? I have," he admitted in the manner of a confession, "been drinking, but not, I think, *that* much."

Claire laughed shakily. "No, I'm afraid it's all my own doing, and I will break the engagement at once if you wish, but let me explain, and then let us...consider whether there is any wisdom in it."

"There cannot be," Graham said at once, but listened to Claire's tale, his expression darkening only briefly when the matter of Benedict Fairburn's inheritance and the institute for orphans came together as one.

"You can't hold that against him, Miss Dalton," he protested. "The institute is nothing to him, nor should it be."

"I most certainly can," Claire said, indignant. "I may not be familiar with the depths of degradation found in London's slums, but there is still a matter of *noblesse oblige,* which I have learned very well in the country. One does not simply gather all the wealth to oneself without considering the welfare of others and still call oneself a goodly person."

"And there is the matter of Society's opinion of you. It will not be favorable."

"Well, I don't care!" It was untrue; Claire cared deeply, and inside shuddered at the thought of people telling unkind lies and laughing into their fans at her. She was not high-enough born to be considered eccentric or too rich to offend. At her rank she would be a laughingstock, or pitied, or both. She—they— might well be ruined socially forever, no longer invited to parties, no longer respected. It could easily be a cold and lonely life.

But the emptiness on the children's faces haunted her more deeply still. The way they hadn't protested when Jack prepared to leave, the way none of them had any expectation of anything more than what the moment gave them, was intolerable. They might grow up in a household scorned by society, but they would grow up warm and fed and loved—for Claire believed utterly that she could love the twins—and that was the more bearable fate. Graham was a nice enough man. She was fond of him and could perhaps grow to love him. Marrying him would not be unpleasant, and it would mean a life for the twins.

Worthington brought the tea, which was almost tasteless with age but was at least hot, and retired to stand outside the door so they could continue their conversation. Bolstered by his presence, Claire concluded with, "I propose we do indeed marry, Mr Graham. My dowry is enough for a modest household, and the twins can live with us in health and safety."

"It's not a sacrifice I can ask you to make."

Claire sat back in her chair, aware of its lack of padding, and considered not only Graham but his phrasing. "You are not asking," she said then. "I'm offering. But I don't think I'm offering to make, or be, a sacrifice, Mr Graham. I must marry, you are pleasant and handsome, and must be wed. The situation lends itself to this solution."

"What if you were to encounter some other gentleman in Society with whom you found true love?"

"Well." Claire's mouth quirked. "I suppose I imagined living in the country, where we would largely be out of Society anyway, but should it come to pass that such a thing were to happen before we married, I suppose I would break our engagement."

"Could you?" Graham asked bluntly. "When you're making it not for me, but for the twins?"

Claire's humor faded and she glanced

toward the tiny, determined fire. "Then I suppose I shall have to not meet anyone more suitable, Mr Graham. Or..." The thought struck her and she looked at Graham's brown eyes, suddenly embarrassed. "Or are you trying to tell me in the kindest way possible that you prefer not to marry me? I do think that you may perhaps still harbor feelings for Miss Hurst."

A dreadful twist of pain marred Graham's features. "Miss Hurst has chosen her path, and in doing so made it clear that if I still have feelings for her, they are not something she has interest in returning. Let us say that my sacrifice would certainly be no greater than yours, and perhaps much lesser. It is, after all, myself and my sister's children you would be saving."

"So we are agreed," Claire said.

"Miss Dalton..." Graham collapsed in his chair, gazing at her with troubled eyes. He looked tired, Claire thought. More tired than she, who had gone sleepless the night before. He looked as though he had carried a burden too long and that now, looking into the possibility of salvation was more than he could bear. It was clear that he was both deeply appalled and enormously relieved by her proposal. The struggle between choosing her virtue and her place in society or the future of his sister's children played out clearly across his handsome features.

"Yes," he finally said, dully. "We are agreed. But Miss Dalton, I think we should be...

circumspect about our arrangement for some time to come."

"If only I hadn't announced it to a room full of Lads last night," Claire said with a rueful smile. "But very well, Mr Graham, I shall be circumspect and I will even ask the Lads to hold their tongues as well, assuming it's not already too late."

Worthington, from the door, as if offering a piece of information that had simply entered his mind without any relationship to the topic at hand, observed that the Lads were all well-known for sleeping late. Claire, smiling, moved to set her now-empty teacup aside, found there was no table upon which to place it, and bent to carefully put it on the floor. When she straightened, it was to say, "I believe Worthington is correct, which means we had best return home so he can send word to the Lads to employ discretion."

Graham set his teacup on the floor, too, and stood as Claire did. Offering his arm, he escorted her to the front door, where, frowning, he paused. "Miss Dalton..."

The expression was too like what had crossed his face when she had asked him about Miss Hurst. Claire put her cold hand against his cheek, then smiled tightly in return. "Good morning, Mr Graham."

He bowed, murmured, "Good morning, Miss Dalton," and she hurried away with the valet close behind her.

They walked for some time before she gathered the nerve to ask a question. "Do you know where Miss Hurst lives, Worthington?"

He cast her a curious look. "Yes, Miss."

"Please direct me there," Claire said with sudden decisiveness. "I shall visit her while you go to…"

"Corral?" Worthington suggested without any laughter in his face, even if his voice somehow conveyed a great deal of it.

Claire smiled. "Yes. Corral. The Lads. Thank you, Worthington. I don't know what I would do without you."

"Soldier on, Miss. You would no doubt soldier on."

Although she would not be inclined to admit it to anyone, Miss Hurst was not especially accustomed to callers. It was largely her own doing. Her remote persona did not incline people toward making friends with her, and it was, in the end, easier than trying to keep up certain appearances at all times. So when her maid announced the second visitor in two days, this time in the form of Miss Claire Dalton, Miss Hurst wondered if this was what married life would be like: intruded upon by callers at all times, although in fairness she could probably not truly consider two visitors on separate days *at all times.*

With Mr Fairburn's visit she had known what to expect. With Miss Dalton's—Claire's, she reminded herself; she had been invited to call Miss Dalton by her given name. With Claire's arrival, she was curious, and that drove her downstairs without more than a cursory glance at herself in the mirror.

Miss Dalton awaited her in the drawing room, where she seemed a spot of warmth amongst the cool colors. Indeed, dressed in layers of cream and brown overcoats, she seemed *too* warm, though when Priscilla took her hands, they were chilly indeed. "Forgive me for keeping my coat on," Claire said. "I've been unable to warm up properly this morning."

"Then sit next to the fire," Priscilla insisted, though she herself took a seat slightly farther away. Its warmth, like exercise and high emotion, brought out blotches on her skin. "To what do I owe the honor?"

Claire, once settled by the fire, looked up with a smile. "You mean, why have I arrived on your doorstep unannounced?"

"I might," Priscilla admitted. "Usually people send cards first."

"They do, but I had a sudden thought and wanted to ask it before I quailed. It's inappropriate."

"I think we established that I enjoy the occasional inappropriate action," Miss Hurst said, then frowned. "Or was that conversation with Mr Fairburn?"

To Priscilla's surprise, Miss Dalton stared, then blushed an astonishing flaming red.

Priscilla stared back, then realized with horror how that comment could have been interpreted, and felt her own face go mottled with color. "Oh *no*, Miss Dalton! I never meant —oh, *no!*"

"Of course you didn't, of course not!" Claire, who was perhaps as red-faced as anyone Priscilla had ever seen, clapped her hands against her cheeks, where they left white marks from the cold pressure. "What a terrible thing for me to even imagine you meant!"

"What a terrible thing for me to imply!" Priscilla said at nearly the same time, and suddenly they were both laughing. Claire held her hands out and, after a hesitation, Priscilla took them and joined Claire on the low, rose-patterned couch.

"You're right," Claire said, "your coloring is dreadful for blushing. Well, let me ask you this awful question while you're still flushed, Priscilla, for it may make you blush again. Do you—oh dear. I can't think of a way to ask it except boldly. Do you still care for Mr Graham, Priscilla?"

A soft breath escaped Priscilla's lips, much softer than she expected, given that her belly felt as if someone had pushed it hard. "He... told you about us."

"After the..." Claire was clearly struggling not to say *scene*, and avoided it only by beginning all over again. "After the party the other night, he came to apologize, and I learned some of your—*his*—story. I couldn't help but wonder if your current difficulties arise from...caring too much."

Priscilla released Claire's hands and went to stand at the window. The view beyond was of a small park; if she turned her head just so, it seemed that the greenery was all that lay outside their home. It filtered some of London's grime away, at least, and the occasional leaping shadow from branches shifting in the wind cut the sunlight and let it fall more gently on her face. She could not imagine that it softened her, but she knew that it flattered; that was usually enough. "You know I am engaged to Mr Fairburn," she finally said.

"I do."

"So perhaps you will hold what I tell you now in the strictest confidence," Priscilla said. She ought not; she knew she ought not. But Claire Dalton seemed to be made of kindness and of concern for others, and Priscilla had been lonely a long time. On the couch, Claire made a sound of desperately curious agreement. Priscilla smiled, careful not to make any deep lines around her mouth as she did so. "The truth, Claire, is that I believe I will never stop loving Jack. He left me with no explanation and I cannot forgive him for that, but neither can I break free of the love he has shackled me with. It has been *four years*," she cried bitterly, "and I thought I had moved past him until I saw him with you at the park. All of my anger and desire for him came to the surface. I have no idea what he said to make me throw lemonade in his face," she confessed. "I only wanted to do something outrageous, to insult and hurt him as he had me. He makes me so angry, and yet somehow I only want to—"

She caught herself just in time, knowing that admitting to carnal desires would be too much, but there was no judgment, only compassion, in Claire's gaze.

"Then why…?" the other woman asked.

Priscilla Hurst, who was proud of all things physical about herself, who kept her carriage strong and upright even in the worst of times, sagged in exhausted despair. "My brother gambles, and gambles badly. We've lost nearly everything. The house has not been stripped bare only because my father gave away a third of our family's company to keep us in it, to keep us looking wealthy. If I don't marry Benedict Fairburn and his fortune, my family will lose everything. Everything, Claire. So you see, I have no choice. I have no choice at all."

But Benedict has no fortune! Claire wanted to cry aloud. It was untrue: he had money, or money enough, and would have a fortune indeed, if only he married Priscilla Hurst. Instead of speaking, though, she looked over the couch at Priscilla, who was, in the end, wrong: blushes might be unattractive to her coloring, but as she'd stood in the broken sunlight speaking of Jack Graham, her whole self glowed with a warmth Claire had never seen before. Her milky skin had become delectable, not only flawless but inviting, and her pale eyes had shone with the fire of diamonds.

Benedict would never see that, Claire thought. He would never elicit that passion in Miss Hurst, and it hurt Claire to know it. And yet she couldn't bring herself to speak out, to tell Priscilla the truth of Benedict's fortune. He thought he was marrying money, ensuring his own future; Priscilla thought the same. Her family would be ruined if she didn't marry him, and her heart would never be whole if she did.

"I'm so sorry," Claire said helplessly.

"So am I. But there is nothing to be done. Mr Fairburn is pleasant, and it will be easy to become fond of him."

Echoes of her own words pierced Claire's breast. They sounded far more dreadful coming from another's lips. Now she understood Mr Graham's concerns — but equally, she understood Priscilla's. There was nothing romantic about the current arrangements, nor any point in belaboring them. Claire had already agreed with Mr Graham that they would not make much of *their* engagement yet, but even if she had been prepared to, telling Miss Hurst now only emphasized that these were all business decisions, made in the name of improving the greatest number of lives. Benedict's family,

Priscilla's family, Jack's family. There were not quite as many people helped here as orphans might be saved with that inheritance, but perhaps it weighted the balance somehow.

It had to, Claire told herself resolutely, and tried not to think of how even a small bequeathment could go much farther in the cold grey institute than it could in London's fine Mayfair quarter.

She rose and spoke, hardly hearing herself as she did so. "He is pleasant," she agreed distantly. "I'm sure you and he will have a satisfactory marriage. Miss Hurst—Priscilla—forgive me again for my bluntness, but I think I should say this. I do not, of course, know the extent of Mr Fairburn's circumstances, but no inheritance is infinite. For all your family's sake, and for Mr Fairburn's family's sake, you had better make it clear to your brother that any new debts he incurs after your marriage will be entirely his to deal with. It is bad enough that he has brought your family to the brink of ruin. He cannot be allowed to do the same with your married family as well."

"He has never been without an income he could idle away as he pleased," Priscilla whispered. "Perhaps a commission can be arranged for him, and he can be made to understand that that stipend will be all that is ever available to him. Perhaps he is only young and rash and unconcerned, rather than unable to stop himself."

"I hope so," Claire said with sincerity, and quietly excused herself from Priscilla's heartbroken presence.

"It is all a disaster, Worthington. Miss Hurst loves Mr Graham still and I had been sure that she and he might be reconciled, but it's much worse than that, for she has no fortune at all, her brother has gambled it away, so she *must* marry Mr Fairburn so her brother's debts can be paid off and her family's business saved, and I fear that without the great-aunt's money, doing all that would leave the Fairburns destitute! There is no happy reconciliation here, Worthington, I simply cannot find it. And the only way Mr Graham's family will be saved now is through me."

Miss Dalton did not appear to wonder how Worthington had finished his missives to the Lads in time to return and walk home with her. Nor did she notice that he carried two packages, one a hat box and the other a stack of fine linen tea clothes for embroidering, upon which a small box of chocolates was balanced: the shopping they were meant to have done. Perhaps Mrs Dalton would have thought nothing of them returning empty-handed, but Mrs Dalton herself never returned from a shopping excursion without at least one purchase. Safer, in the valet's opinion, to play into her expectations, and therefore wave aside any potential questions. Besides, the shopping had been the work of a moment, although his small pool of personal funds was somewhat depleted after the week's efforts. Still, young Master Charles tended to be generous with his coins, insisting Worthington keep a bob or two when an errand had been completed, and it would be little enough time before his savings were flush again.

He said nothing to Miss Dalton about any of this, or indeed about any of the topic upon which she spoke, understanding that she needed to pretend she poured her heart out to a wall, or some other unhearing, impassive object. He did, however, hear, even if he tried not to judge. Upon arriving home he sent Miss Dalton to show off her new hat and share the chocolates (she gasped gratifyingly at their presence, admiring both Worthington's taste and foresightfulness), and asked Master Charles for an hour of two of his own.

Charles, half awake and groggy after the celebration at Benedict's the night before, was only too glad for the opportunity to sleep longer yet, and granted Worthington his personal time with a happy groan. The last the valet saw of him was one foot stuck out of the covers whilst the rest of him, from calf to crown, burrowed deep into duvets and pillows again.

It would not do, Worthington decided, to spread general rumor. Each of the participants in Miss Dalton's disaster was inherently worthy and he had no desire at all to see any of them ruined. But it was not terribly difficult to catch a Hurst footman—they were not so pinched that they had let all their servants go yet—and to congratulate the footman on the family's upcoming success in marriage.

The youth swelled with pride as if it was his own marriage, then held that swollen breath as Worthington agreed it was entirely splendid. "But," he murmured in a confidential aside, "I must admit I feel it's a bit of a shame about the orphans, though, don't you?"

The boy's eyes bugged at this hint of previously unbeknownst gossip, and his struggle to pretend as though it was common knowledge whilst also working the details out of Worthington was nearly laugh-worthy, save that laughter would have ruined the whole game.

"Oh yes," Worthington said very solemnly. "The inheritance all rides on Mr Fairburn's marrying, you know," which of course everyone *did*, and allowed the youth to press on with, "Oh, aye, but I've never got it straight about the orphans—?" without quite swallowing his own tongue with excitement.

"The aunt has a soft spot for them, you know. A kind and good-hearted woman, is Mrs Nancy Montgomery. If the young sir doesn't marry, her fortune will go to their support, and there's some thought that it might anyway. Ah, I shouldn't have said that. Don't pass it on now, do you hear me?"

"Oh, yes, sir!" blurted the breathless footman,

and immediately remembered some errand that had to take him back home that instant.

Worthington smiled at the lad's retreating form, then returned home to get young Master Charles out of bed for the day.

Chapter Twelve

It was a full two mornings later that Miss Priscilla Hurst was announced at the Fairburn household. Benedict was (unusually) awake already, and dressed, and indeed entirely prepared to meet his intended even at the unlikely hour of eleven o'clock in the morning.

His first thought, upon entering the drawing room, was that she did not look well. Indeed, it put all other thoughts out of his mind. He rushed to where she sat on the couch, dropped to one knee, and looked into her pale, wan face. No, not only pale: Miss Hurst was by nature pale. Now even her natural milky coloring seemed to have sallowed and her skin tightened over her bones until she looked pinched; her hair, well-arranged in suitable curls that ought to have flattered her face, was straw-like, all its luster gone. The ice pink of her gown no longer looked suitable, but rather as if someone had played a cruel trick, deliberately choosing a hue one or two off from that which would flatter. Even through gloves, her hands were cold. Benedict raised them to his lips and in real concern, cried out, "My dear, whatever is wrong?"

Miss Hurst, unable to meet his eyes, turned her profile to him. With the new tightness of her skin, her perfect nose became too sharp and her lips disappeared in a thin, unhappy line. "I must tell you something, Mr Fairburn. Something that may change your affections for me."

Benedict thought instantly of Graham, his loathing roaring back to life. The cad had to be responsible in some way for his darling's misery, and he would have her happiness back if it came out of Graham's hide. "Nothing you could say will change my affections."

"I have no fortune."

Benedict wobbled upon his one knee, righted himself, then gave up and sat without dignity upon the floor to gape at his fiancée like a doe-eyed cow. "I beg your pardon?"

Pained embarrassment slipped over Miss Hurst's face as she glanced at Benedict, sprawled on the floor like a child. "Oh, do get up, Mr Fairburn, I cannot look at you like that."

Uncertain how well his legs would respond —they tingled dully, but had no other distinct feeling—Benedict rose slowly, making certain to keep one hand on the arm of the couch and then the back of one of the deeply winged chairs until he was able to ensconce himself in the chair. "Not that your fortune affects my desire to marry you," he said as woodenly as the chair, "but what are you talking about, Miss Hurst? Your family is wealthy, and my mo—"

A faint smile did little to restore Miss

Hurst's beauty. "And your mother was unable to root out even a hint of scandal? Yes, *my* mother is exceedingly good at managing gossip, and even better at managing a household. There is no outward sign of our ruin. Not yet, at least. My father and grandfather were both inclined to keep as much wealth tucked away in the salt cellar as in the banks, and so what has gone out has been steadily replaced, all in the manner of well-accounted business. Those who watch these kinds of things might believe we are in a momentary dip, waiting for the ships to come in, but in a very little time it will become clear that the funds cannot be replenished."

"But—what has happened?"

"My brother gambles."

Benedict fell back in his chair, gazing at Miss Hurst without seeing her. "I knew—I had heard," he said. "I had been given the impression that he had been—been cut off."

"He has now been," Priscilla said quietly. "Too late for the family fortune, but…as I said, my mother is exceptionally good at managing gossip."

"Yes." Benedict spoke without hearing himself, his thoughts aswirl. Her lack of funds did not, he supposed, change anything, save that as a new husband he would likely be expected to save the Hurst family from ruin. He did not, in truth, know if his aunt's estate would stretch that far, and said as much.

"Then they will have to retire to a more modest lifestyle," Miss Hurst said quietly. "We —I—*you*—would not be expected to support my brother; that much has been made clear to him. We...have harbored some hope of a commission for him," she admitted, still quietly. "But that would be an act of generosity and not one I could expect of you."

Benedict's gaze sharpened on her. "You might have asked that anyway. You might have married me without confessing to any of this. Why tell me, Miss Hurst? Surely your parents wouldn't want you to."

"No. But my grandfather would have. Never enter a business deal dishonestly, he would have said." Miss Hurst tried for another smile and failed. "But there is something more."

Graham, Benedict thought again, and braced himself.

"I've heard rumor, Mr Fairburn, that if you do not marry before she dies, your aunt's fortune will go elsewhere."

A knot formed between Benedict's eyebrows. Miss Hurst was confounding this morning. If that was a sign of things to come he would either spend his life in pleasant challenge or unpleasant frustration. "Yes, it's true. She's in her dotage, I suppose, and has got it into her head that if I don't marry before her death that she'll leave the lot to a school for orphans."

He might have struck her with lightning, so abruptly did she straighten. "So that is *true*?"

"I'm afraid so. A terrible waste, so I admit it's hastened me along the road to marriage, but Miss Hurst, I cannot allow you to think that it has in any way bolstered my affections for you. I should have been taken with you regardless, for your unconventionality and your honesty." Benedict spoke with enough conviction to nearly make himself believe it, but Miss Hurst only looked more troubled.

"I'm sorry to hear you say that, Mr Fairburn. If your affections were conceived for purely financial matters I should feel less dreadful over what I must say."

The breath stopped in Benedict's chest, his heart itself suspended between one beat and the next. His voice, when it came, was thin, though why he was so alarmed he could not say. "Pray, do not feel badly, Miss Hurst. Whatever it is must be said. Please. Do not leave me in suspense."

Miss Hurst gathered herself splendidly, color returning to her skin so that she looked at least healthy again, if never flushed. "I am fond of you, Mr Fairburn, and I must marry for financial reasons and for the safety and health of my family. But I do not have to marry *you*. Nor can I in conscience do so, when I know that our marriage could so profoundly damage the hopes and chances of those far less fortunate than even I, in my dangerous state, am. I must, therefore, break our engagement, and I can only hope that you will not suffer too long from the disappointment."

The thud of Benedict's heart matched the beat of every word spoken by Miss Hurst. Despite the blood rushing through him he felt slow and thick, his words measured by disbelief. "Do you mean to say that you refuse to marry me over a school of wretched orphans?"

"That is precisely what I mean to say." Miss Hurst was apologetic but firm, and failed to sound in the least bit heartbroken herself. "I hope you can eventually forgive me, Mr Fairburn. I believe I should depart now. I will show myself out."

"No, no, you must not." Benedict, somewhat surprised his legs would bear his weight, stood and wobbled toward the door with Miss Hurst on his arm. Almost on his arm: they held the proper form, his elbow for her hand, but she did not so much as touch him, not even the most feather-weight of embraces. He escorted her down the hall in this intimate yet remote manner, and at the door slid his hand under hers without touching her. There was no effort on his part as she effectively lifted her own hand to just below Benedict's lips, where he murmured, "Miss Hurst," and allowed her to leave.

No sooner than the door closed behind her than did he fall upon it, his shoulders against its breadth, his chest heaving, his feet splayed wide to press his torso back so the door might support him when he no longer trusted his frame to do the job. Great gasps tore his throat as emotion crashed through him, and he could not with any certainty name that emotion. Sorrow? Relief? Anger? Disbelief? Shock? Insult? All of those and more, he thought, though why anger and insult should lie as bedfellows with relief and delight was all but incomprehensible to him. He could not rationally be both infuriated and glad to be released from his engagement, but then, this was an age of sensibility, not rationality.

Benedict's knees finally gave way and he slid down the door, his coat rucking up in the back. He lowered his head into his hands, fingers knotting in his hair, and there he sat, wheezing with conflicting sentiment, until Amelia's startled voice cried, "Benny? Dear heavens, Benny, are you well?" and his sister flung herself to her knees beside him.

"I do not know what I am," he replied thickly, and to his surprise felt thin tracks of water spill from his eyes as he blinked finally and lifted his gaze to meet Amelia's.

She grimaced at the sight of him, the brief expression conveying that he looked worse even than he imagined. "Benny, whatever has happened?"

"I have been jilted, Amy. Miss Hurst has broken our engagement."

His sister's lips parted in astonishment, then instantly pressed together in anger. "What a fool. She was never worthy of you, Benny. Forget her at once. Whatever could her reason be?"

A sharp laugh escaped Benedict's throat. "The demmed orphans, Amy. The same demmed orphans that Miss Dalton is so concerned with. What could they possibly matter to women of their class?"

Amelia, who knew more than she dared tell, stood and offered her hands to Benedict. He took them and she pulled him to his feet, brushed his tears of disbelief away, and murmured, "Perhaps you should ask one of them, Benedict. Perhaps you should ask one of them."

"A note for you, Miss," Worthington announced, and offered Claire a silver tray upon which rested a single envelope with her name written upon it in a strong masculine hand.

Excitement and dread thrilled through Claire all at once, though she said, "Thank you, Worthington," in a nearly steady voice, and accepted the envelope with hands that hardly trembled. It had to be from Mr Graham, but missives took on greater portent when their contents could relate to the most titilating of scandals, a secret engagement. Claire broke the seal — simple wax, unmarked by anyone's sigil, and unfolded the letter, her gaze flying instantly to the signature.

A frown pulled her mouth down and she looked to the top of the letter, making certain it was addressed to her. It was indeed: *Dear Miss Dalton,* it read, and below that, *I hope that you will do me the favor of a drive in the park with me this afternoon. I will call at 2 p.m. if that suits. I await your response,* and then, bewilderingly, below *that* lay the dark and certain signature of one Benedict Fairburn. Claire looked at his name for some time without comprehension, only realizing how long she had studied it when Worthington finally said, "Miss?" in a tone connoting only a reminder that he was there, and no curiosity at all.

Claire wondered how he could possibly do that so well, when he certainly had to be as curious a creature as any other human. Eyebrows lifted, a stupor shaken off, she said, "Please call for my maid, Worthington. I shall dress for a drive in the park this afternoon. Wait: has it been raining?"

"No, miss. The weather is unseasonably pleasant, although it is rather cold."

"Excellent. Then ask Lucy to set out my clothes, and return to me. I shall have a letter for you to have delivered."

"Miss," Worthington said agreeably, and went away while Claire penned an acceptance to Mr Fairburn's invitation. She could not imagine what he could possibly want. She had insulted him thoroughly, and expected no overtures of reconciliation. Were he not a friend of Charles's, she doubted she would ever see or speak to him again, which was certainly for the best.

Oh, but Charles. He *was* a friend of

Charles's, and it was likely her cousin had intervened, not wanting trouble between his family and his friends. Well, for Charles's sake she could be civil, even if she thought Benedict Fairburn to be among the lowest of the low.

He arrived promptly at two and, although he was unquestionably the lowest of the low, Claire, clad in a lightweight, softly yellow dress and a fetching blue overcoat, was pleased to see that Mr Fairburn was dressed as finely, and indeed nearly matched her in his buckskins and powder blue tailcoat. They murmured polite greetings as he helped her into the gig, and settled himself before clucking to the horse, a fine bay mare whose coat shone and who swished her short tail proudly. Claire uttered a compliment about the beast, which Fairburn accepted before falling into a polite silence the entire distance to the park. Claire, increasingly astonished by his unwillingness to speak, kept her complete attention on the passers-by, the newspaper-sellers, and the businessmen moving purposefully through the streets.

After half a turn around the park, the polite quiet had begun to border on absurd; after a full circuit, Claire broke the silence with a mix of incredulity and insult. "You drive nicely, Mr Fairburn, but I am beginning to have a care for your wits. Does a cat have your tongue?"

Fairburn flinched so guiltily Claire wondered if he had indeed planned an entire drive in unbroken silence. He spoke with the rough voice of one who had not been prepared to use it. "No, Miss Dalton. Please forgive me. I have been thinking about our altercation a few nights ago and have been unable to find a delicate way to broach the topic."

"I see. Well, if you expect me to apologize I believe you should instead return me to my home at once. I stand by my statements."

"No," Fairburn said hastily, "no. Much the opposite, in fact. I had hoped you might clarify them somewhat. Please, Miss Dalton, might we walk a while? I wish to understand something, and although this horse is capable of walking for miles unattended, I should hate to somehow be the cause of difficulties due to my lack of attention."

"Certainly," Claire agreed, and, remembering her intentions of being civil for Charles's sake, kept the opinion that Fairburn preferred to cause difficulties deliberately, rather than through inattention, to herself. They alighted from the carriage and Fairburn handed its care over to a smartly dressed youth who led the ensemble to a post as Benedict offered his arm to Claire.

She smiled a decline. "I think I am safe enough if we keep to the paths, Mr Fairburn. Now, you wanted me to…?" Because while she remembered what he had asked, it seemed unlikely that he was eager for another tongue lashing, and that he would not have chosen such a public space if that was his expectation.

"I want to understand why this institute for orphans is so important to you. I do not wish to discuss my part in it, only to try to grasp why any young woman of means would feel so passionately about a passel of unfortunates."

Surprised, Claire walked quietly for a while, searching out the answers she could give without betraying Jack Graham's secrets. Not that they would need to remain secrets much longer, but for his sake—and her own—it was better that the question of the twins not be revealed until after they were married and settled. "I do not know how you pass your time, Mr Fairburn," she finally said. "I do not suppose young gentlemen are expected to do good works with and for the poor in the way that young women are. You have different expectations placed upon you: politics, soldiering, hunting."

Fairburn gave her a quick smile. "A pastime some young ladies share, I hear."

"Yes," Claire said rather seriously, "but not to half the degree that gentlemen do. I have too many other duties to attend to, and among those has always been to help the poor. Many of the families in our township feed themselves with a small garden, but they must still bargain for bread and meat if and when they can. I have brought many a leg of mutton or shoulder of pork to a family who has not had meat in months, or soups and breads to a widower whose pride will not allow him to seek help. These are not bad people, Mr Fairburn, they are only poor, and the only reason that they *are* poor is because they have no money."

"If they were worthier, they would be wealthier. That is the nature of wealth."

Benedict sounded so sanctimonious that a fire lit in Claire's breast. "That, Mr Fairburn, is preposterous. How can you possibly say an infant or a child is unworthy? It is not the fault of a child that it is born to poor parents, or to parents who are ruined, or even if it is born out of wedlock!"

"But those children grow up to be criminals, Miss Dalton," Benedict said patiently.

Exasperated, Claire whirled toward him and stamped a foot. "Often, yes! But that is because they lack food, warmth, clothing, shelter and must do whatever is necessary to obtain those things! Have you ever seen an infant steal a loaf of bread, Mr Fairburn? No! A father steal one for his starving child, yes, but the child is innocent of anything but hunger! How many loaves of bread do you require on *your* table before you are willing to give one to a hungry child? Answer me, Mr Fairburn! This question demands an answer!"

Fairburn shifted uncomfortably. "None at all, I suppose. I won't starve if I give a child some bread."

Satisfied, Claire relented a little. "You wouldn't starve if you gave up your bread *every* day to a hungry child, which is what I mean to say to you about the institute. You have bread already, Mr Fairburn. You have an entire table full of food. That is what *your* wealth, the wealth you already have, gives you. But you insist that your aunt's wealth must be yours as well. More bread for your table, when you already have enough. And yet you say to me that you have earned your aunt's bread too, and that you will not give it to a hungry child."

"That is not at all what I said."

"It is precisely what you said," Claire said gently, "and it is why I am so very angry with you. Even if I had not seen this institute myself I would think of the families at home who have lost a father to accident or a mother to illness and who have been reduced to nothing because of it, and I would disdain you for your greed. You could be better than that, Mr Fairburn. You *should* be better than that."

Claire Dalton twisted his words with a politician's skill. Benedict tried not to scowl at her and felt he nearly succeeded, but she took one thing he said and made it into something else entirely, and he couldn't entirely shake the suspicion that she was right. "Do all women feel so strongly about these matters, Miss Dalton?"

"Any person with a conscience ought to feel so strongly about these matters," Miss Dalton snapped. "It is not a feminine concern, Mr

Fairburn, even if the care of unfortunates is often left to women. It should be a concern of all of Society, and yet I hear little discussion of it in politics, and in popular writing none so much as Mr Bentham approaching the matter at all. Oh," she said in sudden evident disgust, "wipe that look away. Women trouble themselves with politics and philosophy too; our lives are affected by them as much as yours are. Allow yourself to forget I said that, if you must. Continue in your belief that females are too delicate to consider matters of state. But if you can bear the difficulty of the thought, consider that our greatest monarch, who ruled longer than any other, was a woman, and see how that settles in your mind."

Her contempt was palpable. It flushed her cheeks and curled her lip until she nearly sneered. Benedict, looking at that unconstrained derision, thought suddenly that it was the most delightful, powerful expression he had ever encountered on a woman's face, and had the overpowering impulse to kiss her.

With deliberate consideration, he did so. His hands captured Miss Dalton's heart-shaped face, turning it up to him with the lightest touch. She could escape, he was certain, if she wanted to. Her eyes rounded, emerald darkening with anticipation, and he brought his face close to hers, waiting an impossibly long, aching moment to see if she intended to retreat.

She did not. Her eyes closed and, with a

glad gasp, Benedict's mouth met hers with sweet and determined pleasure. Her lips were soft, compliant, and then, even more deliciously, demanding. His hands cupped her face, her fingers slid into his hair, and for the most enticing moment Benedict had ever known, they were as one.

Then she broke away with an appalled cry, stared wildly at Benedict and, blushing with shame, ran from him.

No sooner had she run than Claire knew she had made a mistake. *Another* mistake: allowing Benedict Fairburn to kiss her had been the first. But he had looked at her so strangely, his blue eyes darker than the sea and a confusion playing about his mouth, that she had forgotten all except him. She had wanted nothing more than the touch of his lips against hers, and as their mouths had met she had felt, wonderfully, as if she was both completing and beginning a journey she could hardly imagine. It had seemed, in that moment, that she had been traveling toward Benedict since the first time she had laid eyes on him, and that the path had suddenly smoothed, all troubles left behind.

And then she remembered that she was engaged, however secretly, to Jack Graham, and a terrible shame had seized her. How could she, who had just lectured Fairburn on morality and conscience, turn her back on those very things so swiftly and with such conviction?

It was not his fault she had been so weak, and so she only ran, rather than slapping him, but in running, she left herself with no way home save her own two feet. She ought to have simply withdrawn, apologized coldly — as Miss Hurst would have done! Oh, Miss Hurst! Claire had betrayed her too, by allowing Benedict to kiss her. There was no chance for her at all, save to hope no one had seen the act of — she would not call it passion. It had been foolishness, nothing more, or curiosity at worst, the curiosity of a young woman who had never been kissed. But only her husband ought to have kissed her, and Graham might cast her away if he heard of her wanton nature.

Somehow Claire made her feet stop running. A woman alone on a walk in the park was perhaps remarkable enough. A woman running pell-mell across the greens was something else, and would be commented upon, as would walking home, although there was no help for *that*. She drew her shoulders back, lifted her chin, and breathed deeply, putting on a performance of propriety that her hammering heart and knotted belly didn't feel. Benedict's kiss had awakened such warmth in her. More than warmth: heat unlike anything she had ever known. Had it been Graham's embrace to waken such desire she might have thought it suitable, but it had been a man to whom she was not, and could not ever be, engaged. Struggling to look careless, Claire left the park without glancing back.

Benedict could do nothing but watch her run; he could not make himself call out, or follow, not when he had disgraced himself and Miss Dalton so thoroughly. He only stood, cold with indecision, until in a sudden heartening action, Miss Dalton drew up, no longer running. In unproven hope, Benedict sprinted forward himself. But Claire's hesitation lasted only the space of a breath or two. Then she walked on, never once looking back. She had clearly not thought better of escaping him, only of drawing attention to herself with her speed. His run faltered into steps, and then stillness as her figure grew ever-more distant.

The bells of a nearby tower rang, informing him that it was the three o'clock hour. That, Benedict thought viciously, was late enough to begin drinking.

Chapter Thirteen

That one of the Lads might come upon Benedict drinking himself to a stupor was always a possibility, but he would not have laid money on Samuel Ackerman being the Lad who did. Benedict had deliberately chosen a pub that lay along the questionable border of Cheapside, far from the fine publican houses and halls the Lads—especially the wealthier Lads—usually haunted. But before Benedict was drunk enough to forget why he was drinking, Ackerman arrived, and in such fine feathers—no inexpressibles this time, but tall, rather soft-looking leather boots, scarlet trousers and a jay-blue coat of immaculate cut —that Benedict was surprised he had made it into the establishment without losing at least his clothes, and possibly his life.

Attired thusly, Ackerman was a bright and shining spot within the dank pub. All eyes were drawn to him, but it seemed to Benedict that there was no palpable air of surprise amongst the men gathered within the pub's dark walls. Instead, it was Ackerman who expressed surprise, pausing at the far end of the bar to take in Benedict's presence as if he were a crayfish crawling unexpectedly along the floor. Benedict waved the most recent of several beers at him in greeting. Ackerman's eyebrows lifted in acceptance and he came to sit beside Benedict, ordering an entire bottle of the pub's best whiskey on the way. They each had two companionable drinks before Ackerman ventured, "Well?" and a roar of frustration erupted from Benedict's throat.

"Ah." Ackerman circled a finger at the barkeep, gathered up whiskey, glasses, and Benedict alike, and maneuvered them all to a grimy table in a corner. There was considerable strength in Ackerman's slim form, more than Benedict expected; Samuel's beauty hardly meant he was as fragile as a women, even if he was as lovely as one. Once situated at the table, one on either side, more drink was poured and two heads, light and dark, bent toward each other while Benedict mumbled his confessions. Not engaged to Miss Hurst. Kissed Miss Dalton. Was an unconscionable beast, according to the latter.

"For kissing her?" Ackerman enquired with real curiosity.

"No," Benedict said gloomily to the pungent golden alcohol in his glass. "I rather thought she liked that, until she ran away."

"Never a good sign, mate," Ackerman said sympathetically. "Go on, then."

"How'd you find me here, anyway? Where're

the rest of 'em? Don't tell me you've spared me all their mockery."

"They'll be along. Hewitt's the only one likely to mock you."

"Hewitt's the only one likely to mock me and mean it," Benedict corrected. "He used to be such a sport. Don't know what happened, except of course he can't abide the soldiers. Jealous as a girl, that one. He was dreadful to Miss Dalton. Worse than me by far. Tried scaring her half to death. I should've knocked him about a bit, that would've taught him. Bit of a duel would've been good for him."

Ackerman, with unexpected authority, said, "A duel's no good for anyone. At best someone ends up hurt, at worst, dead, and it seems that despite the stories, women don't care much for men fighting over them."

Benedict reared his head and fixed Ackerman with as gimlet an eye as he could manage. It would have, he reflected, been easier had there been only one Ackerman, but the angelic face seemed to have doubled, and both swam idly in Benedict's vision. "That sounds like the voice of experience," Benedict accused the middle-most eye of the two faces, trusting that Ackerman was in that area somewhere. "What's this, Sam, have you got shtories — *stories!* — you're hiding from ush Ladsh? Us. Ladsh. Ush?"

Ackerman lifted the whiskey bottle and considered its contents. "I'll tell you after we find the bottom of this bottle. Do you like her?"

"The bottle? It's fair enough. 'Coursh, whiskey burns your taste away with the firsht shot, so the rest of it could be bilgeswipe."

"Miss Dalton, Benny. Do you like Miss Dalton?" Ackerman's rare and brilliant smile was so appealing that although Benedict rooted around in his soul for some degree of embarrassment at the misunderstanding, there was none to be found. Still, he waggled a severe finger at Ackerman.

"I don't go around kisshing girls I don't like, and neither should you, Sham. Do you?"

"I admire Miss Dalton extensively," Ackerman said solemnly, and Benedict placed a poorly-aimed kick at the other Lad's shin, under the table. His toes caught a chair leg instead and he lacked the sensitivity to yowl, though the connecting toes cracked loudly enough to be heard. Ackerman winced and glanced below the table. "I hope you'll be able to walk on that later."

"What should I do, Sham?"

"Limp," Ackerman suggested. Benedict had just enough wit to not try kicking him again, and Ackerman relented by pouring Benedict another drink. "Decide what you want the most, I suppose, Fairburn, and then try to get it. If you fail, accept that, but by God, try."

A vigorous nod began somewhere around Benedict's waist and worked its way up until his head bounced with it a few times. "Capital idea, Ackerman, shplendid. What do I want?"

"That's for you to determine, not me. Drink up."

Benedict did, squinting at Ackerman's glass. It was still full, though he couldn't remember Ackerman refilling it. A suspicion began to trickle in around the whiskey, but the bottle was more than half empty now, and a trickle was not enough to stand against the tide of alcohol. "What do *you* want?"

Ackerman's more usual shadow of a smile curved his mouth. Just as well, Benedict thought; the full smile affected even men, as was proven by the fact that Ackerman had used it only minutes ago to distract Benedict's pique from...whatever it had been. But he listened attentively anyway. Ackerman, for all his foppish clothes and distinctly visible presence, was a rather private man, and Benedict was unsure they had ever spoken alone and so extensively before. "I want to be admired for my wisdom and insight rather than my face, of course," Ackerman said lightly. "Just as any beautiful woman might wish to be."

Benedict's eyes widened and he leaned in, dropping his voice to what he imagined was a conspiratorial whisper. "Ackerman," he said in these near-stentorian tones, "are you a *woman*?"

Unexpectedly, Ackerman burst into laughter and stood. "Come along, Fairburn. Time to go home. You're drunk. Go home, sleep it off, and decide what you want to do with your life when you wake up."

"I'm leaving Town for a while," Benedict announced to this recommendation. Ackerman, eyebrows elevated in interest, slid himself beneath Benedict's arm and steered him out the door before replying, "Oh? Right now?"

"*Yesh,*" Benedict said with a decisive roll of his head that nearly toppled them both. "Shtraightaway. I musht get my head clear. Maybe do shome hunting."

"Fairburn," Ackerman said, suddenly no-nonsense, "I forbid you to hunt in this condition. If you have any thought of it at all, I will take you home myself and stand at your bedside until unconsciousness claims you."

"N-n-no," Benedict promised, not so much stuttering as emphasizing. "I have the carriage. I shall drive it out and hunt when I am shober."

"You are not driving anywhere," Ackerman informed him, but now armed with the knowledge of Benedict's carriage, sought it out and poured Benedict in before taking the driver's seat himself.

It was not an especially long drive to the Fairburns' in distance, though in class and architecture it might have been a different world. Benedict was, despite this, utterly insensible by the time Ackerman arrived at their gates. With a distinct sense of self-preservation, he opted to hand both reins and heir over to the first available footman, and to himself slip away into the evening without further ado.

ff

"What do you mean, Fairburn has left Town?" Charles demanded petulantly. "Why? Where has he gone?"

Samuel Ackerman, who had arrived at an unusually early hour already smelling of whiskey, although his faculties did not seem to be impaired, sprawled casually across the smoking room's finest couch as if it was his own, with one scarlet-clad leg hitched over its arm and the other foot stretching along the floor. He lay with one arm folded behind his head, the whole of him propped up on pillows (half of which he had stolen from other seating), and waved a lazy, graceful hand in the air. "Hunting, he said, although I cannot imagine what for."

"Sam," Charles said, trying now to sound severe, "sit up. You look like a Cyprian."

"Shall I paint my lips and offer kisses?" Ackerman pursed his lips in offering and shifted a few inches, enough to suggest the impression of sitting rather than lounging. "It doesn't matter where he's gone, Charles. He's gone off to clear his head, and I thought you'd want to know. You like to keep track of us."

"Someone's got to." It wasn't true, of course. They were all grown men, quite able to keep track of their own lives. But it soothed Charles to imagine they were an unchanging lot whose occasional deviations from the usual meant nothing. Except Fairburn, in becoming engaged, had already deviated terribly from the typical. A small knot of concern worried at Dalton's belly when Fairburn's sudden departure was added to this mix.

It would have reassured him greatly, of course, had Ackerman said Benedict *intended* to leave, but Ackerman, on his walk from the Fairburn residence to the Dalton house, had considered that explanation and rejected it. With half a bottle of whiskey in him, the last thing Fairburn needed was Charles playing the agony aunt over him. Besides, Ackerman was convinced that Fairburn fully intended to leave once he had regained consciousness. It was not his place to thwart that, no matter how much Charles might have preferred him to. "Look at it this way, Dalton. A man who runs away to the country isn't one who's getting married soon, so your Lads will remain intact a while longer yet."

"He has to get married," Charles snapped. "His inheritance depends on it."

"And yet he's left Town. Something to do with your cousin, I believe, if you want to know the whole of it."

"For heaven's sake, Ackerman, my cousin and Fairburn have nothing to do with one another, especially after that disagreement at his house the other night. Don't be absurd."

"My apologies, Dalton. Come on, let's go out and I'll buy a round so we can forget about it."

"I'll need more than a single round," Charles

warned, but the invitation sounded promising, and soon they were out the door, neither of them having noticed Claire pressed into a hall alcove outside it.

Mr Fairburn had left Town. Ackerman's pronouncement echoed in Claire's ears and somehow pierced holes in her heart. She had spent the afternoon enclosed in her room, fingertips all too often brushing her lips in warm memory of Benedict's kiss. Again and again she had convinced herself that she couldn't dwell on that one mistaken moment. Again and again she had come back to it, until finally she had decided that he could *not* have kissed her so beautifully if he did not in some way care for her, and that she *would* not have responded if she did not herself in some way return that affection.

Which meant that she was shortly to marry the man that Priscilla Hurst loved, and Miss Hurst to marry the man that she, Claire Dalton, loved. Fortunes or not, practicalities or not, business or not, such marriages could only be considered foolishness. Having come to this conclusion, it became apparent to Claire that she must speak to Benedict again, perhaps to explore the depths of their passion for one another, though even the thought itself caused her to blush. So, with her courage gathered, she had come downstairs with the intent of going to visit Amelia and the hope of encountering Benedict there. Instead, she had learned through the half-open smoking room door that Mr Fairburn cared so little for their encounter that he had left Town.

Claire remained where she was, pressed into an alcove she had hidden in when Charles and Mr Ackerman had left. She had feared encountering them or being accused of eavesdropping. Now she could not force herself to move.

How could he be so callous as to leave? How could *she* have been so foolish as to imagine that kiss meant something to him? Thank heavens she had not gone at once to Mr Graham to confess her sin. That kiss would now have to be her darkest and best-kept secret, the one she would take to her grave as Mrs Graham.

Mrs Graham was an idea that filled her with neither delight nor horror. It was simply a practical, if not precisely prudent, decision to positively affect the greatest number of people she could. She enjoyed Graham's company and imagined the children, once certain their new-found country lives would not be snatched away from them, would be anywhere from intolerable to delightful, as children tended to be regardless. And if it was to be done, best she shake herself loose from the alcove and tell her aunt and uncle as soon as possible.

Still, she thought, deep within, as she made herself move, how *could* he have left Town?

At the door of the sitting room Claire hesitated and looked at her aunt and uncle almost as if for the first time. Aunt Elizabeth, in magnificent maroon silk as she sat with a book under a good light, was the image of a gentlewoman, powerful in her own way. Uncle Charles, reading his papers, was a slight man whose hair appeared to have migrated into his sideburns. His gaze was like his son's, mild and lazy, though his smile was readier than Charles Edward's. He dressed fashionably, probably due to Aunt Elizabeth's influence rather than his own inclination. They had been good to her, more generous than even family had to be. Claire smoothed a hand over her skirt, feeling the grain of silk and thinking of Madame Babineaux's care in costuming her. Claire was grateful to her aunt and uncle, and found that she hoped she would not disappoint them.

Both of them looked up as she entered the room, Uncle Charles flicking his papers down and offering one of those ready smiles. "Claire. You look lovely tonight."

"Thank you." Claire inhaled deeply. "I have an announcement to make."

Aunt Elizabeth's spine, always straight, straightened further, and her expression went wary. Claire felt mildly offended, and yet feared her aunt had reason to be cautious. Uncle Charles, however, only looked curious, which lent Claire some confidence.

"It has not been done entirely properly," she said in a rather small voice, "as Mr Graham has not spoken to you, Uncle Charles, much less my own parents, but I should like to tell you that we have agreed upon an engagement, and hope for your blessings."

A silence met this announcement. A silence and a distinct lack, Claire felt, of looks exchanged. Either her aunt and uncle knew each other's thoughts intimately or Uncle Charles fully intended to leave all the marrying business to the women, as it was Aunt Elizabeth who slowly closed her book and did not otherwise change expression. "Mr Jack Graham, you mean? Of whom I have heard less than flattering tales these past weeks?"

"Not from me," Claire said, suddenly stout in defense of both herself and Graham. "Most of it—all of it—is misunderstandings, which I myself have been allowed to understand. I do not regard them as impediments to marriage."

If she had not known better she might have thought she saw humor spark in Aunt Elizabeth's eyes. "Ah," her aunt said. "Well then. Surely any objections we might have are irrelevant, then."

As quickly as it had come, Claire's defensiveness fled. "Of course not, but at the same time, my mind is entirely made up."

"Well, come in and sit down, Claire, and let us hear all about it. How did he propose? Was it gentlemanly? What are his prospects? Who are his friends? How does he know Miss Hurst? And do you love him?"

Claire sat obediently, then gazed at Aunt Elizabeth with increasing horror. There had been gossip a-plenty regarding Jack Graham and Miss Hurst, but to find Aunt Elizabeth knew Miss Hurst by name still came as a shock. And Claire could certainly not admit that *she* had actually made the proposal, which left her stymied for answers on more than half of Mrs Dalton's questions. "I like him," she said to the last, and to her surprise heard Uncle Charles grunt in disapproval.

Blushing with astonishment, she turned to find him looking as startled at the sound as she was. "Forgive me, my dear. That was intolerably rude."

"And yet," Aunt Elizabeth said in the tone of one who expected to hear the reasons for intolerable rudeness.

Uncle Charles squinted, making him once more very like his son, although Claire couldn't imagine Charles Edward giving Aunt Elizabeth a skunk-eye, which was what Uncle Charles's expression slid toward, as if he suspected he had been played like a fish on a line and that Aunt Elizabeth was the expert angler. However, in for a penny, he went in for a pound, addressing Claire directly: "It's good that you like him, my dear, as liking someone often lasts longer than the first flush of love.

But you are young and — forgive me — wealthy enough to choose without being *so* wealthy as to be fortune-hunted. You have some degree of luxury in that you might be permitted to pursue love. I do not like you abandoning that opportunity so soon."

Claire thought of Benedict Fairburn and crushed the thought all at once, not knowing she betrayed herself with a blush. Her aunt and uncle did exchange glances then, but she imagined they were only in agreement, and cried out, "I am abandoning nothing! This is my decision, and if I am so perfectly balanced between independence and fate, then let me choose liking that will last rather than the heartbreak of failing love!"

A second glance was exchanged before Aunt Elizabeth said, "Well, your Mr Graham must at least speak to your uncle, and better yet, to your own father. I will write immediately. I am sure your parents can be here within the week. We shall host an engagement party ten days hence and have it published in the papers the following day, but in the meantime I believe we should have a small and private celebration ourselves. After all, it isn't every day that my niece finds herself engaged, and I, for one, am most eager to meet your young man.

"Tomorrow?" she asked Uncle Charles in a conciliatory fashion, and as swiftly said, "No, of course not, tomorrow we are engaged to have supper with the Talbots. The day after, then. Charles can invite the Lads and we shall struggle to balance the tables. I suppose Miss Hurst must attend," Aunt Elizabeth said, giving Claire a gimlet eye, "if we believe all parties can behave themselves, and Miss Fairburn; that will be a start. Who else would you have, Claire? Only your nearest and dearest now, for we won't want to spoil the announcement for Society at large."

"I believe you've already hit upon my intimates, Aunt Elizabeth." Claire felt rather like Uncle Charles had looked a moment ago: as if Aunt Elizabeth had somehow played her, and she was certain neither how nor what, exactly, her aunt was accomplishing.

"Well then," Aunt Elizabeth said briskly. "Mrs Fairburn, perhaps, as she is a good friend of mine, and her older daughter, Mrs Durrell, as well. We shall simply have to arrange for Mr Durrell to have irresistible plans two nights hence so he isn't obliged to attend and skew our numbers further."

"I could join him," Uncle Charles offered in a voice intended, Claire thought, to sound noble, but succeeding mostly in sounding hopeful.

Aunt Elizabeth reached over to pat his knee. "That's very thoughtful of you, my dear, but I'm afraid as Claire's eldest male relative in London you'll be obliged to attend."

"Ah. Yes. Of course." Uncle Charles turned his face away from Aunt Elizabeth and dropped Claire a solemn wink that made her smile. "Go on," he said to her. "You've said your piece tonight. Surely a young woman has more to do than sit and make polite conversations with her elders during the height of the Season?"

"Oh. Yes. Or, rather, no, Uncle Charles. I thought I would have a light supper and go to bed early. I'm afraid I didn't sleep well last night." Or at all, but Claire could hardly say that aloud. It would lead to all kinds of suppositions.

"The excitement of becoming engaged," he said wisely. "I recall being in a stupor for days after your aunt agreed to become my wife."

"Really," Aunt Elizabeth said dryly. "Stunned with joy or the drink, my dear?"

Uncle Charles's ready smile lit up mischievously. "Joy that could only be expressed through the exuberance of drink, my dear. Go along, Claire. We'll see you in the morning."

"Thank you, Uncle Charles. Good night, Aunt Elizabeth." Claire escaped with the sensation that it had all gone far too easily, and yet was too relieved to care.

No sooner than the sitting room door closed behind Miss Dalton did Mrs Dalton say, "Worthington," in tones even dryer than the ones she had just applied to her husband.

Worthington stepped in from the hall, where he had lingered beside the open door despite the young Master Dalton's departure some time before. Mrs Dalton took up a fan engraved with swans, tapping it against her lips as she regarded the valet. "I should like to ask how you came by the intelligence that you shared with us, but I fear I would sleep less well from the knowing. Still, I must thank you. I believe I could not have responded so evenly had I not been warned beforehand of Claire's intentions. I only wish we had had more than a moment's notice."

This last was said with a suspicious stare that Worthington met with perfect equanimity. He could, of course, have warned Mr and Mrs Dalton several days ago that Claire seemed headed for an unwise engagement, but up until he had glimpsed her in the hall, whey-faced at the announcement that Mr Fairburn had left Town, he had been fairly certain the matter would sort itself out. Previous to that, the Daltons had not needed to know; and upon that moment's arrival, he had taken it upon himself to steal a few seconds of their time and inform them of his suspicions. He had left the sitting room only one step ahead of Claire's arrival.

"Not at all," Mr Dalton said as he took up his papers and a port with equal amounts of decisiveness. "If you'd had time to plan your attack you'd have driven her back against a wall and she'd have held her ground against all objections. Now she'll be squirming at your compliance, Lizzie, and start to wonder if she's making a terrible mistake."

"And how do you know so much about how young women will react?" Mrs Dalton asked, though not in a particularly complaining tone.

Mr Dalton lowered his papers to smile at her. "I married one, didn't I? Some things you don't forget, my dear. Some things keep on working."

Mrs Dalton favored him with an arch look, then returned her attention to Worthington, whose own attention moved from the fire which he had, to all appearances, been studying with mild interest as the lady and gentleman of the house spoke to one another. "Have you any further insights or warnings for us, Worthington? Anything about Mr Graham's character we should know now? Any way to dissuade her from the match?"

"I believe Mr Graham's character is not the problem, ma'am. Indeed, if it isn't bold to say so, I quite approve of him. He is, however, penniless, and I believe the marriage is entirely to his convenience and not at all to Miss Dalton's. Not that he is pressuring her. I believe she feels this is the right thing to do. However, I think I should also mention that Mr Fairburn has left Town, Mrs Dalton. He will presumably be unavailable to attend the party two nights hence."

Mrs Dalton's eyes narrowed thoughtfully. "I see. Thank you, Worthington. I had not realized Mr Fairburn's relevance in this discussion. Is there anything else?"

Worthington considered what information he had overheard from Samuel Ackerman's discussion with Charles Edward, and replied, "Only that I should think Miss Hurst would want to know that Mr Fairburn will *not* be in attendance before she makes her own decision as to whether she herself will be."

The corner of Mrs Dalton's mouth lifted a scant amount. "I *see*. Worthington, you are a treasure and no doubt entirely wasted on my son. See to it that I add something to your wages."

"Ma'am." Worthington bowed and, regarding himself dismissed with the uncouth mention of money, departed.

Chapter Fourteen

If only, Claire thought, she could go hunting. Even riding, but within London the only places to ride were the streets or the parks, and one of those was both too filled with people and—depending on where she chose to go—too dangerous. The other, while obviously more suitable, was so very...*tame*. There was no wildness in the park. It was clipped, trimmed, mowed and swept, with pleasant pathways to keep to, and people braving the winter chill to take some exercise. One could not ride pell-mell over them, even on a known jumper that would easily clear the blankets and the people sitting upon them.

But even riding lended itself to a certain freedom of thought rather than the vigorous application of mind and body that hunting could demand. Claire was not overly interested in the kill. It was the ride and the awareness of the land, the watching for signs of prey, the judging where it might be flushed out and the pursuit that she longed for now. It would consume her, leaving no room for other thoughts, and for the past two days, Claire

Dalton had wanted to do anything but think. Now the day of the family engagement party was upon her, and the larger one would be a week hence. She hoped to be married as soon as possible afterward, so that she might occupy her time with duties rather than thoughts. Where *was* Benedict Fairburn?

"Ah!" Betrayed by her own mind, Claire clapped a hand over her mouth and hoped no one had heard the burst of frustration. Honestly, it was intolerable. She was accustomed to taking exercise in the country, if not in the form of riding and hunting, at least in her walks to and from the village and to the friends and tenants she visited with. She had become too accustomed to carriage rides in London, and felt that if she did not *move* soon she would fly apart from agitation.

"Miss?" Her maid Lucy appeared in the door, concern crinkling her pretty brow. "Did you call for me?"

Claire nearly indulged in a groan, and put some effort into modulating her tone so she didn't snap at the girl. "No, although now that you're here, Lucy, I wonder if you would gather my coat and shoes. I must take some air."

"Of course, Miss." Lucy bobbed a curtsy and scurried off, leaving Claire to gaze out her window into the gardens. They were of moderate size, generous for a townhouse, but they would not do at all for Claire's restlessness. It would have to be the park, and she would walk there, as the idea of another carriage ride filled her with a desire to twitch.

Lucy reappeared with Claire's favorite coat and a pair of beautiful yellow slippers that were entirely inappropriate to extended walking. "Boots, please," Claire declared. "I expect to be gone some time and must not exhaust my feet with the party coming up this evening."

"You ought not go out and exhaust yourself at all," Aunt Elizabeth said, passing by the door. She had been pleasantly interrogative about Jack Graham for the past day and a half, never pressing Claire beyond that which she wished to say. Claire, who thought of her aunt as formidable, was made somewhat uncomfortable by this. It felt as though Aunt Elizabeth had a hidden agenda, a suspicion made worse by the knowledge that she, Claire, had one herself. Her aunt and uncle—indeed, all of Society—could not be allowed to hear of Graham's poverty or, far worse, his ruined sister and the twins until after the marriage had taken place. She and Graham had discussed the topic at some length, concluding that they would retire to the country immediately upon marriage. Claire's dowry would be comfortably sufficient to keep them, when the costs of Town need not be considered, and then Jack's townhouse could be sold or rented for further income. The children would join them in the country a few weeks or months after they were settled. It would give the newlyweds time to put about a story and prepare the quiet town of Bodton for two unexpected arrivals. It was the best plot they could come up with; the one least likely, they felt, to lead to ruin.

Not a word of which she could say to her aunt, at whom she only smiled. "I'm sure I'll feel better for the exercise, Aunt Elizabeth. I promise to be invigorated and vivacious for the party tonight."

"Well, take Worthington with you," Aunt Elizabeth recommended. "A young lady should have an escort, and if you tire he can arrange a carriage home. That's a very pretty dress, Claire. You look lovely." With this compliment she took her leave, and left Claire with the odd feeling she was under-dressed and should change into something more attractive for her excursion.

She was becoming irrational. She shook herself, accepted the low-heeled brown leather boots that Lucy brought her, and found Worthington waiting at the front door for her whether she wanted him or not.

As it happened, she was pleased to have the valet with her. Worthington was an amiable companion who expected no conversation between classes, but was willing to engage in it if Claire so desired. With his escort, she trotted down the steps and into London.

The air was still dirty, the streets still stench-ridden, the noise still tremendous, with carriages rattling and horses neighing, with men calling to one another and women talking as maids shouted after children who ran to and fro with no care for their own safety. It was easy to remember after only a block why one took a carriage in London if one could, but by that time Claire felt as if returning for the carriage would show a lack of commitment. She strode on, and strode indeed, more eager for the exercise than a ladylike pace. Worthington, behind her, didn't protest at her speed, which allowed her to conclude it was not unseemly.

It was nearly as fast to walk to the park, in the end, as it was to drive: the snarls of traffic were more easily evaded on foot, and several times Claire found herself outpacing, being outpaced by, and again outpacing carriages that could not move as lithely as she. Had she noticed that earlier, she would have walked more, weather permitting. At least she knew it now, and could apply her knowledge for the remainder of her time in London.

The park seemed somehow more inviting when approached on foot. Worthington in her wake, Claire entered with the intention of making at least one full circuit. Others were of the same mind, although they took a more leisurely pace, and after rushing past half a dozen walkers, Claire thought that in order to not draw attention she should perhaps slow down. She moderated her stride, focusing her gaze on the stretch of green ahead and to the right. A gathering of young men were playing cricket there with more application to hilarity than accuracy, although a big fellow appeared to be taking his duties as bowler quite seriously. Claire slowed further to watch them, smiling as a disagreement presented in overly dramatic gestures and laughing voices broke out, then startled as the bowler left the field and, upon approach, proved to be Ronald Vincent.

A second glance showed her that one team was half made up of Charles's Lads. Charles himself, whom Claire had presumed still asleep, was among them, and gave a shout and a wave upon seeing her. Claire, forgetting herself, waved as vigorously in return, then folded her hand down hastily. One might greet someone thusly in the country, but in London it would be remarked upon.

Indeed, Mr Vincent, damp with perspiration and fascinatingly undressed in his shirtsleeves alone, offered a bow and remarked upon it: "Miss Dalton. Forgive me for being bold enough to say so, but it's refreshing to see a lady remember she can make a gesture bigger than a mouse's."

No sooner than the words left his mouth than he looked mortified. The very first memory Claire had of Mr Fairburn flashed through her mind: his fine seat on a horse, his cloak falling about him carelessly, the brilliance of his blue eyes—and the condemning phrase that had left his lips: *I've found a mouse in the garden!*

"I see the Lads have shared that story. Don't

worry," Claire said with a laugh as Vincent's expression grew increasingly stricken. "I'm beginning to think I ought to find a way to make something of that name. What special talents do mice have?"

"They creep into places they are not expected, and make themselves at home there, as you have crept into all of our hearts," Nathaniel Cringlewood volunteered as he, too, joined them. Like Vincent, he had the healthy glow of exercise, and his shirt, made of much finer material than the large man's, clung to his torso in a startling and distracting manner. Claire blinked away, looking for somewhere safer to rest her eyes, and found Samuel Ackerman, as undressed as the rest of them, looking rather like a young Adonis under the blue morning sky. The light caught on a still-pink vertical scar, no more than two inches long and quite straight, at the front of his right shoulder. Claire stared at it curiously without even realizing she was doing so until someone tossed him his coat and he threw it over his shoulder, hiding the scar.

"Tut, Claire, staring at Ackerman like that," Charles said cheerfully. "He's pretty, but he's brazen, cousin, running about undressed when there are women about. I should pummel him for sullying your innocent gaze with his brazen ways."

"Ah," Claire replied somewhat absently, "no, Charles, I think that's unnecessary...."

A burst of laughter met her protest and she blushed, but laughed as well. Ackerman gave an apologetic shrug accompanied by his devastating small smile, and if Claire had felt there was anything to be forgiven, it would have been. It was not possible to be upset at a man so beautiful. Indeed, she felt rather like the belle of the ball, surrounded by so much male vigor. Even Hewitt had lost his perpetual sneer in the aftermath of sport and looked very appealing with his black hair shining in the morning sun.

O'Brien, who had somehow got his jacket on faster than the rest and looked slightly more presentable than they did because of it, stepped in beside Claire and offered his arm. He was no less flushed than the rest of them, his own black hair having lost all its shape and falling appealingly into his dark eyes, but unlike almost all the rest, he clearly felt his dishevelment was no determent toward offering his escort. "I saw you walking, Miss Dalton. At the pace you kept, I'd say you ought to join us for the next game of cricket."

"*O'Brien!*" Vincent said, shocked, but the Irishman laughed him off even as Claire wrinkled her nose.

"I very much doubt anyone would approve of that, Mr. O'Brien. I do think, though, that you Lads should come to the country and visit when Mr Graham and I are married. I may not be able to participate in your matches, but I would be pleased to ride on a hunt with you all."

She could not have dulled their mood more thoroughly if she had cast cold water over them. "Graham," O'Brien said with a sniff. "You ought to have married one of us, Miss Dalton."

Claire disengaged her arm from his and stood looking up at him. At all of the Lads, for they were gathered together, dark heads and fair, light eyes and dark, faces from pleasant to sublime, bodies all vibrant with exercise, clothing from passable to quality, all of them taller than she, all of them arrested in the moment, and to them all she said, quietly, "None of you asked."

Claire had, Charles supposed, made some kind of departing remarks, because she left with Worthington on her heels, but there had been a collective intake of breaths amongst the Lads at her entirely salient point, and none of them had heard much beyond their own heartbeats after that. Even *he* had not, and he, as her cousin, was the least likely to have been stung by her remark.

It was O'Brien, generally irrepressible, who said, "Do you suppose she would have had one of us?" but he sounded stunned rather than lighthearted. Five Lads and Charles still looked after Claire as if she had suddenly become a different creature entirely, one to be regarded in a new light.

"If she's marrying Graham, it's not money

she's after," Hewitt said, "so I suppose she might even have taken you, O'Brien, if her wits are dull enough to like a pretty face and no prospects."

O'Brien swung on his heel, visibly torn between insult and flattery. Hewitt was not a man to judge another man's beauty falsely, and had never, in Charles's memory, offered so much as that back-handed compliment to O'Brien. On the other hand, it *had* been back-handed, for O'Brien was not, so long as he remained a friend of Charles's, without prospects. But Hewitt did not intend to let O'Brien stew on whether he should accept the courtesy or call out for a fight, instead meeting O'Brien's half-offended gaze straight on and finishing, "She'd never have had *me*."

"Nor should she," Cringlewood said to Hewitt, "as you've been inexcusably rude to her."

"At least I haven't falsely flattered. *Two* first dances at her coming out, Cringlewood, really? Half of Society thought you were sweet on her."

"But Miss Dalton did not," Cringlewood said stiffly. "Besides, it was the first dance of the second set, at the second ball."

"Still a first da—"

"What do you mean about the money?" Charles asked before further bickering could break out.

Hewitt shrugged stiffly. "You told me to look into Graham. He wins a bit at the tables, and as far as I can see, that's all the fortune he's got. No servants, though he's clever about keeping the gardens maintained. Does it at night so no one sees it's himself. Rarely a light on in the parlor window, or anywhere else in the house, for that matter. Does all his socializing outside of the house. Never visits a Cyprian or a whore, either." A thin smile revealed his teeth. "Maybe he's a better choice than O'Brien after all."

There was no stopping the scuffle, after that. O'Brien seized Hewitt's shoulder and spun him around to meet O'Brien's fist, which knocked Hewitt the rest of the way in a circle, and to the ground. Vincent, with the air of a prudent man, stepped up beside O'Brien and looked down at Hewitt in mild expectation.

Hewitt, on an elbow in the grass, pressed the heel of his thumb against the trickle of blood at his lip, eyed the two soldiers standing above him and the discreet distance taken by the other three men. Then, sullenly, he got to his feet with a muttered, "Apologies."

A gentleman would have offered his hand in acceptance of that apology, however resentful. Neither O'Brien nor Vincent were gentlemen, though, and all Hewitt got for his effort was a short nod from the Irishman. It was, Charles thought, pretty nearly all Hewitt deserved.

Ackerman, as if the altercation hadn't even taken place, said *sotto voce* to Charles, "Will Fairburn be there tonight?"

"What? No, I don't think so. Why?"

Ackerman shook his head and finally

slipped the jacket on over his shoulders. "Thinking about which of us she might have had, is all."

No woman in her right mind could have said such a thing to six men and kept any degree of dignity. Well, five men: Charles hardly counted. So Claire had fled upon the utterance, completely unaware that to the gentlemen she had left behind it had looked not like a retreat, but a scathing gauntlet thrown to the earth by a worthy opponent who could not be bothered to see if any of those she challenged was man enough to retrieve it. So it was with a trembling sense of shame that she allowed Worthington to hire a carriage to take her home after all, and with all the gathered remnants of her pride that she went upstairs to begin the process of dressing for the evening's party.

Marie, Aunt Elizabeth's maid, came to do Claire's hair, and with a rough and sudden gesture Claire agreed to the cutting of her hair that Marie had spoken of the first time they had met. Only a while later, Claire was quite pale beneath a cunningly curled fringe, which — Aunt Elizabeth had been right — framed her forehead perfectly and made her large eyes look positively enormous. A touch of rouge for her cheeks and a little rose salve for her lips made her look fresh-faced rather than ghostly, and finally Madame Babineaux brought forth a gown Claire had not seen before.

Claire's lips parted with astonishment and Madame Babineaux assumed a tight, pleased smile that bordered on smugness. "Madame," Claire whispered. "Madame, this cannot be for me. This is...princely."

"Bah!" the Frenchwoman burst out, and could nearly be said to be laughing. "No prince would look well in this dress, Mademoiselle. It is queenly, perhaps, but not princely. Come. Eat something before we dress you, Mademoiselle, because I shall have to strike you dead if you spill anything on this fabric. It is worth more per length than you are."

Claire, for the first time in hours, laughed, and to the dressmaker's surprise, stood and embraced her. "I *believe* that it's worth more than I am. Thank you, Madame. I look forward to wearing it."

She also looked forward to food, which surprised her; she had thought herself beyond hunger after the humiliating incident at the park. In truth, when provided with a thick soup and sliced pork she fell to it with a good appetite, and ate with the awareness she would not likely have another opportunity before midnight. The tenderloin seemed to feed both her stomach and her soul, yet haunted her with the awareness that marriage to Jack Graham might only rarely see such fine cuts of meat on their plates. Of course, neither would marriage to several of the Lads, which thought came to her with such rue that her embarrassment over the earlier confrontation finally faded. Besides, she could not be embarrassed at all while wearing the dress Madame Babineaux had made; that dress required confidence, and to be less than confident was to do the dressmaker's work a disservice.

Light faded in the west as she finished dressing and was replaced by street lamps as the guests began to arrive. From the top of the stairs, with her door open, she heard voices she knew: Graham, Charles, Mrs and Miss Fairburn, and in a clump, several of the Lads, their voices indistinguishable in the din. Minutes later, sounding as if she had arrived by herself, came Miss Hurst, and after her, a few voices Claire didn't know. Friends of the Dalton family, Amelia Fairburn's older sister, and whomever else was necessary to balance the table, no doubt. It was strange, waiting to be presented. It felt like — it *was* — waiting to be the center of attention. She would have to become accustomed to it, as it would be her lot for tonight and at the more formal engagement party next week, all the way through, she supposed, to the wedding. Claire looked at her gown and wondered how Madame Babineaux could possibly improve upon it for future gatherings. Those who were here tonight would surely comment if she wore the same dress again.

"Claire?" Aunt Elizabeth spoke from the door. Claire turned, suddenly nervous. Aunt

Elizabeth smiled and came into the room, her hands extended to clasp Claire's. She drew Claire into a gentle embrace, set her back, examined her, and finally murmured, "You look wonderful, Claire. Mr Graham will be enthralled. He arrived early and spoke to your uncle," she added. "He seems a fine young man. Handsome and with, I am sure, many other qualities less readily visible. Are you ready?"

"I suppose I must be."

"No," Aunt Elizabeth said with surprising candor. "If you're not certain, Claire, an engagement can always be called off. There's no shame in that."

"There are twenty-five people downstairs expecting it to be announced," Claire reminded her. "I can hardly disappoint them."

"No matter what you do, you will not disappoint anyone," Aunt Elizabeth said firmly. "Come. Let us see how it all plays out."

Together they descended the stairs, Claire doing her best to not lean heavily on Aunt Elizabeth's arm. She had always supposed — hoped — that she might all but float into her engagement, feeling barely tethered to the world, as if she rode in a marvelous hot air balloon. Instead she felt quite prosaic and practical. She was not unhappy, but neither was she overjoyed.

This, she supposed, was what marriage was really like, and she ought not be dismayed by beginning in a realistic manner. Aunt Elizabeth paused in the hall outside the drawing room, where Worthington stood ready to open the door. Her aunt turned her toward the hall mirror, allowing her to gaze at herself in the hall mirror and take one deep, steadying breath. Then, as if a match had been struck, Claire put a smile on her face, bright, sweet, delighted. She could not tell, from the mirror, whether it was a lie, and if she could not, certainly no one else could.

Thus masked, she nodded. Worthington swept the door open and announced her as if it was a grand ball, not a private party in her uncle's home. A curious, respectful, admiring hush fell over the room as she entered.

Jack Graham stood prominently within the room, the foremost person her eye should fall upon. Claire offered a cursory glance accompanied by a reflexive smile, and looked beyond him into the tussle of Lads.

Two dark heads were amongst them: Misters Hewitt and O'Brien. The air left Claire's breast and did not, for some reason, seem willing to return. A little disbelieving, she searched for Miss Hurst, once again barely seeing Graham, but yes: she *had* heard Priscilla's arrival, and, inexplicably, she *was* alone. Benedict Fairburn was no more at her side than he was amongst the throng of Lads.

He had not come. He had not come for her. He had not even come for Miss Hurst, which was by all reasonable intelligence a far greater insult than failing to appear on Claire's behalf. And yet Claire had been certain, somehow, that he *would* be there. That the kiss they had shared — terrible secret, to be forgotten! — had meant something to him and that he would have returned from his peculiar holiday in order to declare his intentions toward her. She had, until that moment, held out hope, and there were two or three among the crowd looking on her who had it in them to see that hope drain away. Samuel Ackerman was one. So was Evander Hewitt, though no one would be less likely to admit that than he.

So, of course, was Worthington, for all that he looked upon Claire's slim shoulders from the back and could not see her attention dart from face to face in the instant after she was announced. He could, however, see the slightest drop of those shoulders, and their subsequent, instantaneous squaring. Very near to him, Elizabeth Dalton sighed. Had he been of a higher social class, Worthington would have caught her eye in shared sorrow.

Fortunately, though, Jack Graham was not among those who saw Claire's dismay, or if he was, he recognized it for the resolution of a woman marrying for practicalities, not love. He could no more hold that against Claire than she might hold his lingering passion for Priscilla Hurst against him. They were of a mind, Jack and Claire, and would do what was sensible even if it did not fill their hearts with romantic excitement.

None of the others saw anything at all, though not one of the Lads could look on Claire and not think of the challenge she had laid at their feet that morning. So the admiring hush of her entrance lingered a little longer than it might have before, as one, Claire and Graham extended their hands toward one another and came together in a chaste embrace of appropriate affection.

Applause, then music, broke out. Claire, laughing brightly if not sincerely, gasped in delight to find a quartet hidden in one corner, then was finally able to see more in the room than Benedict's absence. It blazed with merry light, candles ensconced in every nook that could support them. From the relative lack of smoke it was clear the Daltons had chosen expensive beeswax for the evening's light, which shone against the walls and reflected in the vast mirror over the hearth, making the room seem large and inviting. The papered walls glowed amber in the candlelight, warming the space even more. The furniture had been removed to the room's edges, allowing for comfortable seating and a friendly square in which to dance. Claire clasped her hands over her heart and spun toward her aunt and uncle, crying, "You have outdone yourselves! I'm afraid you couldn't possibly do more for us, Uncle Charles, Aunt Elizabeth! Surely our formal announcement next week will be staid by comparison."

"It had better not be," Uncle Charles said cheerfully. "I've hired a hall to house the thing, as we'd never all fit into these walls. I expect all of Society to be in attendance."

That, Claire thought, sounded perfectly awful, and was relieved when Graham requested a dance and she was able to forget about the future for a while.

Benedict Fairburn stalked up the stairs to the Daltons' home and knocked briskly, his gloves folded into a bunch in one hand. The door did not open instantly and he rapped again more strenuously, as though doing violence to his knuckles would cause the staff within to leap to their job with greater alacrity. Several seconds passed and he was about to strike a third time, this time with a lecture for whomever answered the door, when it swung inward to reveal Worthington.

The valet was forever expressionless, conveying great emotion with no more than the quirk of an eyebrow or the twitch of his mouth. This time both mouth and eyebrow spoke volumes of surprise and nonplussedness, though his actual words were an entirely agreeable, "Master Fairburn. Do come in. The Daltons are in the drawing room."

"All of them?" Benedict threw off his coat. "Even Miss Dalton?"

Worthington caught the coat with the ease of

long practice. "Indeed, sir, even Miss Dalton."

"Thank you, Worthington." Benedict strode past, half aware of laughter from the rooms within, but did not so much as stop to check his cravat in a mirror before bursting into the Daltons' drawing room like a man who belonged there.

Every eye came straight to him, which was precisely as he expected. What he did *not* expect was that there were some thirty people in the room, exclusive of a string quartet and servants. Each and every one paused in their activities to look toward the door with interest. Benedict's blood turned to ice, freezing him in the door frame, then began to thaw under the heat of a quickened, horrified heartbeat.

Miss Dalton was there, of course, a radiant star in shimmering yellow trimmed with green lace. Her fringe had been clipped short—shockingly, fashionably short!—and her eyes, always large, were perfectly enormous beneath the new, becoming fringe. She gazed at him as if he were some beast risen from the depths to scar what should have been an hour of grace.

She stood with Jack Graham, had, in fact, been *dancing* with Jack Graham, until Benedict's entrance had silenced even the musicians. Graham looked very fine as well, although he couldn't hold a candle to Miss Dalton; no one could. Unlike Miss Dalton he didn't appear filled with dread, but merely startled.

That same surprise lay across the faces of

nearly everyone else in the room. The Lads, all save Ackerman, looked astonished at his arrival. His mother and sisters, who amongst them wore more jewelry than all the other women in the room put together, were all more pleased than surprised, but Charles's mother, Mrs Dalton, wore a look of great neutrality that Benedict knew could spell danger. Most dreadfully of all, Miss Priscilla Hurst, whom Benedict would not have expected to see again, and whose normally reserved expression now held even greater dismay than did Miss Dalton's pretty face, was there. She, like Miss Dalton, was attired beautifully. Indeed, it was possible that Miss Hurst, in light blue, *did* hold a candle to Miss Dalton after all, although hers was a cooler kind of beauty.

Benedict took all of this in, and, fumbling for propriety, acquired a desperate smile. "Forgive me," he said in a hoarse whisper. "I… seem to be terribly late."

"So you are!" Charles said, with an all-too-false boisterousness. "Thank goodness, Benny. We Lads were about to have a celebratory drink, and it wouldn't have been the same without you."

He understood Charles's speech, and yet it took a terribly long time to comprehend it all. Then, with effort, Benedict replied, "Of course it wouldn't have been," as jovially as he could, and began to move toward the gathered Lads. But despite what he believed were his intentions to join the Lads, Benedict's feet stopped him in front of Miss Dalton, where he said to Graham, "Forgive me, sir, but may I cut in?"

A ripple of silence swept out from that question before Graham gave a short, almost sideways nod of his head, smiled at Miss Dalton, and stepped away. Benedict presented himself in the pose Graham had abandoned, and the musicians struck up the music again, allowing Benedict to sweep a stunned Miss Dalton into the dance.

For several measures he did not even try to speak. Nor did Miss Dalton, whose gaze fastened on him as though she might see into his thoughts, within his heart—things which, as it happened, Benedict very much hoped were on display.

"What," Claire finally whispered, as hoarsely as he had moments before, "are you doing here, Benedict? You left town after—after!"

"I had important business to attend to," Benedict blurted. "It could not wait, not after—after!" The memory of her kiss seared him now that he allowed himself to think on it again; the softness of her lips, the warm scent of her hair. Her hair! "You've cut your hair!"

"I have," Claire said very formally, almost accusatorily. Benedict scrambled to understand why, then realized the appropriate thing to say: "It looks very well. Your eyes are unparalleled."

Claire, without humor, said, "Indeed, I should

hope they are parallel, else one has taken to wandering, which would be alarming," which was so reasonable and obvious that Benedict blushed at the clumsiness of his compliment. "I only meant—"

"I know what you meant."

"Yes. Yes, of course you did. Miss Dalton—Claire—" Every word was a quick, quiet explosion, spoken only when he was close enough to talk to her alone. The other dancers were trying, none too subtly, to listen in, a fact which made Benedict cringe every time he opened his mouth. This was not how he had anticipated this meeting playing out, and he could see no way at all to draw it back to the script he had intended.

Then suddenly the dance was over; he had chosen poorly, cutting in at the end of the set. Claire curtsied formally and excused herself before he had the chance to ask for a second dance, leaving Benedict bereft and alone as the floor cleared. He retreated to find Ackerman giving him a look of frank expectation. Benedict spread his hands as if to ask what he could do, and Ackerman directed his attention across the room, to where a visibly trembling Claire had taken refuge in Jack Graham's arms. The whole populace of the room seemed to be looking back and forth among the three of them, ready to shatter with anticipation. Miss Hurst, not precisely alone, as she stood with Amelia and Benedict's mother—they were three of a kind,

Benedict realized with a shock. Miss Hurst was a pale version of his mother and younger sister, and appeared as fragile without as Benedict felt within; as fragile as Claire looked in Graham's arms. She met Benedict's eyes briefly, then, as if unable to look away, returned her attention to Claire and Graham.

Graham murmured something to Claire, then put his arm around her waist as if in support, and drew a breath that called everyone's attention to him. As if, Benedict thought bitterly, anyone was already *not* paying attention, but now they were doubly so.

"It is no secret why we are gathered here tonight," Graham began. He had a fine voice, Benedict realized irritably. It held the ear, just as Graham's pleasant face held the eye. Benedict hated him, and could do nothing about it. "But I should like to make the announcement a formal one now. Ladies and gentlemen, our friends and family, I am happy to tell you that Miss Dalton has accepted my propo—"

Miss Hurst shrieked, "*No!*"

Chapter Fifteen

There had been music, Claire realized: soft romantic music, played to accompany and emphasize the announcement Graham had been in the midst of making. There had been music, and she became aware of it because it ended with a shocking violin squawk that underlined Miss Hurst's outburst.

Graham's hands turned icy in Claire's, though her own had gone so cold it was a wonder she could tell. His heart must have stopped entirely, she thought, or maybe started working in reverse, drawing all his blood back into it, for him to be so cold so quickly. They did not look at one another, both frozen into immobility. Perhaps, Claire decided, they had been struck with Miss Hurst's legendary cool gaze so strongly that they had become sculptures of a man and a woman, carved of ice.

The whole room had been struck by ice, in fact: not a single breath had been drawn in the eternity since Miss Hurst had cried out. Not even Miss Hurst was breathing: she stood as though a blow had been struck to her belly, her body curved around a pain she could not hide.

One hand stretched toward Graham as if seeking support, and the second time she spoke it was a broken whisper, a desperate plea: "No. Jack, I know everything. I know about Juliet. I know about the children. I always have. I only waited for you to tell me, and you left me instead. Please, I cannot bear this. I do not care. I do. Not. Care. I cannot live without you, Jack. I cannot let you marry Claire, I cannot stand by and watch another woman raise the children. I swear to heaven that I will take the children myself and flee to America if I must, begin a new life there, but I *will not see this happen!*"

Terrible things came to life inside of Claire: hope and dread, each of them as awful as the other. Here was the chance for everything to be made right; here was the chance for ruin. Her own ruin as much as anyone's, for—

"*Children?*" Aunt Elizabeth's voice cracked across the room, shattering the silence that held everyone else. "Jack Graham has *children?*"

A heartbeat too late Priscilla Hurst recognized the downfall she had laid for others and cried, "No! No, they are not his—!" and Uncle Charles bellowed, "You don't mean to say they're *yours*, girl!? My *God*, Fairburn, what kind of woman are you marrying?"

"I'm not," came Fairburn's faint rejoinder, and that was no better than before: equally outraged, Uncle Charles demanded, "Cast her off at the first sign of trouble, will you? What sort of man are you?"

"I broke with him!" Miss Hurst cried, choosing first to protect his reputation, then, belatedly, adding, "The children aren't mine," as so much of an afterthought that she was generally believed, though the room was already filling with the din of excited gossip. By the time the story left the room — and it would — Claire feared half the Lads would be implicated as fathers and she herself —

She herself was now visibly engaged to a man who had some kind of scandal, perhaps utter ruin, attached to his name, and yet Claire could not yet hold to that particular horror. Something else had *her* attention, and she dropped Graham's hands to whirl toward Benedict Fairburn. "What? *When*?"

"Three days ago," Benedict said helplessly. "The day I asked you to drive with me in the park."

"And you didn't *tell* me?" Claire knew she sounded as hysterical as Miss Hurst — well, nearly — but she could no more control her voice than the other young lady could. "You allowed me to believe that — that — !"

A modicum of wisdom stilled her tongue; she was already engaged to one man who was now saying, as loudly, slowly and clearly as he could, to anyone who would listen — which was no one — that, "The children are my sister's. Oh, Juliet, I am so sorry to darken your name now, but to keep silent would be worse!

She was ruined, the unwed mother of twins," he proclaimed to the room, then shot Claire a slightly wild glance, pleading for her silence as he made an attempt to salvage his family's honor by claiming something that lay far from the truth he'd told her: "and my family ruined in trying to care for her. I have nothing," he said directly to Priscilla, who again cried, "I don't *care!*"

They were a sight, Claire thought unclearly. Miss Hurst's color was high and blotchy, not at all beautiful. She stood what seemed an impossible distance from Claire and Graham, though it was no more than a handful of steps. She had not yet dropped her pose of pleading, one hand reaching. Now Graham stood similarly, as if striving to cross a terrible divide. Claire was nearly between them — as she had been for weeks, she thought, and laughed aloud, sharply. Between them, but she had already turned away from Graham. Her back was nearly to them both, the two of them visible to her only if she turned her head sharply to see them. It was as if she had already shut herself away from them. She felt very alone there, a sensation worsened by the fact that Benedict stood within a circle of Lads, as if they held together and protected their own in the very worst of times.

Indeed, *everyone* else seemed to have some kind of support: Aunt Elizabeth and Uncle Charles veritably clung to one another as if one might have apoplexy and the other, vapors, but Claire could not say which might have which. The Fairburn mother and elder sister were unified, gaping with splendid profiles from their son and brother to the woman to whom he was no longer engaged. Amelia Fairburn looked terribly guilty, her hands pressed against her cheeks and her eyes enormous above them, as if she'd known more than she could tell about the entire dreadful situation.

Miss Hurst compounded matters by crying, "I have nothing either!" to Graham. "That is the irony of it all! Once my grandfather's successes might have offered us all safety and comfort, if only you had not left me without a word! But it's too late now, the money is all gone, I have nothing left but my love for you! I cannot bear it, Jack! I will not live without you!"

An astonished gasp rose up, most loudly voiced by Benedict's mother. Claire could all but see the furious calculations going on in Mrs Fairburn's mind as she attempted to determine how to sort it all out with the least damage to the family name. How she could not have known was beyond Claire, and yet clearly she had not. Surely the Fairburn women had wished to discuss the wedding with Miss Hurst, but then, perhaps Priscilla had demurred upon the topic when pressed, under the sensible assumption that she should not have to be the one to tell Benedict's family of the relationship's end. Perhaps, Claire thought dismally, Benedict had still harbored hopes of repairing the engagement, and had kept its demise largely to himself. Or perhaps he had been so devastated at its end he had left London entirely without telling anyone. And yet that same day he had kissed Claire! She thought she would swoon with the exhaustive emotion of it all, except to do so would add even more fuel to gossip's fire.

Indeed, as party attendees were gathering together, gleeful with the acquisition of gossip, she thought it best not to feed that any more at all, if possible. They were already half-shouting to one another, inventing new details of the scandal to pass around Society circles. Even the musicians huddled together as one, discussing whether the risk of being known as gossips would affect their employment prospects adversely or if they would indeed be all the more in demand if they let it be known they had actually *been* at the most scandalous party of the Season.

Only Worthington also stood alone, and he, of course, was not someone upon whom Claire could throw herself for comfort or in hopes of defense. His gaze, though, when it met hers, was tremendously kind and supportive, as it had always been.

"Then marry me!" Jack Graham cried out, and dropped to one knee before Priscilla Hurst. "Dear God, Pris, marry me! If it must be nothing but each other at the last then let it be so! I will always love you!"

Miss Hurst burst into tears and flung herself into Graham's arms, sobbing an assent that left Claire twisting with happiness and horror as the meaning of it all sank in. Hurst and Graham had simply cast it all away in their passion. It was admirable and profoundly romantic, if one was not among the things cast off. To be jilted by one's fiancé was bad; to be jilted publicly, dreadful. To be jilted publicly, for another woman, with the hint—no, not hint, but *certainty*—of scandal attached....

Claire was ruined. It came home to her with a gentleness that was almost worse than a blow. Standing over Graham and Hurst, she tried and failed to imagine a way out. No one would have her, not now. Not under these circumstances. The most she could hope for would be to return home as quietly as possible and pray that the gossip faded before she died an aged spinster. If she lived quietly enough it might not affect her brother George's prospects for marriage, though she would clearly have to give up hunting and any other behaviors that were in the least bit unusual. If she was fortunate, perhaps the elderly and the poor at home would not turn their noses up at her visits, so that she would not be entirely without companionship, but she could never again hope for friends and acquaintances of her own age or class.

Graham had drawn Miss Hurst to her feet

and they now stood locked in a desperate embrace, kissing more passionately than Claire had even imagined possible, never mind witnessed. Appalled, she looked elsewhere, then, like everyone else, found her gaze drawn back to the entangled couple. The Lads—everyone, in fact—had shifted positions to watch them more clearly. The better, Claire supposed, to spread gossip, although she would not be sharing in that particular vice ever again.

"Miss Dalton," Evander Hewitt murmured at her side, "I realize that the circumstances are somewhat extraordinary, but I should not like to see this confusion blown so far out of control that you find yourself bereft." His tone was so unlike that which she was accustomed to that Claire looked at him, astonished to find his angular face and blue eyes sincere. Far more sincere, she thought, than she had ever seen him before; it reminded her that she had thought him handsome at first, even if he was a terrible cad.

Cad or not, it was Evander Hewitt who offered her the thread of hope she had not even imagined existed. "I hope you will not find me too bold, Miss Dalton, if I ask now if you would do me the honor of becoming my wife?"

Benedict Fairburn seized Evander Hewitt's shoulder, spun him around, and punched him in the jaw as hard as he possibly could.

Hewitt's eyes crossed and he fell soundlessly. Soundlessly indeed, as it seemed to Benedict that there had been a great and terrible roar in the room, a noise so large it had quieted everything else. Hewitt was merely one more quiet thing in the aftermath of that sound. Benedict's throat was suddenly sore, and he had the dreadful suspicion that the roar had been his own voice, unable to contain his frustration any longer.

"Here now," Ackerman said in some surprise, "that's twice today he's taken a hit like that. Perhaps someone should call for a doct—" His last word was cut off as Vincent clapped a large hand over his mouth and in so doing, dragged him a critical step or two away as Benedict, panting with choler, whirled toward Ackerman as well.

Deprived of a second interference, Benedict turned to Hewitt, beside whom Claire Dalton had knelt. She looked between the two of them in astonishment, though, as fire flared in her green eyes, it was clear that emotion was about to give way to another. "What—!?"

"He doesn't love you the way I do, Claire," Benedict said desperately. "He doesn't love you at all. For God's sake, say you'll marry me, not that louse. You must say you'll marry me!"

For a few seconds Claire remained where she was, lips parted in amazement, though not, Benedict feared, delight. He had rendered her dumbstruck, which was not exactly as he had imagined this going. But then, neither was blurting out a proposal in front of dozens, all of whom were now holding their breath as if afraid a single inhalation would draw attention and have them then sent from the room. Benedict was vaguely aware of this, but could no more have dismissed them than turned his back on Claire Dalton, who now rose with the slow, deliberate grace of a dancer.

"I do not require rescue," she said in a voice so controlled and smooth that although all evidence lay to the contrary, Benedict found himself inclined to believe her. Her jaw did tremble, though, as she continued, "I believe I have made it clear, Mr Fairburn, that we are of sufficiently different minds on topics of importance that I could not possibly consider you as a partner in marriage. I am sorry for the break betwixt you and Miss Hurst—" and here Claire couldn't stop herself from glancing at Hurst and Graham, who, although still locked in a kneeling embrace on the floor, had noticed the activities going on around them, and were staring wide-eyed between Claire and Benedict just as everyone else was, "—but I am quite certain," Claire continued with determination, "that you will find a bride of sufficient—practicality—to wed you and ensure your aunt's fortune will be yours and yours alone. I, however, will not be that bride."

"Oh, hang the money!" Benedict howled. "Where do you think I've been, Miss Dalton? I have been to see my aunt, and have told her that I must refuse the inheritance!"

"*What*?" Mrs Fairburn's voice proved a fine contralto capable of shaking the chandeliers. Almost every gaze in the room snapped to her, including Benedict's, although he saw that, beside their mother, Amelia stood with her fingers pressed to her lips and her eyes bright with encouragement. Their mother, however, was nearly as white-faced with shock as Miss Hurst was by nature, and her eyes bulged with horror. "You will go to her at once and tell her you are a young, impetuous fool and beg her forgiveness!"

A feeling of faintness passed over Benedict as he considered the unforeseen possibility that he had not only refused Great-Aunt Nancy's fortune but that he might well have also gotten himself disinherited from the Fairburn money. And yet it was entirely too late, not only because he had been politely decisive with his aunt, but for reasons of far more importance to him now. "Forgive me, Mother, but I will not. There are, it seems, those who need the money far more than we do."

He turned to Claire, who had not, after all, looked toward his mother; she was gazing at Benedict in something he almost dared hope might be considered adoration, and it was to that rising emotion he spoke. "I am blunderingly slow," he said, wretched with apology. "A better man might have understood at once that your argument was full of merit. I, however, had to hear it twice, from two women of greater heart and worth than I myself am, and then had to recognize my own true feelings for one of those women before I began to truly understand.

"Miss Hurst," he said suddenly. Both she and Claire jolted, and Benedict realized in dismay how this would seem if he didn't speak quickly. "I must thank you for breaking with me," he said swiftly. "Had you not I would never have come to understand what I now do. I wish you and Mr Graham all the happiness in the world and I beg you, Miss Dalton, to hear me out."

Breath rushed from between Claire's lips as she gave a diminutive nod. Benedict nearly sank to the floor in relief; that could have gone badly. He was not, it appeared, at all skilled at romancing the fairer sex. "I was very angry with you," he said in embarrassment. "You made me see myself as a lout, only interested in bettering myself, and I feared your vision of me was the true one. It is uncomfortable to look in the mirror and see the man looking back at you as shallow and unworthy. I apologize without reservation for the way I treated you, and for leaving Town so abruptly. Speaking to Great-Aunt Nancy was the only way I could think to prove myself a better man than you had come to view me as. The only way," he confessed, "to prove to *myself* that I was a better man than you believed.

"And in truth, Miss Dalton, without the burden and duty of her inheritance weighing on me, I am more certain of myself than I have been in months, perhaps years. I know now that I do not want to marry for money, but for love. I know the inheritance never meant anything to you, but for a time it meant something to me, so I can only hope that you might see this as some measure of my love for you, Miss Dalton. It no longer means anything to me. All that matters is the hope that you will give me the chance, now that my fortune is not wedded to my, er, wedding...."

He was hopeless. He ought to have asked O'Brien, as silver-tongued an Irish devil as ever there was, to speak for him, or at least write out what he ought to say so that he could study it and not sound like such a fool. It was too late now, though. He had bungled his way through it all, and finished up, in his estimation, equally as poorly. "It may well be that I have nothing to offer but myself, as Mother may well disinherit me after this, but if you think I could make you happy in any measure, I beg you again, Miss Dalton, to consider me for your husband."

There could be little more miserable than standing before one's entire family, all of one's friends, several passing acquaintances and most of one's hopeful's family whilst waiting for that hopeful to make an answer to a proposal. The room was dreadfully hot and Benedict's heart pulsed at an unnatural rate, so that his hands were inclined to tremble at his sides. He didn't dare clench them, afraid Claire might take the gesture as a threat, and so instead he stood and shook like leaves in the wind and tried not to feel the weight of three dozen interested gazes upon himself and Claire Dalton. The Lads were not even wagering on the outcome. Benedict tried to tell himself that this was due to real concern for his well-being, though he suspected it was more the imposing silence: they couldn't whisper bets to one another without being overheard, and that would be beyond the pale.

It was more astonishing that his mother said nothing, though he didn't dare look her way to find out what was causing her to be so discreet. Perhaps she approved of Miss Dalton. Perhaps, more likely, the desire to preserve her friendship with Mrs Dalton was causing her to hold her tongue. Benedict became aware he was holding on to these fleeting, distracting thoughts in an attempt to ward off his own fears as Claire's silence grew more protracted.

Her gaze had not left his face, but he could read nothing of her thoughts on her own lovely features. She was flushed, cheeks rosy and green eyes shining, lips parted, but her expression, while becoming, registered no more than the astonishment she had first presented. Perhaps he had been mistaken. Perhaps her kiss had not been warm and welcoming. Perhaps her anger over the source of his fortune had been simply altruistic. Perhaps it had nothing to do with him. Perhaps she was astounded because she had never imagined or wanted his proposal. Perhaps her wonderment was now calculated as she struggled to find a way to reject him in front of three dozen onlookers. He was very nearly ready to retract it all when she finally spoke.

"Well," said Miss Claire Dalton in considering tones, "if you are disinherited, at least we will have my dowry to rely on...."

Before Benedict could fully understand the import of those words, another roar filled the room. This time the Lads descended upon himself and Claire, pressing them together, lifting them into the air, and bursting into uproarious cheers when, laughing with shy delight, Claire Dalton leaned over and kissed Benedict on the mouth in front of everyone.

The wedding, Worthington felt, was a profoundly satisfactory event. Miss Dalton—now Mrs Fairburn—was radiant, clad in cream silk trimmed with innumerable delicate flowers, and young Master Fairburn looked equally dashing in formal black with sharp-cut tails. The mothers-in-law had outdone themselves and each other, wearing handsome rich jewel shades and admiring one another almost as much as they admired their children. The Lads had made a preposterously long line of men to stand for Benedict; Miss Dalton had been obliged to call upon Miss Hurst, Miss Fairburn, and an entire host of young ladies from the country to stand up for her due to Master Fairburn having so many on his side.

Worthington had observed this all from a discreet location near the rear of the church, which was beautifully arranged with holly and bright ribbons. Christmas had passed, and the air was invigorating and not, this early in the day, heavy with rain. The sky, when the newlyweds emerged beneath it, was blue with slates of grey threatening the horizons, but the winter sunlight warmed petals that were flung over the bride and groom by well-wishers.

A very old lady, her white hair piled high above a face filled with many fine wrinkles, sat imperiously in the carriage at the end of the church walkway. She wore a splendid grey silk gown with a hood and ribbons at elbow, wrist, and throat, all wholly old-fashioned, casting back half a century in style, and suiting her splendidly. Its aged formality was also entirely at odds with the bright and rather wicked smile that broke over her face as Benedict Fairburn came to an astonished halt a few steps from the carriage. "Great-Aunt Nancy?"

"I certainly hope so!" Mrs Nancy Montgomery leaned forward to offer her grand-nephew her hand. He kissed it and she seized his fingers, pulling him up the carriage steps with an obvious strength that belied her aged figure. Benedict grunted in surprise, got his feet under him in the carriage, and turned to offer Claire Fairburn, who stood in pleasantly astonished confusion, a hand into the carriage. She climbed up and sat, still stupefied, which appeared to be entirely to Mrs Montgomery's satisfaction.

"Claire, my aunt, Mrs Nancy Montgomery. Great-Aunt Nancy, it's my honor to introduce you to my wife, Claire Fairburn."

"I'm delighted to meet you," Claire said. "I had no idea you would be here. I thought—"

"That I was dying?" Great-Aunt Nancy demanded loudly enough to be heard everywhere. "Yes, well, I had to do something to get Benny married off, didn't I? I had no idea he would do so well, young lady, but I've been itching to meet you since he showed up on my doorstep to cast away my fortune." More quietly, but audible to Worthington, who attended to the Daltons' carriage only a few steps away, she continued, "I understand you've been to St Sophia's."

"Yes," the new Mrs Fairburn replied, startled. "How did you know?"

"Miss Beacham, who runs the Institute, was a friend of mine," Mrs Montgomery said softly. "I knew her when she was a girl, long before the scandal that ruined her and her family. I've helped her through the years, but I've never felt that I'd done enough. Perhaps I'm no better than you said my nephew was," she said with a sharp look at Claire, who forbore to comment. "I suppose I would have let the money go to Benny and felt only a twinge of guilt, had you not interfered, though I've always known I could have—should have—done better. So I believe you've made all of our family better, Mrs Fairburn, whether you meant to or not."

"Thank you," Claire said, though it was unclear if the comment had been intended as a compliment.

Still, Mrs Montgomery smiled, then suddenly leaned forward conspiratorially. Worthington was obliged to move to the horses' heads and fiddle with their bridles to overhear the remainder of the conversation. "I have a house in Town, you know," she said. "A house I never use, having tired long ago of the politics and snubs of Society. I am giving the house to you, Benny. A wedding gift," the old lady said in triumph as the newlyweds fell back in gasping astonishment. "Indeed, I have been somewhat bold, and have, over the past few weeks, taken the liberty of having the house refurbished and furnished. You will forgive me if I insist on driving there with you this morning, so that I can see you see the house for the first time."

"Of course," Benedict murmured disbelievingly. "I remember your townhouse from my childhood. I remember the gardens, Aunt Nancy. They went on forever. The house was tremendous."

"It still is," Great-Aunt Nancy said in delight, "only now it's modern and finer than ever. Now, Mrs Fairburn, the house is, of course, yours as well, but I have been considering your activities and your influence on our family and I have decided to make you a wedding gift of your own. I am giving you a sum of ten thousand pounds, Mrs Fairburn, to do with as you wish. Be as generous and wise with it as you have been with St Sophia's — yes," she said with satisfied asperity, "I know what assistance you've offered the institute since your engagement — and I shall be pleased beyond measure."

The new Mrs Fairburn went white, then red, then flung herself forward to embrace Mrs Montgomery with obvious strength. Mrs Montgomery looked both flustered and thrilled, patting Claire's shoulders in pleasure. Claire sat back, holding the old woman's hands and smiling until tears ran down both their cheeks, and then, without warning, stood in the carriage to carol, "Priscilla! Mr Graham! Come here at once!"

Mr Fairburn caught her waist to keep her balanced as the Grahams approached. Priscilla and Jack had married in a quiet ceremony before Christmas, and had come to the Fairburns' wedding attended by two blond children who regarded the wealthy, healthy world around them with a mixture of suspicion and wonder. Claire seized Priscilla Graham's hands, pulling her into the carriage with them. Benedict found himself obliged to scoot over as Jack Graham climbed in behind her. The children, not intending on being left behind, clambered up as well, one in Graham's lap and the other in Benedict Fairburn's. Graham looked comfortable with the burden; Fairburn, somewhat shocked. Worthington felt his mouth twitch, schooled his features, then let the smile crook his lips after all.

Claire held the Grahams' hands with tight grips, declaring, "I know that you have purchased passage to America already, and although I will miss you terribly, I understand why you want to go. You will not, though, go penniless. I insist that you allow me to present you with something to start anew with. Five hundred pounds will ease the way, will it not? I insist," she said again, and anything else she might have said was lost in a sudden cry and embrace from Mrs Graham.

"Oh dear," Mrs Montgomery murmured in clear amusement over the joyous sobs, "perhaps I had better increase the size of your wedding purse, Mrs Fairburn, if you're going to be *this* flagrant with it."

"I'll try not to be too rash," Mrs Fairburn promised, beaming. "Oh, please let us see the house, Great-Aunt Nancy? I can imagine no greater joy than seeing it through your eyes."

"Nor I than seeing it through yours. Driver," Mrs Montgomery said regally, and with a shudder and lurch, an over-full carriage bumped down the street to the sound of cheers and shouts. The throng of well-wishers followed them a goodly distance, celebratory songs and laughter filling the morning air. Splendid indeed; better than splendid. Worthington, forgetting himself, smiled after them, and patted the nearest horse's nose.

"I believe," Charles Dalton said cheerfully, at Worthington's side, "that you've polished that bit long enough, Worthington. I don't think it could gleam any more if it was made of gold."

Worthington glanced at the well-shone bit and cleared his throat. "You may be right, sir."

Dalton smiled. "It's all right, Worthington. You're allowed to have an emotion or two, or even be caught listening once or twice."

"I'm sure I wouldn't know what you mean, sir," Worthington said as neutrally as he could manage, and Charles laughed.

"No, I'm sure you don't. It all turned out all right, didn't it, Worthington?" Dalton looked after the departing carriage with more sense of contentment than Worthington had hoped to see from him in the aftermath of the wedding, and spoke as one satisfied with the situation. "They'll be happy, and Claire gets on with the Lads, so we won't be too disturbed by one of our number getting married. And it even ended well for the Grahams and those children. It's all turned out splendidly, hasn't it?"

"So it has, sir. So it has."

Look for more of the Lovelorn Lads in

Seducing Samuel

coming soon!

Acknowledgments

Bewitching Benedict has been a long time in the making, and I want to give a particular shout-out to Leigh Ann Malloy, Chrysoula Tzavelas, and Tara Lynch for reading an early draft approximately a thousand years ago and assuring me that, yes, in fact, I could write a Regency romance with no magic in it *at all*. Carl Rigney also requires special thanks, for reasons he knows and which shall remain secret to the world at large.

I had a splendid editorial team for this book in Mary-Theresa Hussey and Stephanie Mowery, and I love the cover art I got through Cora Designs. I'm looking forward to a whole host of seven Lovelorn Lads books gracing my shelves with their help. (Eventually.)

My son is going to be astonished and perhaps vaguely offended that I got another book sorted while he and my husband were off gallivanting in America (at age 7, he's the only person able to keep track of what I'm working on as clearly as I can!), but I sure will be glad when you boys are home with me again. I love you both.

About the Author

According to her friends, CE Murphy makes such amazing fudge that it should be mentioned first in any biography. It's true that she makes extraordinarily good fudge, but she's somewhat surprised that it features so highly in biographical relevance.

Other people said she began her writing career when she ran away from home at age five to write copy for the circus that had come to town. Some claimed she's a crowdsourcing pioneer, which she rather likes the sound of, but nobody actually got around to pointing out she's written a best-selling urban fantasy series (The Walker Papers), or that she dabbles in writing graphic novels (Take A Chance) and periodically dips her toes into writing short stories (the Old Races collections).

Still, it's clear to her that she should let her friends write all of her biographies, because they're much more interesting that way.

More prosaically, she was born and raised in Alaska, and now lives with her family in her ancestral homeland of Ireland, which is a magical place where it rains a lot but nothing one could seriously regard as winter ever actually arrives.

She can be found online at:

mizkit.com

@ce_murphy

fb.com/cemurphywriter &

tinyletter.com/ce_murphy (a newsletter, by far the best place to get up-to-date information on what's out next!)